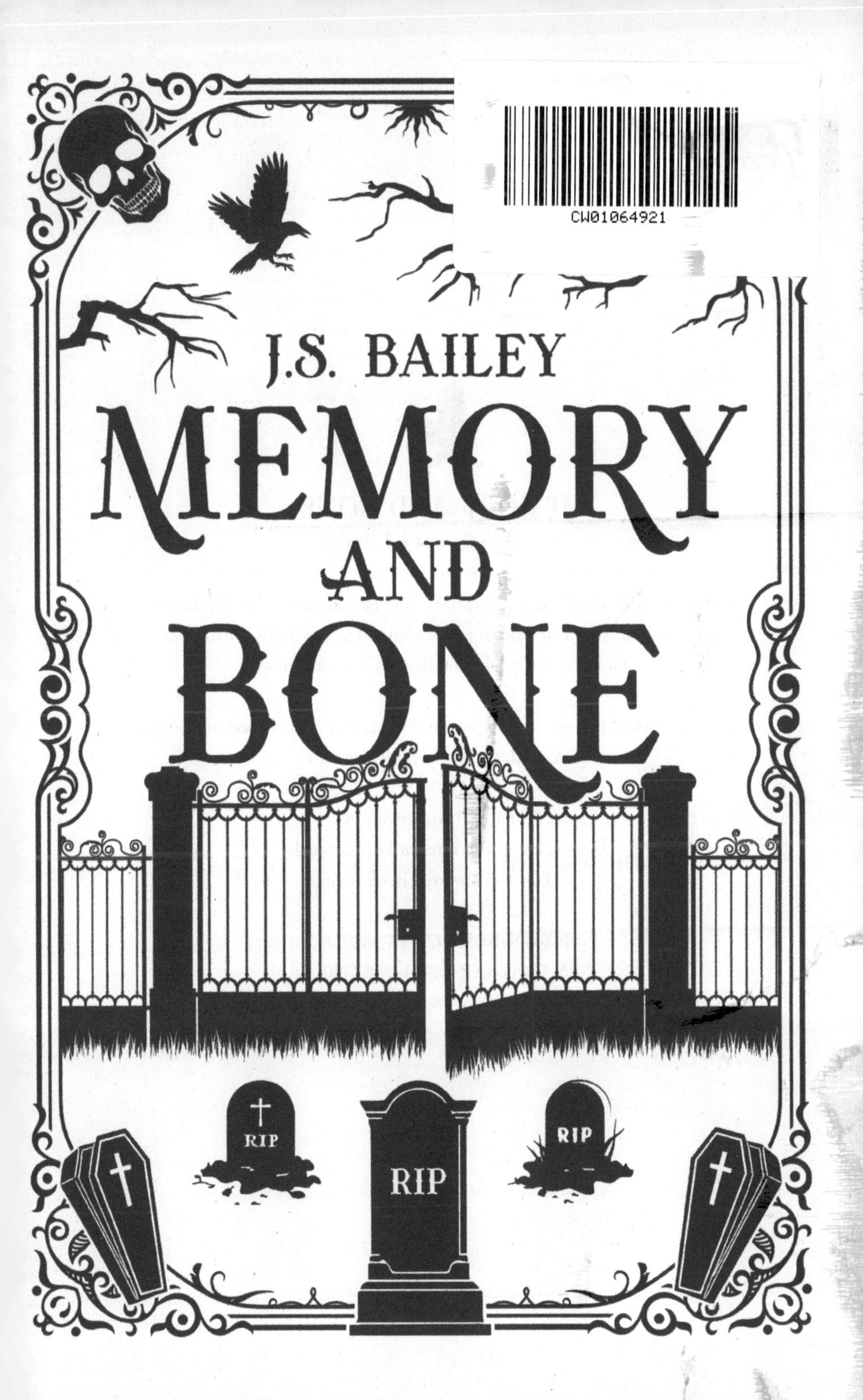
CW01064921
J.S. BAILEY
MEMORY
AND
BONE
RIP
RIP
RIP

MEMORY AND BONE

Edited by Lyndsey Smith
Cover Design and Interior Formatting by
We Got You Covered Book Design

ISBN (paperback): 978-1-7367790-7-1
ISBN (hardcover): 978-1-7367790-8-8
ISBN (ebook): 978-1-7367790-9-5

J.S. BAILEY

MEMORY AND BONE

CONTENT WARNING

The book you hold in your hands is a supernatural horror novel containing graphic depictions of violence and paranormal activity. For a list of specific trigger warnings, please see the end of this book.

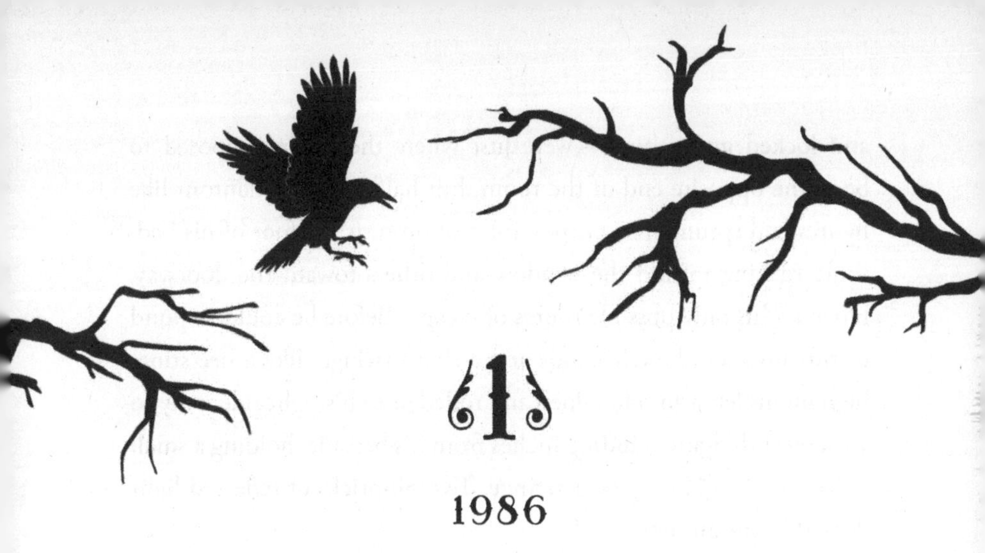

1

1986

A creaking floorboard woke him from a restless slumber, sending figments of dark dreams slithering into oblivion.

He gradually regained his bearings. Beside him, to his left, was the window facing the quiet street. Sheer drapes hung limply from their rod, muting the light from the moon and the streetlamp below.

He stared at the alarm clock on the bedside table just below the window, supposing the sound had really been the house settling on its foundation. It was foolish to worry. Children became frightened by these things, not him. The years of lying awake, calling for his mother to come save him from the creatures in the dark, had long since passed away.

Yet something still unsettled him. His bedroom felt almost alive, like a monster holding its breath. Dare he roll over and see its dripping teeth?

No, he chided himself. That wasn't quite right. The only monster here was him. And yet…

He closed his eyes with the hope of drifting back to that world where the troubles of the daytime melted into afterthoughts.

But then a low voice said, "Get him."

He lifted his head in alarm and, for the first time since waking, peered around the room. The requisite furnishings—dresser, desk, and locked gun cabinet—were just where they were supposed to be at the opposite end of the room, but half a dozen phantom-like figures had sprung into purposeful motion near the foot of his bed, some rushing toward the window and others toward the doorway, blocking his only possible routes of escape. Before he could respond to this invasion, he felt hands and a sharp twinge, like a bee sting, high on his left arm. He yelped and rolled onto his right side, only to see a seventh figure standing inches from his bedside, holding a small object that could only be a syringe. Two pinpricks of reflected light floated in the air: eyes.

"How did you get in here?" he croaked. It was the first logical question to ask. He already knew the "why."

The phantoms had grown still again. Blood rushed through his veins, fear pushing his heart to the limit. Sour sweat oozed from his skin. Perhaps they wanted to stand in the dark, waiting in silence until he went mad.

He tried to sit up, to reason with them, but his body only flopped as if made of rubber. The figure next to him made a gesture with one featureless hand. Three of the others broke away from the rest, one joining the first figure and two coming around to the bed's opposite side.

The gun cabinet across the room from him might as well have been in a different galaxy.

Without warning, four sets of arms grasped him and flipped him onto his stomach. His own arms were wrenched behind him, held in place with the wrists crossed.

He could hear the telltale rip of duct tape tearing from a roll.

The drugs from the syringe coursed through his veins, weakening him more and more with each passing second. He couldn't stop the phantoms from binding him. Cloth was placed over his head—a sack?—and the phantoms wrapped more tape around his ankles before lifting him from the bed. His head banged against the wall as they jostled him down the stairs. He cried out to deaf ears.

A squeak, a gust of air. They were taking him outside! An engine idled nearby while a staticky radio played some Led Zeppelin song. A car door opened, and they shoved him onto a sticky, leather seat.

The phantoms climbed in beside him.

Doors slammed. Seatbelts clicked. Someone killed the radio. The car lurched, moving away from the curb.

Tears stung his eyes. This couldn't be happening! It had to be a dream, a nightmare, his own imagination torturing him while he slept.

But one could not imagine the terror crippling him or the coarse fabric scratching his face, the throbbing in his head where he'd hit it on the wall.

He knew these feelings were real and that he would not end this night alive.

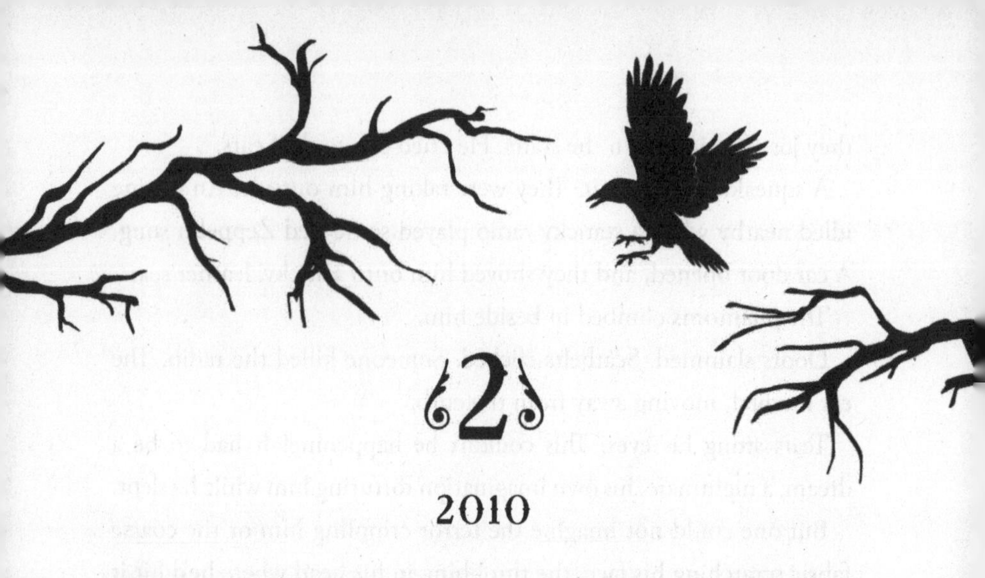

2

2010

Jessica Roman-Dell read the eviction notice twice, then stared across her apartment's living room in a daze. Words like "nonpayment" and "vacate the premises" flitted through her head. Words she'd always associated with other less fortunate people. Not her.

She wasn't entirely sure how things had come to this. Jessica had worked *hard* to carve out this space for herself. The apartment wasn't fancy. It was just the right size to house her and her growing collection of ghost hunting equipment. Unfortunately, her bank account was *not* the right size to fund even that meager lifestyle. Hence the eviction notice.

Jessica picked up her cell phone and made a call.

"Hello?" came a woman's curt voice.

Jessica coughed lightly. "Linda? It's Jessica."

The phone grew suspiciously quiet in her ear.

"I got your letter," Jessica tried again. "I…wondered if we could try to work this out."

"We've already had this conversation, Jessica."

She scrunched her eyes shut. "You said you'd be lenient since I lost my job."

"That was four months ago! I haven't seen a cent from you since then. I have bills of my own to pay, you know."

"I'm not trying to make excuses." Jessica barely held back an unwanted wave of tears. "I just haven't been able to find another j—"

"Then borrow the money from someone and pay them back later. If I don't see your check within the next three days, you're gone."

A click in Jessica's ear told her the conversation was over.

She lowered the phone and stared toward the window without seeing it. This lull in her life was stretching on for much longer than she'd expected, and getting worse by the day. And it wasn't like she could just walk up to her friends and ask for several thousand dollars; they barely got by as it was.

And her family? Forget about it.

Chewing on her lip, Jessica picked up her phone again and dialed another number. A man answered it on the second ring.

"Hey, Jessica. What's up?"

She inhaled deeply and said, "Wayne? I have a *huge* favor to ask you."

Jessica was *supposed* to be packing that night, but she'd gotten a last-minute call on her cellphone from Ellen Shoushanian, who'd asked Jessica if she wanted to come investigate her house that evening for "spooky things," as the older woman had put it.

Jessica, sitting in a cleared island amid a sea of her scattered belongings, looked from the mound of folded clothing she'd been piling into a box to the cat-shaped clock she had yet to unhook from the wall. It was five thirty.

"I can be there at six," she had said.

Now it was nearing ten o'clock, and Jessica found herself praying for something interesting to start happening before she died of boredom in Ellen and Vince Shoushanian's moldy basement.

Ellen's words from hours earlier drifted through her thoughts.

"Things are constantly moving around by themselves whenever Vince and I have gone out," she'd said to Jessica. "Would you believe that I've found the remote in the back of the deep freeze three times? Vince swears he had nothing to do with it. But nothing's as odd as the time we came home from church one morning and the spice rack was sitting in the middle of the stairs."

Jessica had considered asking them if early-onset dementia might be the culprit since ruling out natural phenomena was a part of every investigation, but she did have some tact. Plus, misplaced objects weren't the only concerns in the Shoushanian household. Vince claimed to have seen the apparition of a young man on multiple occasions, and both he and Ellen swore they had heard lively conversations coming from empty rooms late at night.

The voices might have been loud radios in passing cars, but Jessica couldn't pin an explanation to the apparition. Hopefully, she would encounter it tonight.

Jessica shivered. She shouldn't have worn flip-flops on this outing. The day had been warm, like so many in October, but the dampness of the basement chilled her. A pipe dripped somewhere close by, making her think of water torture, and she yearned for a ghost to appear to distract her from the sound.

She picked up her thermal imaging camera and panned the room for the umpteenth time, looking for any anomalies in temperature which might indicate the presence of a spirit. The only yellow-orange heat signatures she could see on the tiny screen came from the water heater and some pipes branching off from it in different directions. She sighed and stared up at the cobwebby rafters.

"If you're really here," Jessica said, "it would be great if you could come out and say hello."

Silence answered her, as it usually did. Investigations like this were frustrating, especially when she sat and sat and sat for half the night, without one single thing happening that could be ascribed to the spirits she longed to meet.

A cricket started chirping in the corner. Now *that* would wreak havoc on her recordings, dammit.

"Are you just being shy?" Jessica asked. "I used to be a little shy too, until I started working at a truck stop. You would not *believe* the bullshit I had to put up with, working there. I lasted there four years, but then the economy went down the toilet, and they said *adios*. Did you work somewhere when you were alive?"

More silence. She lifted the thermal imaging camera from her lap again and gave the room another sweep. *Nada.*

This was starting to look like one big waste of time, just like her mother had always told her. She supposed she could have stayed at home doing something more productive, like eating microwaveable burritos and watching *Mystery Science Theater 3000* for the five hundredth time.

And packing. She really needed to get going with that before Landlady Linda threw all her things out onto the lawn.

"Did you have family?" Jessica asked the hypothetical ghost. "Mine are real winners. I mean, my sister's cool, and my dad is all right but pretty absentminded. But my parents really shouldn't have had children. They didn't call me on my last birthday. I turned twenty-one on New Year's Day. I guess they might have been sleeping in, or something." A birthday card containing a check for twenty dollars had arrived in the mail from them a week later, signed only by her father. She used the money to buy more frozen burritos and counted out the remaining change to put in her gasoline fund.

"Can you tell me what your name is?" she continued.

If the ghost replied, she couldn't hear it.

"My name's Jessica Roman-Dell. It's a weird last name, I know. Nobody really knows how it ended up hyphenated like that. I had a great-aunt who was big into genealogy, but she's gone now."

She waited five more minutes for a response yet heard nothing aside from dripping and chirping. With any luck, the digital voice recorder she'd set on the floor had picked up some kind of ghostly dialogue that had been below her hearing threshold.

Jessica rose from the uncomfortable chair and went upstairs to see if she'd have better luck in the kitchen. At least it would be warmer, and there would be no leaking plumbing or obnoxious crickets to distract her.

She struggled to see, ascending the dark stairwell into the living room. A candle had been left burning in the adjoining kitchen, and the light from its feeble flame cast eerie shadows over the walls.

Both Shoushanians had left to spend the night at their daughter's house so they wouldn't interfere with the investigation. Now, though, she wished she had an actual human to talk to.

"I've got a couple friends," Jessica said to the air. "I haven't known them for too long, but they're fun to hang around. They don't ever want to tag along with me on nights like this, though."

Wayne Thompson frequently used the excuse that the sight of him might frighten away any self-respecting spirits, and his younger cousin Sidney Miller had her own very understandable reasons for keeping away from the dead.

Jessica switched on her night vision camera, set it to record, and placed it on the kitchen table, then retreated several steps so she'd appear in the frame. "Hey, folks, it's Jessica Roman-Dell, your Friendly Neighborhood Ghost Hunter. I'm currently investigating a seventy-year-old house here in southern Ohio, but I'm not having a lot of luck tonight. What's new, right?"

The candle on the table made a loud *pop*, and Jessica jumped, then smiled sheepishly at the camera.

"No word on if anyone has ever died here; the owners just don't know one way or the other," she went on.

A soft, muted squeak echoed from the second floor.

"What was *that*?" Jessica snatched up the night vision camera and tiptoed to the staircase, where the noise was louder but still barely more perceptible than a whisper. She took the stairs one at a time, taking care not to make too much noise, lest she frighten whatever caused it.

Jessica arrived in a short hallway that had a hardwood floor. A door on the right stood ajar, and a thin ribbon of silvery light spilled from the gap.

The squeaking came from that room. Before she could chicken out and go running back downstairs—which would surely disappoint her ninety-seven YouTube subscribers—she pushed the door open the rest of the way and went inside.

Jessica's emotions made a split-second metamorphosis from anticipation to embarrassment. In a cage beneath the window, a hamster raced merrily on his exercise wheel, having the time of his life.

"I think," she said to the camera, "I'm going to call it a night."

Wayne Thompson sat at the wrought iron patio table on his deck, frowning at the spreadsheet displayed on his laptop screen, when the squeak of a door and soft footsteps made him look up.

His cousin Sidney Miller stood in the warm glow of the porchlight, where a swarm of moths swirled in a mindless frenzy. The single bulb brought out the shine in her red hair, which she'd tied back into a bun and adorned with a pair of black chopsticks crisscrossing in an X-shape. Wayne's own hair was as dark as fresh coffee. They might have been related, but they hardly resembled each other at all.

Sidney stepped away from the moth cloud, slid a Camel Menthol cigarette from its box, and stuck it between her teeth, then patted the pockets of her black skinny jeans. "Do you have a lighter?"

Wayne had lit a citronella candle, warding off any mosquitoes that might still be hanging around this time of year, and left the Bic lighter lying on the table next to it. He tossed it to her, and Sidney snatched it from the air one-handed.

"What's that face for?" she asked once the tip of the cigarette glowed orange. A curl of smoke rose into the night air.

"You know those are going to kill you," he replied, trying not to cough.

She shrugged and stared thoughtfully toward the dark yard. They'd had this discussion before, of course, and had reached a similar non-conclusion.

Wayne did have bigger problems to worry about right now. He returned his attention to the computer screen, where his financial situation was laid bare in a grid of columns and rows. "Can I talk to you for a minute?" he asked.

She rolled her eyes at him. "I'm not going anywhere. What's up?"

Wayne ran a hand through his hair. "You know how hard I try to budget things around here, right?"

"Of course. I'm only allowed to use one napkin during dinner and one square of paper if I pee."

His eyebrows rose.

"I'm kidding, Wayne. So, what's the bad news?"

He let out the sigh he'd been holding in since he'd run the numbers. "Everything just keeps costing more and more money. It wouldn't be so bad if they'd given me the raise they'd promised…Would you be okay with paying me an extra fifty a month? It would help cover some of it."

Sidney remained silent. She crossed the deck and leaned against the wooden railing. "I'll see what I can do."

"If you can't come up with the money, you could try giving up your death sticks. You're going to give me black lung disease if this keeps up much longer."

She threw him a sneer. "Asshole."

"Bitch."

They grinned at each other, but only for a moment. It felt strange and almost sacrilegious to be smiling again...though it had been over a year now, so why shouldn't they try?

"Seriously, though," he said. "Let me know if it's too much trouble, and we can work something else out."

"I understand." Sidney exhaled a noxious nicotine haze. "If I have to, I'll start using half a square of toilet paper."

Using the table for support, Wayne pulled himself to his feet. The shift in position made his calves chafe beneath his black and blue flame-patterned ankle-foot orthotics. "On that note," he said, "I'm going in."

Wayne limped across the deck to the back door. His way of walking was often referred to as a "scissors gait," a term that made him envision himself as a giant, anthropomorphic pair of shears. Wayne Scissorlegs. The horror!

After depositing the computer on a clean section of the Formica countertop, Wayne shuffled over to the refrigerator and grabbed a Mike's Hard Lemonade out of one of the crisper drawers. He pried off the cap and took a long, satisfying gulp. Alcohol might not have fixed any of his problems, but it sure made him feel a little better about them.

He heard the *squeak-click* of the back door opening and closing a few minutes later. Sidney strode into the kitchen and threw her cigarette butt into the corner wastebasket.

"I thought Jessica was coming over tonight," Sidney said. "We were going to watch *Corpse Bride* again."

"She didn't tell you? She's packing."

Sidney frowned. "For what?"

Wayne took another sip from the glass bottle. "She's being evicted from her apartment."

"Aww, that sucks. She's not moving back in with her parents, is she?"

"Um, no. She's staying here."

Sidney's eyes grew round. "You *didn't*..."

"You're friends with her too. What's the problem?"

"We don't have any extra bedrooms! Unless you were going to move all your gym equipment to the basement?"

"Your room is pretty big. We'll make do."

Sidney folded her arms. "Look, I like Jessica. But you might have consulted me before assigning me a roommate who spends most of her free time talking to dead people. What if she accidentally conjures the Cincinnati Strangler in my bedroom, or something?"

"I didn't have a lot of time to mull it over. She was being kicked out in three days. And besides, this is only a temporary arrangement."

"If you say so."

Wayne finished the Mike's and set the bottle in the sink. "Besides," he said. "I know my house isn't haunted. Everything is going to be fine."

3

A cascade of leaves drifted from towering oaks and settled around the granite markers documenting the birth and death dates of those moldering six feet below.

Though Jerry Madison once marveled at the beauty autumn brought to the world, it no longer interested him. This fall looked the same as the previous one, which looked just like the one before it. It was as if time progressed in a circle, repeating itself over and over again without end.

He stood a distance back from the crowd of mourners gathered in the cemetery that morning. All he could really see were the backs of people's heads. A gray-haired minister stood next to the casket at the front of the congregation, reciting prayers for the newly deceased. The man paused every few lines to deliver somewhat un-pious bouts of ragged coughing.

A mother and her young son stood about five yards away from Jerry. The woman's head was bowed, but the toddler stared out at the headstones with an expression of childlike curiosity, his baby-blue eyes twinkling in the sunlight. He caught sight of Jerry and smiled in the way the truly innocent do.

Startled, Jerry took a step backward.

The boy giggled. "Funny man!"

"Shh!" His mother bent down and scolded her son in a whisper.

"What did Mommy say about not talking?"

"But he scared of me! Look, someone hurt his hand." The boy stared at the inflamed cut on the back of Jerry's hand, where Abigail had thrown a knife at his face long ago and he'd held his hand up to protect himself.

Shit. Jerry raked his mind for more pleasant matters to contemplate so what the kid had seen would go away. Fortunately, he hadn't been thinking about the other thing, too, because the kid surely would have gone into hysterics. Though it might have made an interesting diversion from the normal tedium.

"Jeremy, be quiet." The woman scooped up her son and held him on her hip, glancing in Jerry's direction with suspicion in her eyes. "You crazy kid." She lowered her head in reverence once more.

Jeremy peeked around her shoulder and made a goofy face at Jerry, who suddenly felt a wave of anger. Why should the boy keep looking at *him*, of all people? It was just like it had always been. They just couldn't leave him alone. The faces. Always watching. Always *mocking*.

Jerry's fists clenched at his sides. He concentrated on *that*, and the boy began screaming, tears running in rivulets down his rosy cheeks. His flustered mother broke away from the crowd, toting a wailing Jeremy off toward the parking lot, the sound dwindling in the distance like a fading siren.

Jerry rubbed his neck. Good riddance.

The ceremony ended a short while later. The grieving family and their kin hugged each other and bade their farewells. The parking lot soon emptied of vehicles, and in solitude, Jerry watched three burly young men shovel dirt back into the grave. The men said little to each other while they worked. They'd probably done this a hundred times and thought nothing of it.

The men finally completed their job and left. Jerry sat down on one of the cemetery benches and gazed unseeingly at the woods surrounding the graveyard. He should leave here, find some other place to lurk about in. But where? Everywhere was nowhere, and nowhere was everywhere. Nothing mattered or would ever matter again.

He didn't know if he should be sad or angry or bitter. Sometimes, he was all three, and sometimes, he was none at all. On rare occasions, he would even think of something pleasant he'd forgotten about long ago, and a spark of joy would light up his whole being, but then he would remember.

It was an endless cycle of emotions. Bitterness felt the worst. It would consume him, like acid dissolving an old coin. *They* had done this to him. If they hadn't, he wouldn't be here at all.

If he could get back at them…

He couldn't take it anymore. Something had to change. But what could he, Jerry Madison, do?

Jerry buried his face in his hands and wept, wishing he could find a way to end his life so the pain of existing would go away forever.

Which, of course, was impossible. Jerry Madison was already dead.

Jessica staggered out of bed, wincing as she stood up. The clock had changed over to midnight the moment she'd pulled into her apartment's parking lot after leaving the Shoushanian place. She'd spent the next hour and a half sorting the rest of her things and piling them into cardboard produce boxes she'd swiped from behind Eleanor Market earlier in the week.

Now, bleary-eyed and exhausted after a night that had been too short, she wished she could brew a pot of coffee—but like everything else, the coffee maker and canister of grounds were boxed up and ready to go to their new home.

She wished *she* felt ready to go.

Jessica went into the bathroom and stood at the sink, examining the dark circles that had appeared under her eyes. Such skin blemishes were a tolerable side effect of the late, uneventful hours Sidney had despised about ghost hunting.

"Jessica," she'd say, "I don't know if you've noticed, but *nothing is happening*. Can we please go home now?"

"Just give me one more hour," Jessica would reply. "Something might happen."

On one of those rare nights when something *had* happened, they'd been sitting in the living room of a sagging house trailer a couple of miles north of Eleanor when a bloodcurdling scream cut through the air, like a machete outside the window.

It took Sidney about 0.2 seconds to grab her cellphone as if to report a murder.

Perhaps unkindly, Jessica had laughed. "It's just a screech owl!" She'd taken the unbelieving Sidney outside and shined a flashlight up into a tree to illuminate the feathered culprit, who then took flight.

If she remembered right, that was the last time they'd ever ghost hunted together. It really wasn't a hobby intended for everyone.

Jessica finished up in the bathroom and then put on the jeans and T-shirt she'd left out before going to bed. She went from room to room, checking to make sure she hadn't missed anything during her fatigued round of late-night packing. Satisfied every last corner was empty of her belongings, she drifted over to the picture window and stared out at her favorite view for one last time.

Her second-floor apartment in Hilltop Villa might have been cheap, but the view was priceless. Half a mile to the southwest, the Ohio River flowed by like a gray ribbon. Most of the village of Eleanor lay below in the flood plain. The green hills of Kentucky rose from the other side of the river, where another village—Iron Springs—sprawled along the riverbank, like a mirror image of the Ohio side.

She drew back from the window, a tear rolling down her cheek. This past year had been one of freedom. There was no greater feeling in the world than earning enough money to actually live on your own and take care of your own bills. Before she'd lost her job at American Dream Truck Stop, she'd even been planning on going to college to study audio visual technology, which was bound to add a professional touch to her YouTube channel.

There came a soft knock on her door. Jessica opened it with a smile and let Wayne inside.

As usual, she felt an inexplicable lightness at the sight of him. Today he wore a peach-colored T-shirt and khaki shorts that showed off his leg braces. He'd put styling gel in his dark hair, and Jessica could detect the faint scent of aftershave.

"You're early," Jessica said, giving Wayne a welcoming hug. "Thanks for taking the day off work to help me."

"Anything for you." Wayne made a quick scan of the room. "I can't believe you're actually done packing."

"You underestimate me."

Wayne adjusted his black-framed glasses and planted his hands on his hips. "What's going out first?"

"We can start with the table. It can lay flat in the bed of your truck."

"Whatever you wish."

Jessica watched with mild trepidation as Wayne bent down and lifted his end of the tabletop off the floor. It hadn't occurred to her he might not be able to handle this.

"Are you going to be all right?" she asked.

Wayne rolled his eyes. "I have cerebral palsy, not brittle bone disease. Now help me lift this thing."

She did as he instructed. Wayne didn't let his disability stop him—one of the many things she'd learned about him over the past few years. Like how his first name was actually Robert but he much preferred his middle name, and that his exact condition was called spastic diplegia.

The spastic muscles in Wayne's legs made it difficult for him to walk, though the braces helped him a lot. Since his balance and gait were poor at best, it would be easy for him to trip on the stairs.

"If you'll remember, *I* volunteered to do this," he said, reading the look on her face.

"Okay, okay," she replied. "But be careful."

She and Wayne made it to the truck without any major incidents. He'd backed it into a handicapped spot and let the tailgate down prior to knocking on her door, and he'd even been thoughtful enough to lay a tarp down in the truck bed to prevent her furniture from getting scratched.

Wayne stopped to catch his breath. "See? I made it."

"Of course you did," Jessica teased, pushing a loose strand of hair from her eyes. "You're more stubborn than a herd of mules."

Back inside the kitchen, Wayne gathered up the detached table legs and held them over his shoulder. Jessica picked up a box of dishes and followed him out the door, staying close in case he needed assistance.

"I went on another investigation last night," she panted, feeling the muscles in her arms strain against the weight of the box.

"And you still had time to pack?"

"Yeah, it was kind of a bust. Ellen Shoushanian asked if I'd check out her house, so I did. I thought I'd have more luck since it's pretty old."

"I always thought her house looked a little spooky on the outside. The wrought iron fence kind of sells it."

"Right? In this line of business, you don't pass up on good deals like hers."

"It's not a business when you don't get paid."

"I'm *working* on it, Wayne. All this free time I've had these past few months is letting me focus on it more."

"Are you going to do it full time now, or what?"

"I'll certainly try."

They deposited their loads into the truck and went back upstairs.

"How many more subscribers do you need before YouTube starts paying you?" Wayne asked, tucking Jessica's wastebasket under one arm.

She felt a little sheepish. "A lot, and people have to actually watch what I post. I've just got to get better content. I don't think too many people like watching me sit alone in the dark, talking to myself."

"I got Cindy at work to follow your channel. She likes those ghost guys on TV."

"I appreciate it."

They spent the next fifteen minutes making more trips back and forth between the truck and the apartment.

"Have you ever considered faking it?" Wayne asked when they paused to catch their breaths.

"You mean, like hiring someone to be a ghost for me? Rattle the pipes, say boo?"

"Maybe."

She folded her arms. "That's being dishonest."

"Just like everyone else on the internet. You'll get more views and followers and start raking in the dough, and then you can live happily ever after."

"Faking it would be pretty obvious. I'm not that good with video editing yet."

He shrugged. "You'll get there."

Jessica thought about it for a minute. She'd always figured the ghost hunting shows that had inspired her were mostly staged. That's why her YouTube channel was going to be different: whatever evidence she found would be the real deal. "I don't know. Faking it goes against my morals."

"It sounds like you need a real ghost to liven things up for you, then."

"Well, if you find one for me, be sure to let me know."

4

The busy morning of loading and unloading Jessica's rusting white Taurus and Wayne's pickup truck came to an end. After the final trip, the two of them stood in Wayne's short gravel driveway. Wayne's front yard consisted of two yellow patches of grass on either side. Shriveled plants in terracotta pots lined the edge of the cement-slab porch.

Home.

"Okay," Jessica said, staring at the house. "Now what?"

"Now we put everything away," Wayne replied, "and then we get something to eat."

It was nearly two o'clock by the time they were completely finished and a pizza was cooling on top of the stove. Jessica took two slices for herself and sat down at the table, staring forlornly at the orange and green gourds Sidney had recently purchased for a fall centerpiece.

"Are you all right?" Wayne asked. He sat across from her, checking something on his BlackBerry.

Jessica shrugged. "I guess so. It's just weird."

"You'll get used to it."

"I really liked my apartment. It was a place I could call my own." She nibbled at her pizza, trying not to burn her tongue. "And now my back is killing me from moving everything."

"I've got Tylenol in the medicine cabinet."

"I'll take some when I'm done eating. Don't take this the wrong way, but I don't know how you do it."

His eyebrows rose above his glasses. "Do what?"

Wayne wasn't generally the type to get his feelings hurt, so it was never an issue to discuss his disability with him.

"You know. You being the way you are but still being ten times more in shape than I am."

"You do know I exercise every morning before work."

"I did some pushups once."

He rolled his eyes at her. "It's never too late to start working out. We can even do it together sometime, if you'd like." He winked.

She pretended to swat at him. "In your dreams."

"Frequently."

The kitchen felt much too hot all of a sudden.

"You know," Wayne continued, "if you really want to get your parents all riled up, you can tell them you're shacking up with a nice older man who wears pastels and gets his nails done every month."

"They know you're not gay."

"I know—that's what would rile them up. Do they know you got evicted?"

"No."

"You should probably let them know."

"They've barely even talked to me since they moved to Indianapolis last year."

His expression softened. "Their loss."

"Yeah, well, it's fine with me." Jessica's stomach tightened. Her entire life had been spent trying to win her parents' approval.

Stephen Roman-Dell taught university-level economics, and Maria Roman-Dell was an accountant like Wayne. She had even worked with him at Reynolds and Korman until both she and Stephen found better work and moved away. Jessica's mother had the chronic inability to show affection, and her father's mind was generally off in the stratosphere somewhere, dreaming of the New York Stock Exchange.

Like many parents, they'd wanted her to be like them. She took great pleasure in denying them the honor.

Jessica and Wayne finished lunch in silence.

"I've been thinking." Wayne rose to put his plate in the dishwasher.

"Uh-oh," Jessica said with a smile.

"No, no, hear me out. You want your YouTube channel to do better, right? So maybe you should start investigating local famous places, and then when people search for them online, your channel will come up. I've heard that Bobby Mackey's and Promont House both offer ghost tours."

"I know, but those have both been done a million times already. Same with Music Hall and The Golden Lamb. I want to do something *different*."

"Keyword search," Wayne said in an ethereal tone, waggling his fingers like a magician.

He did have a point.

"I suppose I could do both," she said. "Mix in the famous places with the unknown ones."

"You've got to admit that 'The Ghosts of Music Hall' sounds more compelling than 'The Ghosts of Ellen Shoushanian's House.' No offense to Ellen."

"True…"

"And if I may offer one minor criticism?"

Jessica was immediately on her guard. "About what?"

"I watch every single video you post. You've been trying hard, I know. But sometimes it comes across like you're trying *too* hard."

"But I have to try hard!" she objected. "How else am I going to get where I want to be?"

"I know you have to try hard," Wayne said. "I get it. But I think your videos will seem more genuine to other viewers if you just try to be yourself."

She blinked at him. Hadn't she *been* being herself? She wasn't putting on funny accents or using pretentious words. Jessica was even using her real name, for goodness' sake!

"You look confused," he said.

"I *am* confused."

Wayne let out a breath. "How do I put it? Just act like you're sitting here, talking to me. And maybe do an introductory video so your subscribers can get a feel for who you are. I really think it will help you."

Jessica chewed on her lip. "I didn't know you were such an expert on this sort of thing."

"Haven't you guessed? I watch a *lot* of YouTube videos."

5

Sidney hadn't arrived home from work yet, so Jessica set up a camcorder on a tripod in their now-shared bedroom and sat down on a chair in front of it so her head would appear in the center of the frame. She cleared her throat—she would edit that part out later—and began to speak.

"Hey, everyone! It's Jessica Roman-Dell, your Friendly Neighborhood Ghost Hunter." She paused, thinking. Just be herself? Here went nothing. "It's a weird day. Sometimes when you think you've got it all figured out, something happens that makes you take a step backward. Things look different from a different standpoint."

Stop rambling, she told herself. *People will get bored.*

"I want this channel to succeed so badly," she continued. "It's my passion, but I've only got ninety-seven subscribers because I just don't know how to make interesting content. A friend of mine has some ideas for me. I trust him, so I'll give them a try. And if anyone watching wants to offer feedback on my videos, please tell me in the comments. Thanks."

Jessica flashed a grin, rose, and stopped the camcorder, then changed into a different shirt, brushed out her hair, moved her chair two feet to the right, and shifted the tripod accordingly. She set the camcorder to record again.

"Hey, everyone! It's Jessica Roman-Dell, your Friendly Neighborhood

Ghost Hunter. I'm not hunting any ghosts at the moment, so I just thought I'd take a little time to properly introduce myself. I'm twenty-one years old and live in Eleanor, Ohio. You'll find it on the Ohio River, east of Cincinnati. It's one of those places where everyone knows everyone else. It's not the richest town, and it hit everyone hard when the bottling plant closed, but it's home.

"I've been interested in ghosts for as long as I can remember. Some of my favorite movies growing up were *Beetlejuice* and *The Shining*. I'm Catholic, so we believe there's an afterlife—I personally believe it's in another dimension, but don't tell the pope that—but what if there's an afterlife here on Earth too? A place where souls get left behind to roam the paths they followed in life. Those paths might be in a fancy old restaurant, a popular concert hall, or even your own living room.

"That's my goal with this channel. I want to prove that ghosts exist. And to do that, I'm going to find one. If you're with me, please like and subscribe. Thank you."

Jessica's cell phone rang as soon as she finished speaking. She let out a nervous breath—that had been a close one!—stopped the camera, and answered it. "Hi, Rachel! What's up?"

"Hey, Jess!" came the voice of her older sister, Rachel Schellenberger, who lived hundreds of miles away in one of the suburbs of New York City. Rachel had changed apartments so many times in the past five years, Jessica could never remember where she currently lived. "How's it going?"

"I asked first."

"I'm older than you."

"Fine. I still haven't found a job, and I just got evicted from my apartment."

"Aw, you should have told me! I'd have lent you some money."

"I don't want to be a burden on you guys. I'll be okay."

"Sure. Who are you staying with? I'm assuming you're staying with someone and not in a shelter somewhere. Oh my God, you're not in a shelter, are you?"

"I'm *fine*, Rachel! I'm bunking with Wayne and Sidney until my luck turns. I'm hoping I'll be able to get my apartment back someday. Fingers crossed."

"Oh, good." Rachel sounded relieved. "So, are you and Wayne…?"

"No."

"That was a succinct answer, if I've ever heard one."

"We're not dating, Rachel. He's just a friend."

"Who you're now sharing a house with. But I digress! I wanted to know if you're coming to the family reunion on Saturday, the twenty-third. Uncle Esteban says we can wear costumes if we want."

Jessica narrowed her eyes. "What family reunion?"

"The Reyes reunion. Mom and Dad are going. It's at Campbell Community Park over in Campbell County. Didn't you get an invite? It starts at noon."

"It must have gotten lost in the mail."

"That figures. But you'd better be there because Eric and I are coming into town for it, and we haven't seen you in ages. We'll probably do some house-hunting while we're here too."

Jessica's heart made a joyful flip. "You're moving back to Ohio?"

"Or northern Kentucky. The city's getting too expensive, and we didn't think it would be the best place to raise a baby, besides."

Now Jessica's mouth fell open. "You are *not* pregnant."

"Ten weeks today!"

"Rachel, this is great!"

"I know! It was our first month trying too. We got to hear the heartbeat at my last appointment. Let me tell you, it is *weird* to think there's an actual human in there. I'm like one of those Russian dolls, or something."

"Or a character in one of those *Alien* movies. Your kid will burst out of your stomach and spray blood across the dinner table when you least expect it."

"Okay, I did *not* need that imagery in my head." Rachel paused, and Jessica could hear other voices in the background. "Hey, I've got to get back to work. Eric and I are flying out there on Thursday, the twenty-first, and we'll be staying with Uncle Esteban and Aunt Sharon for the weekend. I'll call you when we get in, okay?"

"Sounds good to me. Love you, and congrats."

"Love you too, Jess. See you next Thursday."

Jessica stood in the kitchen, rummaging for snacks, when Sidney stormed through the front door and slung her black, faux-leather purse onto the countertop so hard it knocked over a couple of pill bottles and an empty cup.

"Bad day at work?" Jessica asked.

Sidney's face was the color of a beet. "Travis was being Travis again."

Travis was the proprietor of American Dream Truck Stop—and the very man who'd laid Jessica off.

"What do you mean?" Jessica asked.

"He got all weirdly religious on me when I mentioned that it was two years ago yesterday that Mom found out she had brain cancer."

"Weirdly religious?"

Sidney sat down at the table. Tears brimmed in her eyes. "We had a customer that looked a little like Mom today. And Travis said that maybe it was a sign from God that Mom was okay somewhere."

"Um...okay."

"And then I told him that I didn't think Mom was *anywhere* other than in...than in her casket. And he told me Mom would be sad that I thought that way."

"Oh, Sidney." Jessica leaned in and hugged her friend. She hadn't known Sidney's mom for long before she got sick, but the woman had been kind. "I'm really sorry."

Sidney balled her hands into fists. "None of it's fair."

"Are you really mad at Travis, or are you mad at the cancer?"

"What, can't it be both? I'm going to my room." Sidney paused. "I mean, *our* room."

It was hard to miss the bitter tone in Sidney's voice. Jessica swallowed. Was it wrong that Wayne had let Jessica stay here? What else was she supposed to do?

Jessica took a bag of chips and her laptop out to the living room to start reviewing the audio files from last night's investigation. It was possible her equipment had picked up something her ears hadn't heard.

Five minutes into reliving the previous evening, Jessica's phone rang again. The number of the incoming call began with "859": Northern Kentucky. Was one of her extended relatives calling to see if she planned on coming to the reunion?

She held the phone to her ear. "Hello?"

There came a few staticky clicks. "Hi, is this Jessica Roman-Dell?" asked a congested, elderly sounding man.

Her brow furrowed. "Yes, this is she. I'm really sorry, but who is this?"

"My name's Al Tumler. My sister gave me your number."

"Who's your sister?"

"Ellen Shoushanian. She says you investigate hauntings?"

"I do!" Jessica felt her chest lighten. "I have a YouTube channel called Friendly Neighborhood Ghost Hunter. I post a lot of stuff on there."

"Have you seen a lot of ghosts?"

"To tell you the truth? No. Sometimes I see weird orbs on my videos, or hear unexplained voices, but that's about it."

The man's soft chuckle turned into a gut-wracking cough that flooded the phone line for the next ten seconds. He cleared his throat. "Sorry about that. Woke up this morning with the granddaddy of all colds. I presided over a funeral earlier today and have been in bed ever since."

"I'm sorry to hear that."

"I'll be okay, young lady. But I was going to say, I'm the pastor at the United Methodist Church just south of Iron Springs. A lot of folks around here think the church grounds are haunted. Specifically, the graveyard."

"That doesn't seem too unusual."

"You've got to understand, it's not just people getting the spooks out there for no reason. Some have seen orbs, like you said. Some see moving shadows, with nothing around to cause them. I've had three different people tell me they saw a black figure, and others have said they feel like someone is watching them when there isn't anyone there."

His description sounded typical of many so-called hauntings. Jessica scrambled for a pen and a scrap of paper, then started to jot down notes.

"Is there any particular time of day when these things tend to happen?" she asked.

"Not really."

"Have you ever experienced anything personally?"

"Not me, but my daughter swore she saw a shadow shaped like a person standing by the church steps a couple years back and snapped a picture on her cell phone, but the shadow person didn't show up."

"Interesting. Is there any history about the church I should be aware of? Untimely deaths, that kind of thing?"

"I don't think so. The church has been around awhile, so who knows."

"I'm assuming you'd like for me to come out there and check things out?"

"If you want to. Ellen said you're trying to make money with this YouTube thing, and I thought I'd lend a hand. You can come out any weeknight. Tonight's fine too, but I won't be there to show you around. Got to take care of this cold before it takes care of me, if you know what I mean."

"I don't have any plans tonight. What's your church's address?"

"It's 876 Hill Road, just south of Iron Springs, like I said. There shouldn't be anyone out there to bother you on a Tuesday night like this. The funeral was over around noon."

"I'll bring my pepper spray, just in case there is."

"Sounds like you've got a good head on your shoulders. But still, be careful out there."

"I will. And Mr. Tumler?"

"Yes?"

"If I do capture footage of ghosts, do you want me to show you?"

"No need. Ellen showed me what to do—I've already subscribed to your channel."

6

As per custom, when she went up to the bedroom to collect her ghost hunting equipment, Jessica tried to persuade Sidney to come along with her.

Sidney, sitting on her bed with a crochet pattern book in her lap and a partially finished crocheted pumpkin in her hands, only lifted her gaze and gave Jessica a piercing stare over the tops of her purple-framed glasses.

"Fine," Jessica said, shouldering her black zippered tote bag. "Be that way."

Sidney rolled her eyes, which were still puffy from crying. "Just be careful, okay?"

"I always am."

The muscles in Jessica's legs protested as she descended the stairs. Not wanting to spend the rest of the evening in pain, she made a detour into the bathroom and swiped a bottle of Tylenol out of the medicine cabinet. She washed two of the pills down with a glass of water and shoved the bottle into her purse.

In the car, she switched on a classic rock station and backed out of the driveway. This might not have been the lofty investigation Wayne thought might boost her channel views, but it sounded much more interesting than squatting in a basement for hours. With as sore as she still felt from moving furniture, she didn't think her body would ever uncramp again.

Jessica glanced at the directions she'd printed off the computer prior to leaving. The highway merged with the interstate several miles up ahead. Then, once she was in Kentucky, she would take the Route 9 exit and follow that all the way out to Hill Road.

As the crow flew, Eleanor and Iron Springs were separated by less than half a mile of river. It took Jessica fifty-five minutes to reach Hill Road.

Hill Road headed due south. Like its name promised, the road—marked by a signpost bent to a forty-five-degree angle by some unfortunate motorist—ascended a steep incline for a quarter-mile and then leveled out into meandering curves.

The woods grew so thick on either side of the road, Jessica had the feeling she was driving down a long, leafy tunnel. She'd spotted a single ranch-style home nestled among golden maples shortly after she made the turn, but other than that, there was no indication anyone had set foot in this part of the tri-state before.

"Kentucky: The Final Frontier," she said to herself. "I claim this land in the name of Roman-Dell."

A white sign on the righthand side of the road came into view after a couple of miles. "Irons Springs United Methodist Church," read the black script stenciled above the service schedule. A battered mailbox emblazoned with the number "876" stood sentry by a blacktopped lane disappearing into the woods.

She swung the car onto the lane. This had to be the most isolated church on Planet Earth. There wasn't even a parsonage in sight. Al Tumler must have been a commuter.

Two-tenths of a mile later, the lane opened out into a vacant parking lot where the faded pavement was interlaced with a web of cracks, some of which had been patched with black squiggles of sealer. To the left loomed an ancient red-brick church bearing a white steeple and stained glass windows. The worn date on the cornerstone looked like it might have said "1862."

To the right, on the opposite side of the parking lot, sat the graveyard Al Tumler had spoken of on the phone. Like Hill Road, all was encircled by a thick expanse of trees looking as though they might have continued forever.

Jessica selected a parking space close to the chain-link fence surrounding the graveyard and shut off the engine. She took a few bites from a granola bar she'd stowed away in her purse, staring at the headstones while she chewed. The closest ones jutted from the earth at haphazard angles, like they'd grown tired over time and slouched to the side to rest. Even from the short distance, she could barely read their epitaphs. They must have been about as old as the church.

She wadded up the granola bar wrapper, stuffed it into her jeans pocket, and crammed her purse into her equipment bag. Time to get down to business.

Unexpected stillness echoed in her ears the instant she stepped outside. At home, the ambient sound of traffic on U.S. 52 could be heard rumbling by most times of the day, but here, the only sounds were the wind and a twittering bird sitting on a branch high in a tree. The forest must have swallowed all other sounds before they could reach her ears.

Leaving her bag on the hood of the car, she held up her digital camera and snapped a few pictures of the front and sides of the old church, then the parking lot and lane. Tomorrow, she would go through each of the images on her computer to see if they'd produced anything unusual.

She returned to her bag and swapped out the digital camera for her camcorder, which she switched on and propped on top of the hood. "Hi, everyone! It's Jessica, your Friendly Neighborhood Ghost Hunter. Today, I'm at the Iron Springs United Methodist Church in northern Kentucky. The pastor here called me and said there have been sightings of orbs and shadow figures, so I'm here to check it out.

It's pretty isolated here, so I don't expect there to be any interf—"

A wave of nausea hit her like a sucker punch to the gut. Jessica doubled over, battling her stomach's overwhelming urge to empty its meager contents onto the pavement. It took all her strength to keep her granola bar where it belonged. Was she coming down with the stomach flu?

Jessica swallowed a mouthful of saliva. No sooner had she done so than the world around her bathed itself in shades of deep red, as if she were looking through a pair of crimson-tinted sunglasses. A distinct sensation of rage crashed over her like a tidal wave drowning the shore. Her hands clenched into tight fists. She had to *kill*...

The bizarre spell passed with the abruptness by which it had begun. The red aura faded away, and her stomach stopped twisting in her abdomen. Rubbing her sweating forehead, she realized the camcorder was still recording.

"Um...hi," she said awkwardly, even though the video was saving to a memory card and not broadcasting to a live audience somewhere. "I'm not really sure what happened just now—I've never had anything like it happen before."

Her heart thudded in excitement. Maybe this was an actual paranormal phenomenon!

"I've done a lot of research on the paranormal these past few years. Some people believe that powerful emotions can be imprinted on the place where they were felt. Maybe a haunted hospital feels full of sorrow, for example. If that's true, then someone stood here once, feeling a rage so deep that they wanted to murder someone. And maybe they did."

She stepped forward and switched off the camcorder.

"Holy shit." Jessica blinked in the evening sunlight and put a hand on her stomach. It was like the nausea had never been there.

Deciding here was a good place to officially start investigating, Jessica slid out a voice recorder and switched it on. "Hi there," she said to the air. "I could feel anger just now. Is there someone here, or was it just an echo? Please tell me, if you can." She let the recorder run for another twenty seconds before turning it back off, planning on using it more once she'd gotten the rest of her things set up.

Jessica rubbed her hands together, trying to reorient herself to reality. Her body did still ache, in spite of the Tylenol, but she would just have to live with it until the first dose wore off. Picking up the camcorder, she pointed it toward the graveyard itself and turned it back on. She would get as much footage on this as she could while there was still enough daylight, then she'd switch over to the night vision model.

Up ahead was a rectangular heap of dirt with bouquets of lilies and chrysanthemums stacked neatly at one end—no doubt from the funeral Al Tumler had mentioned. She panned the camera to the left and then to the right.

Her heart rattled as it skipped a beat.

She was not alone.

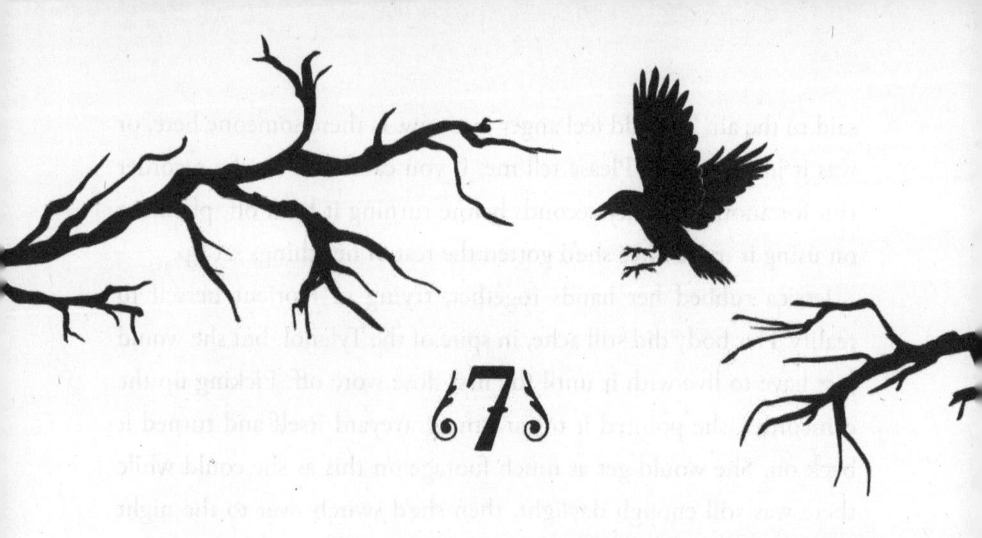

7

A solitary man dressed in the dark shades of mourning slouched on a concrete bench, seemingly unaware he had company. He must have stayed behind after the funeral, too stricken to go home and start life without his loved one.

Quietly, Jessica lowered the camera and tucked it back into her tote bag. It might be rude to investigate while the man was still here—Al Tumler wouldn't have known someone would stay so long after the funeral ended. But if the man had been here long enough, he might have seen some of the shadows or orbs, or even experienced the strange echo of rage she'd felt in the parking lot.

She made her way toward the man on the bench, trying to ignore the nagging pains in her muscles. "Excuse me," she said when she was about ten yards away from him.

The man gave no indication of having heard her. She couldn't see his face—was he asleep or stone deaf?

She continued toward him. "Hi! Sir?"

He neither turned around nor flinched.

Jessica's approach brought her up to his left side. "Hello!" she said, waving to get his attention. "Can you hear me?"

The man swiveled his head in her direction. His icy blue eyes widened. "You were talking to me?" he asked in the soft voice of someone who spent much of their time browsing a library. He couldn't have been that old—maybe mid-thirties at the most. His dark brown hair was disheveled, like he'd forgotten to run a comb through it before the funeral, and he wore a black button-up shirt and black slacks that desperately needed ironing. Two prominent dark circles below his eyes spoke of a chronic lack of sleep.

Jessica gave him what she hoped was an understanding smile. "Who else would I be talking to out here?"

"I've seen people talking on phones. You do the math."

He had a point.

"I'm sorry to bother you."

"It's okay." He glanced down at his hands, which lay folded in his lap. A partially healed gash sealed together with three black medical stitches marred the back of his left hand.

Jessica felt an inexplicable sense of unease at the sight of the wound. "I can leave, if you want me to."

A faint smile lit up his pale face. "You're not bothering me. Quite the opposite, in fact."

"Are you sure? I thought you might be paying your respects."

He gave her a quizzical look.

"The pastor told me there was a funeral today," she added.

"Oh, that. It wasn't anyone I knew."

Then why was he here? "So...do you come here often, then?" she asked, having taken a step in reverse without at first realizing she'd done so.

"You might say that. What's in your bag?"

Jessica unconsciously slid the canvas straps higher on her shoulder. She hoped he wouldn't try to take it from her. "It's got my equipment in it. I'm hunting for ghosts."

"You're kidding."

"Nope! I've got a thermal imaging camera, K2 meter, camcorders, voice recorders... You name it, I've probably got it. I'm trying to grow my channel on YouTube."

A crease appeared in the man's forehead. "What's that?"

"YouTube? It's a website where people upload videos. It's been up for about five years now, but I know it's going to get even bigger. If my channel gets enough followers and views, YouTube will start paying me. I'd like for it to be my full-time job."

"Right," he said after a long pause. "And you think finding a ghost will make this happen."

"It can't hurt. I've got to give my viewers something exciting so they keep coming back for more."

"What sort of thing would you consider exciting?"

"You know, ghostly lights, shadows, apparitions, disembodied voices, that kind of thing. A few months ago, I was investigating a house out in Ripley and recorded a voice saying, 'Let me out!' It's gotten the most views out of anything I've posted."

"And how many is that?"

"About five hundred. I don't know if it was a ghost or not, but I don't have any other explanation for it."

The man seemed to mull this over for a moment or two. "I don't mean to insult you, but I can think of far more exciting things than spooky voices."

"Such as?"

He smiled. "You could come across severed limbs, bleeding torsos, entrails spread across the ground…"

Jessica took another involuntary step back from him. "I hope to God I don't find anything like that out here."

"Don't worry. Tonight you won't. What's your name?"

Jessica briefly considered inventing an alias for the evening, in case the guy was a psychopath, but instead, she opted for honesty. "I'm Jessica Roman-Dell. And you are?"

"Jerry Madison." He did not offer a handshake. "How will you know if you've found a ghost?"

"If I find a bunch of glowing orbs floating in the air, I'll know for sure it isn't the birds and squirrels doing it."

"An excellent deduction."

"Are you making fun of me?"

"Why would I do that?"

"I don't know. A lot of people think ghost hunting is bogus. Like chasing a fairytale."

He nodded. "That's understandable. I never used to believe in it myself. There's heaven, there's hell, and nothing in between but this lousy lump of rock we call home." He gave a short laugh. "And Earth might as well be a hell in itself. What did you say your name is?"

Jessica hesitated. "I told you already."

"Jessica, yes. What's your last name?"

"It's Roman-Dell."

"Is that common?"

"I doubt it. The only Roman-Dells I know are my immediate family."

"Interesting." Jerry remained silent for several moments. "Why did you decide to look for ghosts?"

"Because I want to grow my—"

"Channel, yes. But why ghosts? Why not aliens, or Bigfoot, or skin-walkers? Or baking, even?"

Jessica laughed. "I'm a terrible cook, skin-walkers don't live around here, I don't believe in Bigfoot, and if aliens exist, they're too far away to ever get to Earth, so there's no point in trying to find one."

"But why *ghosts*?" he pressed.

She thought about it. Why, indeed? "It's just something that's always struck a chord with me. I'm drawn to it like...like a moth to a flame, or something. I think it's neat that souls can linger behind on Earth after death. There's so much they could tell us, if we could only hear them."

A flash of hurt appeared in Jerry's icy eyes. "'Neat.' I haven't heard that one before."

"Maybe that wasn't the best way to put it. So, um, I'm going to start investigating now. It was nice talking to you."

"Have fun," he said. "I won't stop you."

Well, that was a relief. Quelling her nervousness when she turned her back to him, she retreated to another cement bench she'd spotted close to the back part of the cemetery, where gnarled pines grew just yards away from the last row of headstones.

Jessica set her tote bag on the bench beside her and rummaged through it. She pulled her cellphone, pepper spray, and keys out of her concealed purse and shoved them into the pocket of her sweatshirt, in case she needed to make a hasty getaway.

Jerry still hadn't budged from his seat and looked as if he had no immediate plans to leave. What if he was a predator, waiting for his next unassuming victim? Other than the pepper spray and maybe the car keys, she had no way to protect herself if he tried to make a move on her. She could kick and shout and maybe hold him off for a minute, if he knocked her pepper spray out of her hand, but in the end, no one would hear her screams.

Another thing nagging at her thoughts was, her piece-of-junk Taurus was the only vehicle in the entire parking lot. That meant Jerry had walked here, and for what purpose? To sit and stare at concrete crosses and angels for hours on end?

His voice repeated itself in her memory. *You could come across severed limbs, bleeding torsos, entrails spread across the ground…Don't worry. Tonight you won't.*

What the hell was *that* supposed to mean? Would she have found such carnage here on some other night? Was Jerry a modern-day Ted Bundy, who lured women to their grisly deaths? What a convenient place to hide the bodies.

Maybe she should just call it quits and come back another day.

But it took you an hour to get here, whined a small voice inside her. *It'll take you another hour to get back, and then your whole evening would be wasted.*

Well…she should probably just get started. She'd keep an eye on him, though.

With the stubborn resolve of a Roman-Dell, Jessica went about setting up her equipment. One voice recorder went on top of a headstone bearing the name: "Edna Schultz (1912 to 1953)." Next, she placed a camcorder on the ground next to the gravel path and angled it so anything walking by would be in full view on the recording.

Jessica turned on her second voice recorder. "Today is Tuesday, October 12, 2010. I'm investigating a haunting at the United Methodist Church near Iron Springs, Kentucky. You can hear more details on the video I took a few minutes ago. I'm going to see if there are any electromagnetic waves present that might be tied to the rage-echo out at the parking lot."

Electromagnetic waves could be emitted by power lines and other electronic devices and had been known to instill a "creeped-out" feeling in some people who encountered them. Many "hauntings" had been attributed to this phenomenon, and for all she knew, it could have caused her to feel sick and hallucinate the red aura.

The setting sun cast long, headstone-shaped shadows that spread over the ground like reaching fingers. Pocketing the recorder, she glanced over at Jerry to make sure he wasn't creeping up on her.

Her breath caught in her throat.

It might have been a trick of the fading light, but it looked like a bluish-purple bruise encircled the man's neck like a gruesome collar, and his face appeared to be covered in dark splotches of broken blood vessels. She squinted to get a better look, and to her relief—though this relief was slim—Jerry appeared unharmed. His gaze drifted in her direction. He gave her a nod of acknowledgment.

As much as she was glad to see Jerry was all in one piece and she wasn't sharing the graveyard with a very fresh, unburied corpse, she couldn't shake her unease. Why wouldn't he just go home? Night was falling, and she had no desire to be alone with him in the dark.

She finished setting up her equipment five minutes later. One last look at the bench told her Jerry had finally left.

Thank God.

She hung the strap of the thermal imaging camera around her neck and made a few laps around the rectangular path while looking at the screen. The sound of her feet crunching in the loose gravel sounded as loud as gunshots in the still air.

Jessica panned the camera back and forth. If the device was going to be her primary indicator of graveyard spirits, she was out of luck. No uncharacteristically cold spots showed up on the screen, and the only major heat signatures the thing picked up were in the shape of two deer grazing near the church. The front of her car glowed orange on the screen, still warm from the trip here.

She planted her rear in the crunchy grass beside the path, got out her night vision camera, and pointed it at her face. "So, not much has happened since my experience right when I got here," she said in a loud whisper, for dramatic effect. "In a few minutes, I'm going to check for EMFs, but first, I'm going to ask some questions to see if any spirits will answer."

She cleared her throat and spoke a little louder, but in a gentle tone.

"Hello! My name is Jessica. I want to be your friend, so don't be scared. I'm from just across the river, and I came here tonight to see if we could talk."

Jessica counted off fifteen seconds in her head before continuing. She could edit out the pause before uploading the finished video.

"This graveyard seems like a lonely place. Kind of ironic, right? There's at least two hundred graves here. That's at least two hundred different lives, full of hopes and dreams and sorrows, come to a quiet end. Are you one of them?"

While she waited for a ghost to reply, she peered toward the woods. They seemed so dark. A person might wander in there and never come out again.

"People say there's a heaven," Jessica said. "I don't see why not; the universe is huge and full of unanswered questions. Maybe some physicist will find it someday without dying first. But if there *is* a heaven, why are you still here? Do you have unfinished business?"

Her phone chimed, and she dug it out of her pocket. Sidney had sent her a text message.

Storm coming through around 9:30, it read. Be careful.

"Shit." Jessica hadn't thought to check the forecast. It had barely rained in ages, and it had to do it tonight?

She looked up at the sky. Stars were beginning to appear directly overhead, but off to the west loomed a thick bank of clouds. A sudden gust of wind caressed her with chilly air.

Thanks for the heads-up, she replied.

"That's an interesting device," said a voice right behind her.

Her blood froze.

It was Jerry Madison.

8

Jessica managed to get her feet back under her and whirled around to face the man. He stood barely three feet away from her, so he must have walked through the grass between the headstones to have approached so silently.

She stuck her hand in her pocket and closed her trembling fingers around the pepper spray. "What do you want?" she asked, stepping away from him.

His eyes looked wild, as if he were on the verge of hysteria. "I've been listening to you talk. You seem very kind."

"Thanks." Jessica didn't dare let her guard down. Jerry had *hidden* from her and waited until she'd been distracted to make his move, which clearly meant nothing good.

"I mean it," he said. His unkempt hair and rumpled clothes frightened her all the more, and she couldn't have said why. "You're kind. Unless it's a lie, but I don't think so."

"I…"

His mouth twisted into a thin-lipped smile. "Are you scared?"

Jessica said nothing. She wondered if she felt as terrified as Ted Bundy's victims during their final moments. Then, cursing herself for thinking of something so ghastly, she nodded.

"Why?" he asked.

"You're going to hurt me."

"Have I given you any reason to think that?" He drew closer to her, his footsteps making no sound.

"What—what else would you be doing out here?"

He folded his arms almost casually and frowned. "You wouldn't understand. I've had a very complicated life."

"Me too, but you don't see me sneaking up on people like this. You want to hurt me."

"If I had planned on hurting you, I wouldn't be standing here, talking."

"Then what do you *want*?"

Jerry reached out as if to touch her, then drew his hand back. "You have no idea what it's like, sitting here day after day after day, knowing that everyone and everything has moved on without you."

"Okay…?"

He spread his arms wide. "Don't you get it, Jessica? This has been my universe for longer than I even know. Sure, I could have left whenever I wanted, but where would I have gone? Heaven?" His laugh sounded bitter. "Don't give me that look. You've gotten exactly what you asked for."

"I don't know what you mean," she stammered. Though she longed to flee, Jessica had become rooted in place, like some stupid damsel doomed to die in the first ten minutes of a horror movie.

He gave her an almost pitying look. "You can quit playing dumb, Jessica."

"Stop saying my name!"

"What did you expect, a dirty sheet with holes cut out for eyes? I'm a *human being*, and I need help."

Jessica swallowed. "Help?"

"Yes! You can see me, Jessica. Keep me company. You can make my punishment more bearable."

"I don't think so!"

Jessica broke into a run. Jerry threw himself at her and hooked his arms around her neck, but instead of dragging her down, he had no weight to him. Which meant…*Oh.*

Jessica clawed at him. It was like trying to snatch fog out of the air. "Get off of me!" she snarled. Her first real encounter with the dead wasn't supposed to be like *this.* He was *attacking* her, for crying out loud!

Jerry hung on tight. Her skin tingled with a biting chill where he touched her. Without thinking, she tore off in the direction of her car, letting out whimpering moans with each footfall. She arrived next to her car, gasping. A mercury vapor lamp next to the church provided enough light for her to see that no weightless man accompanied her.

When had he released his grip? Had he even been there at all? Of course he had. A lingering iciness raised gooseflesh on her neck.

Jessica dug her keys from her pocket and succeeded in opening the car door without dropping them from her shaking hands. Once inside, she slapped the automatic lock button. She leaned back and closed her eyes, willing herself to breathe.

The foolishness of her actions hit her then. A person devoid of flesh and blood could pass through metal and glass as easily as she moved through the air.

A voice spoke by the window. "Please help me, Jessica. I don't want to be here anymore. Surely, you can understand that."

She peered out the window to try to pinpoint his location. All she could see were headstones and trees. No black-clothed figure lurked in her field of view.

A part of her wanted to stride back outside and start over with Jerry. So, he was a ghost. Which was exactly what she'd been looking for, right? Then why was she so damned frightened?

Before she could make a decision, the car dissolved around her in a burst of red. She was sinking into an ocean comprised of blood. Voices shouted in the distance, as if she and those speaking stood at opposite ends of a vast canyon.

¡Mataste a mi nieta!

¡Vete a la verga!

Though Jessica knew some Spanish due to the Reyes in her blood—her mother was half Mexican—the overwhelming sense of terror that had taken hold of her suppressed her ability to understand the words.

The sea of red morphed into shadowy faces lit from behind. She could feel their emotions like they were her own. Pain. Grief. *Hatred.* All directed at her.

She didn't want to see the faces. If she didn't look away, they would get inside her head and nest there like rats, gnawing away her sanity piece by tattered piece.

Make it stop, she prayed. *Make it stop, make it stop, make it—*

Everything around her grew darker. The faces had gone. She tried to straighten herself out but found she could barely move—she was trapped in a small, enclosed space, like a casket.

Panicking, Jessica sat up and cracked her head on something solid. The glove box! She must have hunkered on the passenger side floor mat, as if that would protect her from restless spirits.

A low rumble of thunder rattled her eardrums. Sidney had said the storm would arrive around 9:30, which meant Jessica had been unconscious for two hours, maybe longer.

She should leave this godforsaken place before another—vision? Hallucination? Whatever she wanted to call it—knocked her out again. The only problem was, all her equipment still sat around in various places outside. She couldn't just leave it all behind; it had cost her thousands of dollars, and she couldn't afford to replace everything.

Jessica had to retrieve it.

She began to sweat.

Jessica looked toward the driver side window. From her crouched position on the passenger side floor, she could only see a swatch of indigo sky. It wasn't raining yet, but it would start soon.

A scraping sound nearby made her jump. "It's just a raccoon," she said to herself. "It found some trash, or something."

Something made a soft thump. It was nothing. It *had* to be nothing. Maybe only the wind, which gusted stronger with each passing minute.

Jessica picked herself off the floor and climbed back behind the wheel. Wind, she could handle. She stared out at the headstones. Nothing moved.

A drop of rain splattered on the windshield and rolled down the glass in a lazy zigzag. Then a second, and a third.

She gritted her teeth. If she didn't hurry and rescue her equipment, her YouTube channel was doomed.

"God help me," she said and clambered out of the car. She tripped over something and fell to her knees. A corpse! No, not a corpse. It was her bulging tote bag, which had transported itself here all the way from the back of the graveyard and filled back up with her equipment too, by the feel of it.

Jerry must have dragged it across the ground for her: the source of the scraping noise.

Jessica carried the bag around to the back of the car and set it on top of the trunk so she could see it better in the lamplight. Dirt and bits of dead leaves clung to the fabric. She brushed it away and undid the zipper.

All her cameras and recorders were nestled neatly inside, as were her purse and Maglite. She let out a breath that wasn't quite relief.

"I guess I owe you one," she said quietly, though how to pay back a dead man was beyond her.

9

1986

His captors drove in silence, and the silence drove him mad. If they'd turn the radio on again, the music might drown out the imagined sound of seconds ticking down to his final moments, but he wouldn't ask them to. They wouldn't have listened.

He had no clue where they were taking him. Somehow, that seemed immaterial. It didn't matter if they killed him in a warehouse or a cornfield—they'd still get what they wanted, and he would still be dead.

As much as he loathed himself for it, he couldn't stop thinking about Abigail. She'd been the inciting incident leading to all of this. If he hadn't met her, he might be married to someone else. Some nice woman who didn't throw dishes and cutlery at him.

He'd be asleep right now, lying on his side with her warm body snuggled up against his chest, and their children—he was sure there would have been two or three of them—would be asleep in the next room, dreaming of sugar plums or whatever kids dreamed about. If he hadn't met Abigail, he certainly wouldn't be stuffed in the back of a car like a slab of meat with his own executioners.

Abigail had been a secretary at the high school where he got his first job. He would never forget the moment he first saw her standing in the office. Her hair was golden, her skin fair as the snow. Her hips swayed with a captivating seductiveness when she walked.

Abigail seemed friendly at first. She paid attention to him, listened to his dreams and he to hers. He'd been blind with infatuation and failed to notice anything amiss.

When he married her, he'd foreseen none of the marital strife that was to come: the fights, the threats, and the tears; the manic highs and the rock-bottom lows; the brutal name-calling and the shattered plates lying like rubble on the kitchen floor.

He'd been a young fool in love, and now, he'd give anything in the universe to rewind the tape of his life and do it over differently.

The car drove over a bump in the road, and his thoughts returned to the present. He flexed the muscles in his shoulders. The tape had been bound so tightly around his wrists, his fingers had gone numb.

He didn't blame his captors for wanting to kill him. After all, he'd made them angry—though what he had done brought him more relief than anyone could ever allow themselves to understand.

He would never have to see those faces again. If he'd had the opportunity to continue, he'd have done so without a moment's pause. The world teemed with faces. Grinning faces. Taunting faces. Faces mocking him in his sorrow and reminding him of what might have been.

He hadn't *wanted* to do it; it was simply a matter of necessity. But when all was said and done and he'd stared down at their lifeless bodies and stuffed the gun back into his pocket, he knew he'd done the right thing.

The big question nagging at him was how his captors had known it was him. He'd made sure each of the faces lay still, and the dead do not tattle on those who kill them. Perhaps the bullets had been traced to his weapon, but in that case, shouldn't there have been a warrant out for his arrest? Breaking into his house wouldn't have been necessary. They could have just knocked on the door with the warrant in hand, read him his rights, and hauled him away.

This could only mean the police had gone above the law and aided in his abduction.

He cursed himself for not having chosen a different weapon. Perhaps he could have used a golf club or a sharp knife; he owned both. However, those were more suitable for a single killing. The use of those weapons would have given the others the freedom to flee, allowing them to torment him another day—and the thought of that horrified him more than his impending death. The faces! Oh, the faces…

The car turned off the road and was now bumping along a gravel lane. Their destination couldn't be too much farther ahead now, since gravel lanes tended to dead-end.

The car slowed to a stop. His emotions bordered on the edge of panic. This was it: the end of the road.

Placing mind over matter in a last-chance attempt to wriggle from between his captors, he squirmed around like a dying worm and received a fist in the nose for his effort. Blood trickled from his nostrils and over his lip. The taste nearly gagged him.

The car door opened. The captor on the left grabbed him under the armpits and dragged him out onto the solid ground. The scent of fresh asphalt filled the air.

More car doors slammed. The rest of the intruders who'd escorted him from his house must have taken another vehicle, and now all seven of them were regrouping to take care of him.

He could only hope whatever they planned on doing wouldn't take very long because he imagined it wouldn't be gentle.

10

2010

Sidney waited at the living room window, anxiously watching the downpour. Heavy sheets of rain spattered the glass with every gust of wind. Visibility on the highways would have been nearly zero in a storm like this one.

Two cars turned onto the street, but neither of them was Jessica's.

She forced herself to step away from the window. Sidney had never been much of a worrier until her mom got sick, and now that's all she ever did. What she really needed was a smoke. A few draws on a cigarette would calm her down. She'd have to wait until it stopped raining, though. Sidney didn't dare smoke inside because Wayne would just go on and on about black lung disease again, as if she were a coal miner and not just a sad young woman who no longer trusted the world to keep her loved ones safe.

She sat back down on the couch and gazed at the black-and-white monster movie she'd found on some obscure channel the antenna picked up, but she just couldn't bring herself to pay attention to it. Jessica should have been home by now. What had happened to her?

"Don't do this to me, Jessica," she whispered. Though Jessica had been her friend only since Sidney started working at the truck stop, sometimes it felt like they'd known each other their entire lives. If some harm had befallen her…

Headlights pierced the curtains. Sidney leapt off the couch, fully expecting to see a police cruiser sitting in the driveway as a harbinger of grim news—never mind there was no public record of Jessica staying here—but instead, she was greeted with the sight of a white Taurus covered in patches of rust. It pulled up close to the house, and the headlights blinked out.

One benefit of expecting the absolute worst was Sidney could never be disappointed.

She unlocked the front door and held it open as Jessica came up the walk with her tote bag.

Jessica stepped onto the mat and pulled her hood back. Her hair was a mess, and she shivered like she'd gone for a swim in an icy pond. "Thanks," she said, placing her bag on the counter and rubbing her hands together as if to warm them.

"I was starting to think you'd drowned out there," Sidney commented, trying to sound cheerful. No need to let Jessica know just how worried she'd really been.

Jessica kicked off her shoes and lined them up against the wall. "It was a close call. I kept hydroplaning. It took me two hours to get back here."

"Maybe you should have parked somewhere and waited it out?"

"No." Jessica went to the fridge and grabbed one of Wayne's bottles of Mike's Hard Lemonade. "Is there a bottle opener around here anywhere?"

"It's in the drawer under the microwave." Unease crept along Sidney's spine. Something here wasn't right. "Is everything okay?" She pulled a chair away from the table and sat in it.

Jessica found the bottle opener and joined Sidney at the table. She pried the lid off her drink, took a sip, and grimaced. Her face was chalk-white. "I don't even know where to begin."

"Did something bad happen?"

"Uh. That depends on your point of view, I guess." Jessica's gaze had gone hollow. "I've made contact."

Sidney blinked. Jessica made it sound like she'd encountered an alien spacecraft making crop circles out in a cornfield.

"With…?"

"The things I've been trying to make contact with for years."

Understanding dawned within Sidney. "Oh my God. Like…for real?"

Jessica nodded. She looked like someone who'd glanced into a mirror and seen a skull staring back at her.

"I mean, this is great, right?" Sidney tried to grin. "You've wanted to see a ghost for as long as I've known you."

"I didn't just see one. I talked to it too. Him, I mean. I'm going to need some time to process all of this."

"Wait. You *talked* to a ghost? Like, carried on a conversation?"

Disappointment showed on Jessica's face. "I wouldn't believe me either. But I screwed up. I had the opportunity of a lifetime, and I *freaked*."

"Just tell me what happened."

Jessica drained about half of her alcoholic lemonade in one gulp. "I was just getting settled in when I saw a guy sitting on a bench out in the graveyard. Mid-thirties, probably. We got to talking, and he said his name was Jerry Madison. He didn't *look* dead."

Sidney folded her arms. So far, it sounded like Jessica had gotten spooked over nothing. "Then how do you know he was a ghost? He could have been some loser pranking you."

Jessica gritted her teeth. "He was weirding me out big time. Like, my car was the only one there, and the place was literally in the middle of nowhere. I…He said he wanted to go with me. And then he *jumped* on me, and he didn't weigh anything. But it was *so cold.*"

Sidney drew her arms closer to her body. She'd never known Jessica to lie. "How did you get away from him?"

"I'm not sure. Maybe he can't really leave that place."

"Were you able to record any of it?"

"I don't know yet. My equipment was on, but I obviously haven't had a chance to look it over."

Sidney rose and strode toward the tote bag on the counter. "Then let's find out!"

Jessica jerked to her feet, eyes full of panic. "No! Not yet. I need time to process all of this. Maybe tomorrow after I've had a good night's sleep."

"But…"

"I know. Call me 'Cowardly Neighborhood Ghost Hunter.' That's what I am, right?" Jessica finished the drink and wiped the back of her hand across her mouth. "You don't know how much I want this to have been some screwed-up dream."

"But this is what you've wanted," Sidney said. *Assuming you're telling the truth.*

She felt guilty for thinking that way. If you couldn't trust Jessica, you couldn't trust anyone. But this was too extraordinary. Could Jessica have been mistaken about what really happened?

Jessica headed toward the stairs without answering her. "I'm going to bed."

Sidney bit her lip, staring at the chair Jessica had vacated, then at the black tote bag.

Had Jessica really met a ghost? Sidney had always assumed that if ghosts did exist, they were just imprints of people left on a place, like characters on a TV screen. That's what apparitions and disembodied voices were supposed to be, right? They weren't supposed to be *actual* people. If actual people lingered on after death, then that meant her mother…

No. Sidney wouldn't even go there. Her mother was gone, buried in the ground. Souls were like dragons. It was fun to pretend they were real. It didn't mean they were.

The tote bag seemed to beckon to Sidney. Jessica might be upset if Sidney rummaged through her equipment without her permission.

Sidney could be careful, though, and put everything back in the bag the way she'd found it so Jessica would be none the wiser.

She closed her eyes. Should she, or shouldn't she? The truth might be terrifying.

The truth might be extraordinary.

"Oh, what the hell." She pulled a voice recorder out of the bag, peered up the staircase to make sure the bedroom door was shut tight, and hit play.

After tossing and turning for an hour in the bedroom she now shared with Sidney, Jessica fell asleep and dreamed she was a man.

She found herself seated at a round table in a bar with three other men in their thirties. Even though nobody had mentioned them, she knew their names: Phil Knippenberg, Andy Schlosser, Garret West. Phil and Andy were maintenance men at the high school, and Garret coached track. More men than women crowded the bar. A live band performing on a stage played Aerosmith's hit "Dream On."

The smell of liquor and clouds of cigarette smoke hung like fog in the poorly lit room. A waitress whose blouse exposed an ample amount of cleavage brought four foaming glasses of beer to their table, left, and immediately returned with an enormous tray of nachos.

Jessica's comrades dug in like starving wolves. She herself had no appetite and stared down at her man-hands, feeling emptier than the deepest void of space.

"Come on, eat something," Andy urged her.

She shook her head. "I ate before I got here." A man's voice came out of her mouth.

"He's probably thinking 'bout that bitch again," Phil said, his mouth full of cheesy tortilla chips dripping with grease. Jessica could tell from the slur in his speech this beer was not his first, or even his second, of the evening.

"I can think about whatever I want to," Jessica snapped.

"Get over it, man," Garret said. "It's been ages now."

"And just how am I supposed to do that?"

Garret gestured toward the bar counter, where a pair of busty women with feathered haircuts were laughing with the bartender. "I'll give you twenty dollars if you ask one of those babes out. Doesn't even have to be a date—just take her home tonight. Hell, let's make it fifty dollars. I'm feeling generous."

Strangely, the thought of taking an unknown woman to bed was somewhat appealing. It had been such a long time, much too long…

No. Never again. Relationships of any kind only led to ruin.

Her hesitation must have been too obvious. Andy let out a chuckle. "He'll never do it because he won't let himself get over dear Abby, am I right?"

Jessica's temper began to build. "I can't just forget what she did, like it never happened."

Phil lifted his glass into the air. "This might help."

"I'd kill myself before stooping to your level."

Phil grinned. "Then go right ahead."

"It was her decision, you know," Garret said. "Some people just aren't cut out for raising kids."

"I would have raised it!" Jessica spat. "I told her that, and she laughed at me."

Phil took a swig of his beer. "It's not such a big deal. You just need to man up and get laid."

"That's harsh, man," Andy started to say, but bile was rising in Jessica's throat, and the next thing she knew, she was on her feet and had her man-hands locked around Phil's throat, fully intent on crushing it. Her chair crashed into the floor behind her.

"You son of a bitch!" she screamed in Phil's reddening face.

Phil tried to speak but couldn't. He reeked like alcohol, and for all

Jessica cared, he could have drowned in it.

Several sets of hands pried her off her victim, and Phil drew back, his chest heaving up and down, fighting for air. "Go to hell," he breathed, murder gleaming in his eyes.

"I'll see you there," Jessica responded. The hands dragged her away from the table and out into the night, leaving her alone in the darkness.

The dream changed, and Jessica was that man again, clad only in boxers, sitting on the edge of a bed. She turned a black revolver over and over in her hands. Six bullets nestled in their proper places. Six shiny passports that would enable her transport from this bleak world to the next.

"God," she rasped in her man-voice, feeling her throat constrict with grief, "if you're really there, if you really care about me at all, you'll make this painless."

She put the tip of the gun in her mouth and pulled the trigger.

The weapon clicked like a child's toy gun. She lowered it, dumbfounded. It shouldn't have malfunctioned. She pointed the gun at the floor and fired a hole into the rug. The sound of the gunshot reverberated throughout the room, making her ears ring.

So, the gun had jammed. It wouldn't happen again.

She returned the revolver to her mouth so she could properly execute herself and pulled the trigger a third time.

The gun emitted another inadequate click. Enraged, she threw the gun to the floor and kicked it across the room.

"Can't you let a man end it all in peace?" she screamed at the ceiling.

Thou shalt not kill, whispered a voice she'd heard long ago in another, happier lifetime.

She started laughing at the absurdity of it all and could not stop.

The dream faded away, and Jessica awoke to a dark bedroom. She had the faint sensation of something ominous slithering around in her mind, but the feeling soon dissipated. Dreams were only dreams, after all. There was nothing sinister about them.

Yet she still lay wide awake in bed for a long time after.

Wondering.

11

Wayne had already left for work when Jessica crawled out of bed, aching, at ten o'clock. Sleeping in that late was not her usual custom, but after the previous evening, she deserved to indulge herself with a little extra sleep.

In the kitchen, Sidney was gulping down a glass of orange juice and holding a half-eaten piece of toast in one hand.

"Running late?" Jessica popped two slices of bread into the toaster. *The breakfast of paupers.*

"Forgot to set my alarm." Sidney placed her empty glass in the sink. "I already called Travis to let him know." She cleared her throat, then glanced toward her feet. "So, how are you feeling?"

"Not great. What about you?"

"Um." Sidney's cheeks darkened.

Jessica didn't like the look in her friend's eyes. "What?"

"I kind of peeked at your stuff after you went to bed last night."

"And by 'stuff,' you mean…"

"You know which stuff."

Jessica did know. "So…did you see anything?"

"No. They're all blank."

Jessica's insides turned a somersault. "Are you sure?"

"Pretty darn."

Jessica's heart plummeted. Not just that there was no longer any recording of her adventures last night, but that everything else was gone too. Unless Sidney hadn't been checking them right…

"Are you sure you'd turned your cameras on?" Sidney asked.

"Yes, I'm sure!" Sidney had to have made a mistake, and to prove it, Jessica snatched a camcorder from the tote bag. She pressed the power button and swung the screen open, revealing a tiny menu.

Yesterday, there had been about fifteen videos stored on the memory card. Today, there were none. "I don't believe it," Jessica said, feeling somewhat dazed.

"Did you back them up on anything?"

"Yeah, it was all saved on my laptop. Except for the stuff from last night, of course."

"Well, have fun figuring out how everything got wiped. I'm heading out." Sidney stuffed the last bit of toast into her mouth, shouldered her purse, and left without another word.

Jessica closed her eyes and counted to twenty. She replayed what she remembered of the previous evening and shuddered. Had Jerry erased her videos and voice recordings? Or had she imagined the whole ordeal and erased them herself?

After breakfast, Jessica showered, put on her nicest graphic tee with the words "I Hunt Dead People" printed across the front, daubed a little makeup onto her cheeks and around her eyes, and set up a camcorder on its tripod in the living room.

"I have a dilemma," she said once the camera was rolling. "I'm not even sure if I should be talking about it here, but I have to talk about it with somebody or I'll scream.

"I went on an investigation in a graveyard last night. I brought out the usual equipment, but something happened, and everything I recorded got erased. I don't *think* my friend would have sabotaged it; she respects me too much. That gives me two options: either I've had a compete mental breakdown, or ghosts know how to manipulate camcorders, and not in a good way.

“That’s right. I met a ghost last night. His name is Jerry. Here’s what happened.”

Jessica spent the next few days settling in to Wayne’s house, editing and uploading the videos that had the fortune of being saved to her computer, and going for long walks through the town of Eleanor, trying to wrap her head around the events of Tuesday evening. As per Wayne’s advice, she even took a day to tour first the Promont House—a Victorian mansion once the home of an Ohio governor—and then Bobby Mackey’s, the haunted nightclub in northern Kentucky supposedly crawling with the restless dead.

The tours were nice, and she did a video summary of each one, talking about her experiences and giving a little history of each location. She uploaded them to her channel, made sure to include the right keywords, and waited for the world to find them.

“How’s Friendly Neighborhood Ghost Hunter doing this week?” Wayne asked over dinner on Friday evening. He and Jessica dined alone in the kitchen, Sidney having gone to hang out with her father and brothers.

Jessica paused to swallow a bite of chicken tikka masala Wayne had prepared himself. “Not bad! I added a little local color, like you said, and I’m up to two hundred subscribers.”

Wayne’s eyebrows rose. “That’s more than double from just a few days ago, right?”

“It is! I mean, I didn’t actually *hunt ghosts* at Promont House or Bobby Mackey’s, but I went there and posted about it, and voila. Any ideas on where I should go next?”

“I’ll have to think about it. But don’t let me dictate all of your decisions for you.” They ate in silence for a few minutes. Then Wayne asked, “So how was the thing at the graveyard the other night? You never said."

Jessica could feel her cheeks changing color. She and Sidney seemingly had an unspoken agreement not to bring up any of the details from Tuesday night's investigation. "It didn't turn out how I'd planned," she said. "I had an equipment malfunction and lost a lot of footage."

"That's a bummer. Do you think the storm might have had something to do with it?"

"I don't really know."

"Are you going back there for a redo?"

Jessica shivered. "Nah. That place gave me the creeps."

Wayne gave her a lopsided smile. "Says the fearless ghost hunter."

"I sure wasn't feeling fearless on Tuesday."

Something must have shown on her face, for Wayne said, "Did something happen?"

She stared down at her plate. "I know you haven't watched my new videos this week. Otherwise, you'd know."

He waited, and Jessica sighed.

"I saw a ghost, okay? I didn't know he was a ghost, and he tried to come with me, and I freaked out. Ironic, right?"

"You talked to this ghost?"

"Just like we're talking right now."

Wayne paled a shade. "Maybe you ought to be careful from now on."

Jessica snorted. "Are you kidding me? I can't gain new followers if I play it safe."

"Then you *are* going back out there for a redo."

"I don't know what I want to do. I'll have to think it over. I mean… you weren't there. I was so scared, like I haven't been since I was a little kid and thought Freddy Krueger would murder me in my sleep. But it was also…" She broke off, unsure of the right word.

"Exciting?" Wayne suggested.

"Yeah. Which makes me really wonder about myself."

An uneventful weekend came and went. Jessica passed the time refreshing her YouTube channel every few hours, watching her subscribers climb one by one. By Monday, she was up to 215 of them. Not bad, but still a far cry from the level she'd need to be monetized.

She sat alone at the kitchen table Monday morning, finishing up her breakfast while she researched more local public places she could tour and then post about, when a voice said, "Good morning."

Jessica jerked backward and let out a little scream. Jerry Madison was sitting in the chair opposite her, his arms folded across his chest.

"No," Jessica said, continuing to back away. "No, no, no."

"You seemed to know more words than that the other night."

She stopped when her back hit the wall, her heart racing with disbelief. Jerry looked like a perfectly ordinary man sitting at the table. Dark brown, disheveled hair, rumpled black clothes, icy blue eyes just a touch out of focus, like someone who preferred to stay in their own inner world rather than reality.

"I can't look *that* bad," he said.

"You can't be here."

He gave her an amused smile. "Can't I?"

"You…You…You're…" *Stay calm*, she told herself.

He's just…a guy. That's right. A harmless guy.

She took the deepest breath of her life and said, "How long have you been here?"

"A while. Getting here took a lot out of me. I had to…recharge."

"Did you delete the files out of my cameras when you moved them?"

"I'm not sure what that means. If I did, it was my mistake."

Seconds ticked by. "Are you just going to sit there all day?" Jessica asked him.

"I can stand, if you'd like."

What a comedian. "How is it I can see you?"

"You must have a special gift. There's certainly nothing special about me."

"Look," she said. "I don't want to sound rude, but there's nothing for you here."

Jerry's face fell. "I told you, I'm lonely. Try spending a couple decades by yourself and tell me how you feel."

"I don't mean *here*, as in this house. I mean here, as on this planet. You're supposed to look for a tunnel of light, or something."

"Some people don't go to heaven, Jessica."

"What could you have done that was so bad? Forget to return your library books on time?"

He narrowed his eyes. "That's my business."

"Maybe if you address it, you'll move on."

"I'm not 'moving on.' End of conversation. Do you understand that?"

"I'd like to help you."

"Then keep me company. That's the most I could ever ask for."

12

Smithfield Park sat at the base of Lookout Hill on the eastern end of town, boasting miles of wooded trails, a fishing pond that had briefly become a part of the Ohio River during the infamous Flood of 1997, volleyball and tennis courts, a picnic pavilion, and a playground and swings for the kids.

Only one other vehicle occupied the lot when she arrived. A man stood at the edge of the pond, casting a fishing line out into the water, paying her no notice.

Jessica adjusted the Bluetooth earpiece she'd swiped off the kitchen counter prior to leaving. That way, any bystanders wouldn't think she was talking to herself.

"*Estamos aquí,*" she said to her invisible passenger, trying to pretend that any of this was normal.

Jerry coalesced into being beside her. "*Sí. Yo veo.*"

"So you speak Spanish too, huh?"

"I studied it in high school. Ancient history. You?"

"I mostly learned it from family. One benefit of being a part-Mexican mutt."

Jerry looked skeptical. "That sounds almost offensive."

"Semi-Latina? My *abuelo* was from Juárez. I think."

Jessica undid her seatbelt. She was halfway out the door when Jerry said, "Wait."

She halted. Jerry gazed forlornly through the windshield at the play area, where empty swings hung limply from rusted chains and dead leaves clustered at the base of a rock-climbing wall.

"What?" she asked. "I thought the park might be a nice place to chat."

"It's fine," he said, recovering. "I'm just not used to any of this."

"*You're* not used to any of this? There's a dead man in my car."

A look of hurt showed on Jerry's face, and Jessica immediately regretted her choice of words.

"I'm sorry," she said. "I shouldn't have said that."

It took several moments for him to speak. "What you need to understand," he said slowly, "is that what's in here doesn't go away." He placed a hand on his chest. "It's the core of who we are. My body is gone, but I'm not. You might say that in a sense, I'm just as alive as you are."

"I guess that does make sense. So…do you want to go for a walk?"

He nodded. "Sure. Let's go."

They left the car and fell in step beside each other. When they passed the playground, Jerry made a point of looking the other way. So, he had an aversion to playgrounds? Interesting.

They entered the woods. Signs describing different plants and animals living in the area had been posted along the edge of the trail, but Jerry showed no interest in reading them.

"Feeling better yet?" Jessica asked him, basking in the autumn glow.

He glared at her. "I hope you don't have plans on becoming a psychologist."

"Sorry."

"One of my brothers was a psychologist," Jerry commented, gazing up at the bit of blue sky visible between the orange and crimson treetops. "But even he couldn't do anything for me. I tried to kill myself. I only survived because my gun wasn't working right."

Jessica wheeled to face him. His words had triggered a memory. "Wait. I had a dream about that the other night. When the gun didn't go off in my face, I tested it on the floor. Were you fiddling around inside my head?"

"Why would I do that?"

"I have no idea!" She realized she was shouting, so she lowered her voice. "That dream about the men in the bar must have been you too—they were both way more vivid than what I usually dream. What were you trying to prove to me?"

"Prove? Nothing. I just want you to understand me. I'm just thoughts and memories. Not all of them good."

"Sounds like my life."

They continued on their way. "Do you care to indulge me?" Jerry asked, after a time.

"About my life?"

"That's what new acquaintances do, yes?"

"I mean, there's not a whole lot to tell. I guess you could say I've always been a little lonely."

"I've seen your friends."

"Sidney and Wayne came later. They're the best things that have ever happened to me. My parents have always been workaholics, so they never paid much attention to me and my sister. Rachel and I played together a lot when we were kids, but school was awful."

"How so?"

Jessica shrugged. "I was always the weird kid taking pictures of everything and scrapbooking it. I'd take pictures of random shit, like people's backpacks or the class gerbil, trying to make it all aesthetic. I've got probably twenty photo albums from back then."

"I can think of stranger hobbies."

"Trust me, I made it as weird as humanly possible. I wanted everyone to think I was so edgy, I even wore a chain on my jeans and armbands that said, 'Cute but psycho.' Then when I got into high school, I started to get obsessed with ghost hunting shows, and then YouTube went online when I was a junior, and my life sort of progressed from there."

"How did you meet your housemates?"

"Sidney and I worked together at the truck stop. Wayne is her cousin. I knew them in passing before that since it's a small town—we actually lived on the same street at one point in time, and Wayne worked with Mom—but once I really got to know them, I realized they're my people."

"Sidney and Wayne lived together as children too?"

"Yeah, Wayne got taken away from his family because of some sort of abuse situation. He doesn't talk about it, and I know not to ask."

"I've seen Wayne walking with a limp."

"He has cerebral palsy."

"I see."

They passed a turnoff for a secondary trail that looped through the trees for a mile. Jessica paused at the signpost, assessing her muscle pain, which still had not abated.

"Are you feeling all right?" Jerry asked.

"Just sore."

"We can sit." He nodded toward a nearby bench.

Jessica conceded. They sat down together and watched as a squirrel dug a hole in the decaying leaf matter on the forest floor.

"So, what's your story?" Jessica asked. "Where are you from?"

"Originally? Cleveland. I came to Cincinnati for college and bought a house in Clarkville, Kentucky, after I graduated. I taught English at Lyle Mercer High School for several years. My parents thought I was being a fool and that I'd never get by on a teacher's salary, but that ended up being the least of my worries."

"Being broke is a pretty big worry to me. I can relate."

"Death tends to change one's perspective on things."

Jessica swallowed. The conversation was getting awkward again. It occurred to her, perhaps the reason the living and the dead did not typically mingle was because of a disconnect in shared experience. "I don't doubt that," she said.

"It changes everything." His face grew pained. "We work our whole lives trying to impress everyone with our fancy clothes and fancy cars, but in the end, the only thing that matters is the choices we make, and unfortunately, I made some very bad choices."

"Well, we all do that, I think."

"Do you realize," he continued, his eyes growing livid, "that at any moment, Christ may appear, and all souls on Earth will be judged before him? That I have *nothing* good to say about myself except that I read my Bible cover to cover half a dozen times and sat in church every single Sunday? Look where it got me!"

"I didn't realize you were so religious."

Jerry didn't seem to hear her. His face contorted as if he were in agony. "No, I'm not sorry. It's all God's fault. He should have seen it coming. If he didn't, how can he be God? How can he be anything?"

Though Jerry was still visible beside her on the bench, his mind seemed to have retreated to a place Jessica couldn't see.

"Can a just God make us suffer so much? He hurts us because he lets others hurt us. If he cared, he'd stop them! I want to make them hurt…" He broke off, glancing around wildly. "Jessica? Jessica!"

He started to rise, like one about to flee in mindless terror, and Jessica grabbed his arm without thinking. Jerry didn't feel quite as cold to the touch as he had during their first meeting.

"I'm right here," she said, heart pounding. "Are you okay?"

He shuddered, and his gaze latched onto hers. "I—I'm not sure what happened. I felt myself slipping. I thought you'd left me." He noticed her holding his arm and frowned. "You're touching me."

She hurriedly let go of him, face flushing. "Sorry."

"No, it's okay."

"What was all that stuff you were just saying about God and

suffering?"

"I'm not sure. Sometimes my thoughts get away from me..." He paused, tilting his head slightly to one side. "May I touch you?"

She could feel her blush deepening. "In what manner?"

Jerry lifted his right hand and held it up, palm facing her. Understanding, she raised her left hand and held it against his, palm to palm. His hand didn't feel solid, yet it had a heavier texture than air.

"Can you feel it?" she asked.

"A little." His expression grew wistful. "You know how when you fall asleep and dream, you can sometimes feel sensations as if they're real, but when you wake up, you know they were just echoes of reality? It's like that."

Jessica curled her fingers, lacing them into his, hoping he would feel some comfort. "Can I ask you a question?"

"Sure."

"How old were you when...?"

"Thirty-three," he said quietly.

"That's so young. Were you sick?"

"Oh, no." His expression turned wry. "I was murdered."

She jerked back from him, clapping a hand over her mouth. "Oh my God. I'm so sorry. I didn't realize..."

"It's okay, Jessica. It happened a long time ago. It isn't anything for you to worry about."

"How did it happen?"

"I'll spare you the grisly details." He rubbed his neck, and Jessica remembered the sight of him on the bench in the graveyard, when she thought she'd seen a dark bruise around his neck and broken blood vessels all over his face.

He was strangled, she thought hollowly. Or lynched.

"I—I think I saw what you looked like at the very end," she admitted. "Last week at the graveyard. It was only for a moment, and then you looked normal again."

"Did you?" He sounded almost bored. "I'm just memories, like I said. I could probably appear however I like if I wanted to think hard enough about it. This is what I normally wore to work."

Jerry made a gesture at his black shirt and slacks. Jessica tried to picture him standing at a chalkboard before rows of jaded high school students, discussing the literary merits of Stoker and Poe.

"So…that graveyard is where you were buried?" she asked.

"Not exactly. You won't find a headstone with my name on it—I'm off in the woods a ways. Nobody has ever found my body."

"I'm sorry."

"I don't need your pity."

"But why would anyone murder you? No offense, but you look like a Goth librarian."

That made him actually smile. "They had their reasons."

They? "Were they ever caught?"

"You might be surprised that I have not had access to the news in quite some time," Jerry said. "But given the fact that my bones are still moldering in an unmarked grave, I'm going to say probably not."

Jessica took his left hand in her right and gave it a squeeze. It sounded like Jerry had a lot of unfinished business to deal with. "You've been through a lot," she said. "I really want to help you, if you'll let me."

"Just don't leave me," he said, sorrow edging his voice. "I don't think I can handle being alone ever again."

13

Jerry faded into invisibility before Jessica left the park. She didn't think he'd left—he'd very likely just worn himself out from interacting with her for so long—but she didn't know the mechanics of it all. Was he still aware of his surroundings if she herself couldn't see him? She'd have to ask him about it the next time he appeared.

Jessica set up a camcorder on its tripod in the living room and began recording her next video.

"Today is Monday, October 18, 2010. If you've been following my videos, you know that I met a ghost named Jerry Madison during my recent investigation of the graveyard at the Iron Springs United Methodist Church. Well, guess what: he followed me home! We talked more today, and he told me a little bit about himself. I'm not sure how many details I should go into here, but let's just say he was from Clarkville, Kentucky, and he didn't have an easy death.

"I know for a fact that that's why he's stuck here. I want to help him move on, but I don't know how to go about it. Maybe he can't accept the fact that he was killed so young, or maybe he wants to see his killer brought to justice. If that's the case, I'm not sure I'm the right person to help him since I'm not a detective. I don't even know how long ago he died. According to him, it's been decades, but how many?

"If any of you paranormal investigators have dealt with anything like this, or have any advice, please tell me in the comments. And don't forget to like and subscribe!"

After her recording ended, Jessica logged into her YouTube account and checked the stats on her most recent uploads. The video where she'd talked about meeting Jerry had garnered about 3,000 views already and had six comments:

@spookybaybee1994 OMG that's so scary

@GodOfTacos86 ur cute

@ParaNormie123 Let's collab!

@JoshJoshJosh YOUR DELUSIONAL

@kinzeetube7 This is the content I crave.

@OatmealTheDestroyer SHOW US THE GHOST!!!

Show us the ghost? Now there was a thought. Would Jerry even be visible on a recording? Either way, he wouldn't like being exploited for her own gain.

But think of the new followers you'll get, whispered a honey-sweet voice somewhere inside her head.

Could she hide a camera and record him secretly? Jerry would probably see her doing it. Better to just skip that whole angle and continue entertaining her growing list of subscribers with tales of her experiences.

Plus, she had to figure out how to actually help Jerry move on, reluctant as he might have been to do so. He thought he would go to hell, but it sounded like he was the victim here. And given his bizarre tirade at the park, he might even be harboring some kind of religious guilt. Had his parents been zealots, pounding the evils of alcohol and sex into him for his entire life?

Jessica thought of her own aloof parents and felt a pang of sadness. What would it be like having a mother and father who actually paid attention to her, even if in a negative way? She did have to give her father some credit because he'd tried. Stephen Roman-Dell would, on occasion, read bedtime stories to her and Rachel, though he'd typically fall asleep in the recliner before he finished the book.

And then there'd been the time Stephen had been teaching her to drive and had her take Interstate 75 all the way down into Tennessee one day, just to get the practice hours in. They'd made it to Gatlinburg, Tennessee, in the early afternoon. Jessica had picked out a restaurant where she and her father had eaten a late lunch. She'd bought a souvenir T-shirt and then took a quick ride up the Space Needle before getting back into the car and heading home.

In hindsight, it had been a nice bonding experience, but Stephen had barely spoken a word. He just didn't know what to talk about when he wasn't lecturing. Her father was a stranger to her, just like her mother.

Jessica shook her head to clear it. There really wasn't any point in thinking about her parents. They'd produced her and Rachel for some inexplicable reason—she knew they weren't unplanned; Stephen and Maria were far too methodical for that—and then went on with their lives as if parenthood had been a mere blip in the grand scheme of things.

She closed her laptop and stretched. The stroll in the woods hadn't helped the pain go away. If anything, walking had made it worse.

Jessica still had a bottle of Tylenol in her purse. She took two pills again and willed them to kick in.

"Okay," she said to the empty house. "What should I do for the rest of the day now that that's done?"

The voice of reason told her she should continue the job search she'd put on hold for the past week. Her well of funds was about as dry as the Martian surface, and she couldn't mooch off of Wayne forever.

Speaking of which, she ought to pay him back for his generosity. Maybe she could do a little cleaning to prove she was a useful addition to the household.

Jessica went into the cramped first-floor bathroom. The tub looked a little dingy, and toothpaste speckled the mirror over the sink, so she could start there. Once she'd finished the bathroom, she could tweak her new video and upload it to her channel.

Snatching a roll of paper towels and two different bottles of cleaner from the kitchen, Jessica thought of more things to talk about on her channel, like the echo of rage from the church parking lot. The original recording where she'd mentioned it had obviously been wiped, possibly when Jerry collected her equipment and brought it to her car. *Almost as if he didn't want anyone else knowing about him...*

She spritzed cleaner in the tub and on the toilet and set to work wiping down the sink while they soaked, mulling over what she knew. Was there a connection between that echo and Jerry's death, or were they completely unrelated? It was a graveyard, after all, and many powerful emotions would have been experienced in its vicinity over the years. The place was bound to be a psychic hotspot. Too bad she'd never gotten the chance to scan for the electromagnetic waves that might be amplifying it all.

Jessica had just started to spray down the mirror when her vision went red and the bathroom disappeared.

A blinding anger permeated every cell of her being. It was all she knew, and all she had ever known. The urge to maim, to hurt, to *kill* burned through her synapses. She knew those who were guilty would finally get their reward, and she would stand in *triumph* over their broken corpses, just like they had always deserved...

Hands grabbed her shoulders and shook her, hard.

Jessica gasped as she came to. Wayne knelt in front of her, face white with fear.

"Oh, thank God," he said breathlessly. "What happened here?"

Jessica blinked and assessed her surroundings. They were in the bathroom between the tub and the sink. Globs of foam oozed down the tub walls, and the smell of the cleaner made her head feel funny.

All she could bring herself to say was, "What time is it?"

"About three o'clock. I got off early today; I thought you and I could just hang out."

Jessica let out a breath. She hadn't been unconscious for long, then. "I…I guess the fumes got to me."

Wayne didn't look amused. He pushed his glasses farther up the bridge of his nose. "I appreciate you wanting to help out around here, but be more careful next time. You didn't mix bleach and ammonia, did you?"

"I don't think so."

His expression pinched, Wayne snatched the soap scum remover bottle off the edge of the tub and scanned the ingredients on the label, then let out a sigh. "Okay. But let's get you into some fresh air."

He helped her out to the back deck, hurriedly returned inside, and reappeared with a glass of ice water. Jessica thanked him and drank half of it in one gulp.

"Feeling better?" Wayne asked when she sat the glass down on the patio table.

"Some." Jessica breathed in deeply, relishing the calming scents of autumn. "I've had an incredibly fucked-up day."

"That seems to be happening a lot lately. I finally got to watch all of your latest videos during my lunch break."

Though she was thrilled Wayne supported her efforts, it still made her feel awkward knowing her friends were watching her paranormal ramblings during their free time. It was like catching one of them reading her diary, even though she was the one who'd put it on display. "Do you believe everything I said in them?" she asked.

Wayne stared at her long and hard. "If it were anyone else on this planet," he replied, "I'd say they were fabricating things to get more views. But it's you, and you don't lie."

"I may occasionally stretch the truth," she admitted.

"Did you meet a ghost named Jerry Madison last week?"

"Yes."

"And you talked to him."

"Yes."

"Then that's good enough for me. So, what happened today that's got you all flustered, aside from fainting while doing chores?"

Jessica closed her eyes, afraid to see Wayne's reaction to what she was about to say. "Jerry is here. He followed me home."

Wayne's expression grew hard. He opened his mouth, closed it, then opened it again. "How long have you known this?"

"Just since this morning. He showed up in the kitchen."

She summarized the day's events, concluding with her fainting spell and the red aura she'd experienced while out cold.

"I don't like this," Wayne said.

Jessica crossed her arms. "It's not like I asked for this to happen."

"It doesn't matter. You're telling me there's a stranger in my house that I can't see, and there's nothing I can do about it because he's lonely and has a crush on you."

"He does not!"

"You're blushing."

"Oh, come on, Wayne. I mean, sure, he's not bad-looking, but I do prefer men who can breathe."

"That's good to know. Did you tell Jerry he needs to leave?"

"I said he should move on, but he said he'll go to hell if he does."

"Now that's interesting." Wayne lapsed into silence, staring out at his yard. "Did he say why?"

"No. But don't you think it's sad for someone to think that way?"

He gave her a sidelong glance. "Have you thought about where you'll go when it's your time?"

"Me?" She laughed, not sure if he was being serious. "If there's a heaven, I don't see why I wouldn't be allowed in. Why?"

He looked away from her again. "If I died right now, I don't know where I'd go."

The smile melted from Jessica's face. "Don't say that. You're one of the sweetest people I've ever known."

"If you say so."

"Wayne..."

"Can we change the subject, please?"

"Fine." Jessica blew a strand of her dark hair out of her face. "I don't think I told you, but I'm going to be an aunt, and the proud parents are flying in on Thursday for a family reunion nobody bothered to tell me about."

Wayne perked up a bit. "Tell Rachel I said congrats. It's the Reyes clan having this reunion?"

"Yep. They do like to throw a party."

"Where are they having it?"

"Some park in Campbell County. Rachel said she and Eric will be staying with Uncle Esteban and Aunt Sharon for the weekend."

"You should invite them over for dinner Thursday night, if their flight lands on time," Wayne said. "They'll make better company than a dead guy."

A quick movement in the corner of Jessica's eye caught her attention. Jerry was leaning against the back door, glaring at Wayne with eyes like daggers.

Jessica gulped. "Um, Wayne? Can you maybe look at the back door?"

The rest of the color drained from Wayne's face. He eyed the door, frowning in concentration. "He's here, isn't he?"

"Yeah."

"What's he doing?"

"Uh...just standing there, watching us. Hi, Jerry." Jessica tried to grin at their unwanted guest, but she knew it came across more as a grimace.

"Is it okay to talk to him?" Wayne asked.

"Sure. Just...maybe watch what you say."

Looking uncertain, Wayne rose and approached the back door as if he were inspecting an undetonated landmine. "I don't like this," he said again, voice sounding small.

Jerry glanced at Jessica, smirking. "Does your friend always act this queer when he's scared?"

That sent a hot rush of anger through Jessica. "Wayne is *not* queer," she snapped. "And even if he were, that shouldn't be an issue."

Baffled, Wayne looked from Jessica to the door and back again. The armpits of his pastel-pink button-up shirt were darkening with nervous sweat, but his carefully coiffed hair looked as fresh as when he'd styled it that morning. "Do I even want to know what he just said?"

"He thinks you're acting queer."

"All right." Wayne put his hands on his hips and stared about six inches to the left of where Jerry truly stood. "Listen, *Jerry*. I don't know what year you're from, but 'queer' isn't the insult you think it is. I happen to enjoy sex with women as much as the next guy—if I come across as 'gay' to you, that's your own problem."

Jerry looked him up and down with disdain. "Times have certainly changed, haven't they? In my day, men who looked like you would be hanging out in discreet bars after work, hoping not to contract AIDS."

Jessica covered her face with her hands. "I cannot believe this is a conversation that is actually happening right now. Jerry, it's 2010. Styles change, okay? And it's not cool to joke about a disease that killed so many people."

"What did he say this time?" Wayne asked, expression growing increasingly sour.

Jessica told him, starting to feel exhausted from her role as translator.

"Jerry," Wayne said, "I'm guessing you must be from the eighties, which—if you didn't know—are just as dead as you."

Jerry's face went apoplectic. Jessica stepped in front of him the moment he lunged for Wayne, but instead of stopping him, he simply passed through her.

It felt like the blood in her veins suddenly changed to ice, and fragments of intruding images filled her mind's eye. Faces of people unknown to her, a yellow house with a For Sale sign posted in the yard, a boy tossing a baseball to another child, a woman hurling dishes out of a cabinet onto the floor…

"What the *fuck* just happened?"

Jessica snapped back to attention. She felt disoriented, as if the deck had turned on its side. "I think Jerry forgot that he isn't solid."

She turned to see where Jerry had gone and noticed Wayne struggling to his feet. She held out her hand and helped him up. "Did he get you?"

Wayne brushed at his sleeves and straightened his glasses. "Something cold smacked into me, and I saw some weird shit. Otherwise, I'm fine."

"Wayne, I'm really sorry about all of this. Here, let me help you inside."

"Not yet. Where is he now?"

"I don't know. I don't see him anymore."

Wayne narrowed his eyes and turned in a full circle, as if trying to spot some anomaly indicating Jerry's presence. "Jerry, if you can hear me, you'd better listen up. This is *my* house. Try to hurt me again, and you're toast."

Later, after the red-haired young woman came home and she and Jessica went up to bed, Jerry drifted into the living room where Wayne was watching television.

The man had changed out of his pretty-boy office clothes and put on shorts and a purple T-shirt bearing the words "Holy Trinity Summer Festival 2008" in white lettering. His black and blue flame-patterned leg braces lay on the floor beside the recliner in which Wayne rested. He stretched his legs out on the footrest, but instead of looking relaxed, the man's jaw remained clenched.

There were three empty bottles of Mike's Hard Lemonade sitting on the end table, with a fourth still partly full.

Jerry stared coldly down at Wayne. What he would give to trade places with this broken man, to breathe and drink and eat again. Did Wayne even appreciate what he had?

"You don't understand," Jerry said, knowing Wayne couldn't hear him. "I'm not angry that you choose to dress the way you do. I'm angry that things keep changing, and I just get left behind."

If this was truly the year 2010, then Jerry ought to be fifty-seven now, sporting salt-and-pepper hair and sagging jowls like his father before him. But no, he would be forever thirty-three, thanks to *them*.

Wayne sat up straighter, more alert. He muted the television and made a visual sweep of the room, his gaze coming to rest surprisingly close to Jerry.

"I may not be psychic," Wayne said in a low voice, "but I can tell you're here. You make the room colder."

Jerry didn't say anything; it wouldn't have mattered if he had.

"I don't know why you've latched onto Jessica the way you have, but you need to lay off it," Wayne continued. "You're *dead*. Yeah, I know you get pissed when someone reminds you of that, but it's the truth, and you have to accept it. The last thing I need is an angry ghost coming along to screw up my life just when I've finally gotten it figured out."

Jerry paced the room, agitated. He didn't really want to hurt Wayne. But maybe he could make Wayne *feel* it. Maybe then Wayne would understand.

Jerry returned to the recliner, reached out, and touched Wayne with his mind.

Wayne gasped. His face twisted in anguish, and he let out a wordless moan that was only a whisper compared to what Jerry had been feeling for so many decades.

"I know it's not a contest," Jerry replied, "but I know I've had it worse than you."

Wayne didn't stick around for long after that. He dried his tears on his sleeve, finished his fruity little drink, turned out the light, and went upstairs with his leg braces tucked under his arm.

Jerry was alone again. Not for the first time, he wandered over to the bookshelves, contemplating whether he should attempt reading something to pass the time, like in the olden days when he'd devoured everything from classic literature to pulp horror novels.

These shelves contained a bit of everything too: Poe, Hemingway, Agatha Christie, some cookbooks, and more. A stack of *Haunted Ohio* books lay horizontally across the tops of the other books, as if recent additions to the collection, and a cardboard box full of thick photo albums occupied the floor.

The top album had a pink cover. Jessica had said she liked to take pictures. Perhaps the box of albums was hers.

Jerry focused all his remaining energy into lifting the album out of the box and onto the carpet. He rested awhile, then mustered the strength to turn to the first page.

Inside the front cover were inscribed the words: "The Life of Jessica Mary Roman-Dell: 2004: Part 1." Instead of the pocket pages he'd expected, these photos were layered with colorful papers that coordinated with the colors in the pictures.

The first page showed pictures of teenage girls sitting at a round table, wearing party hats. Jessica had written: "Fifteenth birthday! January 1, 2004. My cousins came over, and we had a blast! Rachel and I ate way too much cake, and we almost threw up from laughing while we were playing Apples to Apples. She'll probably be mad if she finds out I wrote this, but what she doesn't know won't hurt her, right? Mom actually took the time to bake a cake this year. Dad bought me a digital camera. I told him I could use it on ghost hunts once I finally get my license. Mom got mad about that, but what's new there? Anyway, this birthday was awesome!"

Jerry leafed through the following pages, growing progressively weaker from the effort. Jessica was right; she'd photographed anything and everything. Interesting trees. Tiny orange mushrooms. A bluebird sitting on a fencepost. People.

Especially people.

Jerry reached the end of the album and quietly closed it. He thought about what he'd just seen and smiled.

He said, "I *thought* so."

14

"We need to lay out some ground rules," Jessica said.

She perched at the kitchen table with a glass of orange juice and a single waffle slathered in margarine. Jerry sat across from her again, his expression unreadable.

"I expected as much," he said in a soft tone.

"So, you admit that what you did yesterday was wrong?"

His jaw clenched. "I *admit* that I sometimes lose control of myself. It's long been a personality flaw, according to my brother."

"The psychologist?"

"That's the one."

"I can look him up if you'd like, put you in touch."

"I'd really rather you didn't."

"Okay, well, you're going to have to get a grip on yourself." Jessica sipped at her orange juice. "Rule one: you don't hurt people. Rule two: you respect our space. This is Wayne's house, okay? You need to behave like any other guest."

"Yes, Mother."

Jessica scowled at him. "I mean it. Wayne doesn't deserve any more trouble. How long are you planning on staying here, anyway?"

"As long as I need to." He gave her a thin smile.

"Riiiiight." Jessica mentally went over the things she'd stayed awake half the night thinking about. "Moving on from that…there's some stuff I want to ask you."

"I can't guarantee that I'll answer."

She ignored that. "What year did you die?"

"1986. Why?"

"Because it gives me more of a guide of what all I have to explain. I realize I've been talking to you like you're one of my peers, but I'm guessing there's a lot you haven't understood. Like my YouTube channel."

"I understand it's something like television."

"Not exactly. You see, when I was a kid, the internet went public. It's like…a worldwide network of computers. People can share things with other people using the internet. Like videos."

"And that's what this YouTube is."

"Basically. People can log onto their computers and watch videos that other users share. My YouTube channel is called Friendly Neighborhood Ghost Hunter. When enough people start following your channel and watch your videos, YouTube starts paying you."

"And that's what you're trying to do with this ghost hunting business."

Jessica nodded. "I just checked last night, and I'm up to 243 subscribers. Still not enough to be monetized, but I'm getting there."

Jerry studied her long and hard. "You want me to help you with this."

"Only if you want to." She didn't mention the voice recorder hidden in her sweatshirt pocket. It had been recording since she got dressed that morning. She didn't know if it would pick up Jerry's voice or not. Call it an experiment.

"Jessica, I'm not some animal here to do tricks," he said.

"You realize I'm going to keep talking about you in my videos whether you make an appearance or not. *Maybe* some of my viewers can even help solve your murder, and then you'll have the closure you need to move on."

"Solve my murder?" Jerry nearly choked on the words. "What's the point of that?"

"Um, I just said. So you can move on. It's obviously your 'unfinished business.'"

Gingerly, Jerry reached a hand across the table and laid it on hers. "Jessica…"

"What? I know you said you think you'll go to hell, but you're just being too hard on yourself. I'm guessing you had overbearingly religious parents who made you feel guilty about everything. I've seen it happen to other people."

"You are an incredibly naïve young woman."

Jessica's face flushed with irritation. "I'd like to think I notice more than other people."

"You remind me of some of my old students." He studied her face. "They had the cockiness of youth too. They thought they knew everything, but they'd only seen a speck of water and thought it was the whole ocean."

"You're not *that* much older than me."

"I was born in 1953. You do the math."

She paused. "Oh. Right."

"You want to know more about me so you can blab it to this YouTube? Tell them this: I was drugged and kidnapped from my home in the middle of the night. They drove me from Clarkville to that graveyard at the Methodist Church. There's a clearing way off in the woods behind the last row of graves. They dragged me there all the way from the parking lot because I was still too sedated to walk.

"When we finally got to the clearing, they bound me to a chair and took the bag off my head so I could look at them face-to-face. Someone came up to me and pulled a rope tight around my neck." He grimaced. "It was awful. The fibers were cutting into my skin, and my throat started to collapse. I thought it would all be over quickly, but before I could pass out, he let go. And then…" He broke off, looking distressed, rose, and darted through the closed front door as if fleeing his own memories.

Jessica scrambled after him, heart thudding. The door squeaked when she opened it, and to her relief, Jerry was sitting at the edge of the concrete-slab porch with his head in his hands.

Fully aware of how awkward this would look to any prying neighbors, Jessica sat beside him and said, "You don't have to talk about it if you don't want to."

"Maybe I *should* talk about it," he said without looking at her. "Maybe if I talk about it, my mind will finally stop replaying it like one endless nightmare."

"Take your time," Jessica said, wondering what could be worse than strangulation.

Jerry remained silent for half a minute or more. "They tortured me," he said in a voice just above a whisper, "and they mocked me while I screamed. And each time they brought me to the brink of death, they'd stop and wait and start again. I begged them to let me go, but they kept at it for hours. And when my body finally gave up, I saw myself from above. I barely recognized what was left of me. They…"

His eyes went out of focus, and dark bruises and broken blood vessels erupted across his neck and face. The entirety of him seemed to ripple, and his clothes changed. He was no longer dressed in his black teaching garb, but yellow smiley face boxer shorts and a filthy white T-shirt that had been shredded down the front, exposing a chest and abdomen mutilated so badly, it was impossible to tell which injury had ultimately killed him.

Jessica's vision wavered when she met his gaze. Thick splatters of coagulating blood caked his hair and dripped down the sides of his face, and the whites of his eyes were hemorrhaged dark red.

She forced her orange juice back toward her stomach, but it seemed to just slosh around in her throat. "You can stop that now," she said, trying not to cry. "I…I see."

Jerry cast his gaze away from her. He closed his eyes and concentrated, and he gradually reverted to his black-clad, bloodless self, then put his face in his hands again. His shoulders shook with inaudible sobs.

Jessica instinctively put an arm around him, ignoring the chill. He buried his face in her shoulder and cried, and she rocked him slowly as if he were a lost child.

If the neighbors saw and thought her crazy, they could get over it.

After a time, Jerry reined his emotions in and pulled away from her. He rubbed his eyes and said, quietly, "The nightmare doesn't end. I have to live with it...and I don't know what to do about it."

Jessica's chest felt tight. "These people *never* got caught?"

"If they did, they certainly didn't tell anyone where they put me."

"Jerry, they deserve the death penalty for what they did to you. What are their names? I can send in a tip to the cops."

"I didn't know all their names. There were so many of them. And some of them may have died of old age by now."

"Can you give me *a* name?"

Jerry's brow creased. "Patrick Smith. You'll find a hundred of them in the phonebook."

Jessica filed the name away for later. "I want you to be honest with me," she said. "Why did a lynch mob go after you?"

"The same reason lynch mobs go after anyone. They thought the world would be better without me in it."

Jessica opened her mouth to pry more out of him when a Camry turned onto their street and slowed as it pulled into the driveway.

Sidney sat behind the wheel a moment, then looked up at Jessica in confusion. She killed the engine and got out. "What are you doing out here?"

"Just enjoying the morning sunshine," Jessica said in an airy tone. "What are *you* doing?"

"It's been so slow at work today that Travis sent me home." Sidney's coloring had gone practically gray. "I'm really afraid he's going to have to close the whole business."

"At least you'll be able to find a different job if you have to."

"Says the unemployed freeloader who's been sleeping in my bedroom all week." Sidney winked and joined Jessica on the porch, thankfully sitting on the side where Jerry wasn't. "I just worry that any other boss wouldn't be as flexible as Travis."

"He hasn't made any more weird comments about your mom, has he?"

"No." Sidney let out a long sigh. "Why are you really sitting out here? You don't look so good."

Jessica turned to Jerry, who sat to her left.

"Go ahead and tell her," Jerry said. "You already plan on telling the whole world."

Jessica swallowed. "Remember how I met a ghost last week?"

"What about it?"

"He's sitting next to me."

Sidney flew to her feet. "He is *not*."

"Don't worry. You weren't sitting on him."

"Do you honestly expect me to believe that a ghost just happened to follow you back here?"

"Not really."

Sidney bit her lip and seemed to be studying Jessica's face. "I know you think it's true," she said. "But this kind of thing just isn't *real*."

"I'm not imagining things, if that's what you're getting at."

"You said it, not me."

"Sidney, come on!"

But Sidney was already striding past her into the house. Jessica followed her into the kitchen, leaving Jerry to his own devices.

Sidney stood at the sink, aggressively filling a glass of water, if such a thing were possible. Tears glistened in the corners of her eyes. "You really believe in this ghost," she said.

"Yes! He was murdered and is looking for some closure. I'm looking for decent content for my channel. We're a perfect match."

Sidney blinked at Jessica as if she'd just started speaking in Klingon. "There's got to be something wrong with you. You're…hallucinating, or something."

"If I'm hallucinating, then Wayne is too. You should ask him about yesterday afternoon."

"Shit. I thought you two were acting weird during dinner. I figured you must have gotten into each other's pants while I was at work."

"Seriously?"

"I've seen how the two of you look at each other when the other isn't looking. Honestly, it's kind of cute, and you have my blessing."

"You're dodging the subject!"

"I don't want to talk about ghosts, okay?" Sidney's eyes glistened. "I've started having nightmares, ever since you told me what happened last week. Only it's not some strange man haunting me, it's my mom."

"Sidney, I say this with the utmost delicateness, but I don't think your mom is a ghost. She seemed to accept what was happening to her. She would have moved on."

Sidney swallowed. "I hope so. Because I can't stand the thought of her being lost somewhere without me or Dad or my brothers, or Wayne, even. Like, what would she do?"

"She would reach out to someone for help, which is what Jerry is doing with me."

"If you say so. I'm going up to my room. Our room. Still can't get used to that."

Sidney ascended the stairs and was gone.

Jessica supposed it was okay that Sidney didn't quite believe her. She would come around eventually.

After putting her breakfast dishes in the sink, she took her laptop to the couch and checked the stats on the video she'd uploaded last night. It had 506 views and four comments:

@ParaNormie123 Sorry, I've only ever picked up spooky voices on my investigations. Are you pranking us? If not, that's super cool. I've always wanted to have a real conversation with a ghost.

@Lacey2840 you need jesus, the bible says not to mess with spirits

@franklinbugbug You should write a book! I'd read it.

@ghostwiththemost666 Murder victim ghosts can be super volatile. You need to tread carefully around this one. I'd be happy to talk with you privately sometime and compare experiences.

Jessica found herself smiling. Now this was engagement! She typed out quick replies to everyone and then remembered the voice recorder was still doing its job inside her sweatshirt pocket. She withdrew it to stop the recording—she'd have to delete the whole last part with her and Sidney—then plugged her earbuds into the recorder's headphone jack and hit play.

Jessica could hear static from when she'd switched the recorder on and muffled crackling as it rubbed against sweatshirt fabric. She'd gone into the kitchen to get breakfast and ran into Jerry waiting for her at the table.

"We need to lay out some ground rules," she heard her own voice say.

"They must die! They must die! They must die!"

Jessica nearly dropped the recorder. That second voice wasn't one she'd heard before. It was deep and rasping and raised the hair on her arms. Jerry hadn't said it. So who had?

She expected her own voice to chime back in on the recording, but that ghastly echo kept repeating itself, as if it were the only thing that had ever been uttered over the breakfast table. Jessica skipped forward five minutes on the track.

"They must die! They must die! They must die!"

"What the hell?"

She skipped ahead another five minutes, hearing only more of the same. The entire conversation between her and Jerry—even the one between her and *Sidney*—was gone, buried under that awful voice.

Jessica sat back, bewildered. What in the world could it mean?

15

"They must die! They must die! They must die!"

Shaken, Wayne paused Jessica's latest YouTube upload and ran his hand over his mouth.

He couldn't ignore the fact Jessica had clearly bitten off more than she could chew with this one, whether she knew that or not. Wayne had barely slept last night after Jerry had shared whatever *that* was with him, down in the living room. The sensation had felt like being buried in a pit with his own filth. Only it hadn't been his filth; it was Jerry's. The ghost had clearly been trying to make a point, though its exact meaning eluded him.

Wayne couldn't sleep tonight either, which was why he'd crawled out of bed at twenty past midnight to browse YouTube again. He'd perused some of his favorite topics—style tips for men and cute baby animals—then noticed he had a notification Friendly Neighborhood Ghost Hunter had posted a new video six hours earlier. He'd watched as Jessica, with bags of worry under her eyes, had described the apparition of Jerry's murdered corpse in full, morbid detail and then played back the chilling recording of that voice from hell.

It would take a month of kitten videos for him to get over that one.

Wayne rubbed his eyes and looked at his bedside alarm clock. It was 12:59 a.m. now. He had to be up for his pre-work exercise regimen in five hours, but sleep still felt far from him.

There came a soft tap on his bedroom door. He twitched, then rose stiffly from his desk—the spasticity in his legs and pelvis was really getting to him tonight. Wayne hobbled to his dresser, slipped on a shirt, struggled back to the door, and opened it.

Jessica stood in the hallway, her hair tousled and her eyelids heavy. She wore a pair of tiny shorts and a baggy Class of 2007 T-shirt, and her toenails were painted blue.

The room suddenly felt very warm.

"What's up?" he asked her.

"I can't sleep."

"Must be contagious."

"Can I come in?"

Wayne let out a breath. "Sure."

Jessica stepped into his room and quietly shut the door behind her. She glanced around, admiring his neatly kept inner sanctum, from the beige carpet to the light blue walls, to the tall floor lamp in the corner, angled over his desk. It was the tidiest place in the house, and not one many ever got to enter.

"You saw my video," she said, nodding at the PC on his desk, where her own face was frozen on the screen.

Wayne sat down on the edge of his bed. "Yeah. Want to talk about it?"

"I think I covered pretty much everything in the video."

"So, Jerry was killed by a mob?"

"It's scary."

"What is?"

"That people can be driven to do…that." Jessica sat down beside him and stared at her feet.

"You need to be extremely careful about what you mention in your videos from here on out," he said. "If one of his killers comes across your video, they're going to think one of the others blabbed to you, and you'll become a target."

"That's part of the reason I can't sleep. And what did Jerry even do in the first place? He won't tell me."

Wayne thought about it. "Do you think he killed someone?"

"I don't know." Jessica frowned. "He doesn't seem the type."

"You'd be surprised at who could kill, given the right circumstances."

"Well, he says he taught high school English. He reminds me of the literary Goths I knew in school."

"Literary Goths?"

"You know, the kids who hung out in the library all day, wishing they were vampires, or something. The ones who painted their nails black and wrote sad poems and pretended to be suicidal for attention."

"The emo kids?" Wayne asked wryly.

"Yeah, only Jerry is a grown man." She paused. "I know he won't leave here until he moves on for good, but that can't happen until we solve his murder, and I can't do that without putting myself into danger. So, what the hell am I supposed to do?"

"That is a very good question."

They sat together in silence for a few minutes. Wayne wondered if Jerry was with them even now, listening, though the room felt far from cold.

Jessica cleared her throat. "So, I hear you really like sex with women."

Wayne snapped back to attention. "Well, yeah." He coughed lightly, fully aware they were sitting inches apart *on his bed.*

"Been a while?"

"Too long," he admitted.

Jessica seemed to ponder that. "I don't remember you mentioning any girlfriends."

He shrugged. "I had a couple in college, and I dated Beth Hornsby from down at the town hall for about six months. They all left me. Couldn't handle the baggage."

"Their loss."

"There's a lot I haven't told you, Jessica."

"You don't have to."

"I appreciate that."

"So…is it hard?" Jessica asked.

"Is *what* hard?"

Her cheeks flushed. "You know. Sex."

Wayne looked down at his bare, inward-turning legs and awkwardly angled feet. He'd taken off his leg braces before bed and leaned them against the bedroom wall. Wayne always felt practically naked without them, especially if someone else was looking. "It's not easy," he said. "Are you sure you want to have this conversation with me?"

"I'm an adult, Wayne."

"I don't want to complicate things between us."

"Don't you think our lives are complicated already? I can handle it."

"Okay, then." He let out a breath. "Some things I just can't do. I generally had to be on the bottom and let them do most of the work. Which did make for some lovely views, I might add."

Jessica's blush deepened. "I'm sure it did. Were you afraid, the first time?"

"Isn't everyone?"

"I wouldn't know."

"I see. Um…why are you asking?"

"Because…" Jessica hesitated, then plunged ahead. "I just want you to know that I'm here. If you ever need anything. You know."

He couldn't help but smile at her. "I'll keep that in mind—preferably for a time when we're both more awake."

There came a soft thump from across the room. One of the leg braces that had been propped against the wall had fallen onto its side.

They both stared at it as if it were a venomous snake coiled and waiting.

"You don't think…?" Jessica asked, rising.

Wayne felt pale. Had that dead creep been here the whole time?

"You tell me," he said.

"I honestly don't know. It could have just been gravity."

"Gravity. Yes."

"Um, Wayne?"

"What?"

"I don't want you to think that I'm throwing myself at you like some virgin in the throes of desperation," Jessica said, "but would it bother you if I spent the night in here tonight? I think we'd both feel a little safer."

She certainly wasn't wrong about that.

"Sure," he said. "Just…let me sleep, okay?"

"Okay."

They climbed into bed and wriggled under the covers like a couple of teenage coeds. Wayne switched off the light, heart hammering at having Jessica in such close proximity. It felt right, though.

Maybe more right than anything ever had before.

Jerry floated somewhere near the ceiling, in the darkness, without form or shape.

The voices wouldn't stop whispering to him. He'd been able to hold them at bay for a long time, but now they were getting louder.

you're so close So Close SO CLOSE

just let go and WE will guide you

stop fighting it will only make things worse Much Worse MUCH WORSE SO CLOSE SO CLOSE SO CLOSE!!!

Things tugged at him with long, grasping fingers.

Jerry curled tighter into himself and waited for the dawn.

Jessica raced through a dark cemetery, into a forest even darker than the surrounding night. Hostility hung in the air like a black smog. She had to get away from them, but they were gaining on her. She could feel them at her heels!

"Jessica..." called a voice from far beyond the trees.

She angled toward the voice and kept running. If they caught her...

"Jessica!"

She jolted awake. Wayne stood at the foot of the bed, wearing mauve boxers and an unbuttoned peach-colored shirt over a plain white T-shirt. His hair appeared to have been recently moussed, and he smelled of aftershave.

Jessica smiled groggily at him. "Good morning."

"Where are my leg braces?" he asked.

"Huh?" She sat up and stretched, remembering she'd spent the night in his room instead of Sidney's. How bold of her!

"I can't find them," he said, frustration mounting in his voice. "And they were *right there* when we went to bed."

"I remember."

"Then where the hell are they? I'm going to be late for work!"

Jessica scrambled out of the bed and looked underneath it in the off-chance they'd been kicked there. "I don't see them."

"I've looked everywhere." He gave her a hard stare. "Jerry took them."

"Why would he do that?"

"Do you have a better explanation?"

Sidney poked her head into the room, her red hair a mass of tangles. "What's going on? Oh!" Her eyebrows shot upward as she looked back and forth between Jessica and Wayne.

"It's not what you think," they said in unison.

Sidney gave them a wicked grin. "Uh-huh."

"I don't have time for this," Wayne said. "Sidney, my braces are gone."

Her expression sobered instantly. "What do you mean?"

"I mean, they were here in my room, and now they're not. Help me look for them, please?"

"Yeah, sure." Sidney immediately knelt and looked under the bed.

"We checked there already."

"Well, they're not in my room. I haven't touched them."

Wayne's eyes flared with anger. "Let's see if they're downstairs."

"How would they have gotten there, if you keep them in here at night?"

"God only knows."

Wayne eased himself down the steps one by one and into the kitchen, making sure he didn't lose his balance and fall. He limped over to the cabinets and started yanking them open, muttering things like, "Cost me a *fortune* to have them custom-made," and "I'll *kill* that fucking ghost."

Sidney turned to Jessica, worried. "Am I the only person in this house who hasn't completely flipped their lid?"

"Probably."

While Wayne continued to ransack the kitchen, the two of them made cursory searches of the entire living room, Wayne's first floor "exercise" room, the mudroom, and the basement, with no luck.

Jessica wondered if Jerry was watching them. Surely this couldn't have been some sick game the ghost had chosen to play. Yes, his moods were about as stable as a two-legged stool, but this was juvenile, even cruel. Wayne's leg braces—the ankle-foot orthotics which allowed him vastly improved mobility—were as necessary to him as a wheelchair was to a paraplegic.

Wayne scissor-walked into the living room and flopped onto the couch. "I don't believe this. I've never been late for work before. Charlie's going to think I'm dead in a field somewhere."

"I'll drop you off," Sidney said without hesitation. "If your braces turn up, I'll bring them to you."

Wayne glanced at the round wall clock ticking seconds away without a care. "Yeah, let's do that. I'd rather not drive without them."

"Don't forget to put on pants before we go."

Wayne looked at his legs, then to Jessica. "Uh. There's a clean pair lying out on my dresser."

Jessica hurried up the stairs into the bedroom, whisked the khaki work pants off the dresser, and glared at the room.

She and Jerry needed to have a talk.

"Are you still here?" Jessica called out as soon as Sidney's Camry left the driveway.

Jerry did not appear, nor did she feel a chill indicating his proximity.

"Ugh." She marched back up to Wayne's bedroom again. Logic dictated the braces were still in the room somewhere since the bedroom door had been shut for the rest of the night. If Jerry had opened the door to remove the braces from the room, they would have heard it.

Jessica checked Wayne's attached bathroom, still hot with steam from his morning shower. Dirty clothes had been piled neatly into a hamper. A toothbrush, toothpaste, a razor, and a comb lay in a perfect row on the vanity. A Glade plug-in beside the sink puffed a nice smell into the room.

But there were no leg braces.

Jessica backed out of the bathroom and faced the closet, which seemed the next logical place to check. *Here goes nothing.*

She slid the closet door aside a little more viciously than planned. It hit the opposite door frame with a thud, sending a precariously placed box tumbling off a shelf onto the floor. A confetti of news clippings and other papers spewed across the carpet.

"Dammit." Jessica kneeled to clean up the mess. She started

stuffing clippings back into the box, when one of the headlines caught her eye.

"Teen Kills Mother in Self-Defense," it read. Startled, she brought the yellowing paper closer to her face so she could read the tiny print.

Police are still investigating the death of a Georgetown woman whose name has not yet been released.

According to reports, she viciously beat her thirteen-year-old son with a fireplace poker when he refused to bring her a glass of vodka and emptied the bottle down the drain. The teen was able to save himself by striking his mother on the head with that same poker. The blow proved fatal. The teen called 911, and his mother was pronounced dead on the scene.

"Extensive evidence indicates that the teen has been subject to horrific abuse for many years," said Officer Harry Watson, who was present at the scene. "He's lucky to be alive."

The teen told police that he suffers from cerebral palsy and that the ankle-foot orthotics he was required to wear were several sizes too small—he had not been fitted for a larger pair and had not been to physical therapy for more than three years. Two other adults present in the household were unable to provide an explanation for this grievous lack of care.

"As grim as this case is," Watson said, "the boy is fortunate to have been removed from such a terrible situation. We can only hope he'll have a bright future ahead of him."

The teen has been placed into foster care. It is unclear if the other adults in the home will be charged with child endangerment and neglect.

The last whisper of breath had left Jessica's lungs by the time she finished reading, and she realized she'd clapped a hand over her mouth in wordless horror.

She read the article twice more, taking it in one disturbing word at a time. Her eyes felt dry, like someone had filled them with sand,

and her ears were ringing.

A key grated in a lock down below. The front door squeaked open, and light footsteps crossed the entryway.

"Jessica?" Sidney called. "Where are you at?"

Jessica crammed all the clippings back into the box and shoved it onto the closet shelf. It took her a few tries to get words out of her mouth. "Up here."

Sidney knew. Had always known and protected her older cousin like a mother bear guarding a cub. Jessica conjured Wayne's face as it had appeared such a short time ago, and a black rage bubbled up inside her. To think someone could have ever hurt him so badly…

She turned to face Sidney when her friend came through the doorway, and the two of them froze, in unison, as they saw it.

Wayne's leg braces were leaning neatly against the bedroom wall, right where he'd left them.

16

"What are you trying to pull?" Sidney asked, her voice hard as granite.

"You think *I* did this?"

"You're the only other person in here! And you *slept* with him!"

Jessica ground her teeth together. "I spent the night in here because we were both scared."

"Ah, so you left me alone and vulnerable."

"It wasn't like that, and you know it. Jerry has to be the one who did this. He doesn't seem to like Wayne."

Sidney's expression went neutral, and she stooped to pick up the braces. "Are you trying to tell me Jerry is jealous that you spent the night in Wayne's room, and he decided to prank Wayne as punishment?"

"I don't know!"

"Jessica, Jerry isn't *real*. Now, I'm going to take these to Wayne's office, and I'm going to come back here and forget any of this ever happened. I swear to God, Jessica, if you do something to hurt my cousin, I'll never forgive you."

"I would never forgive *myself*," Jessica spat. "I care about him just as much as you do."

"We'll see about that." Sidney vanished into the hallway and clomped down the stairs. In less than a minute, her Camry coughed to life and faded from earshot, rattling down the street.

"What happened?" Jerry asked.

Jessica whirled. Jerry sat at Wayne's desk, eyes out of focus again.

"Why did you take Wayne's leg braces?" she demanded.

Jerry frowned. *Frowned*, for crying out loud! As if he truly had no clue.

"He wears them on his legs," Jessica said, as if explaining it to a particularly stupid kindergartener. "They help keep his feet and ankles stable so he can actually walk, and I think it's completely horrible that you would hide them as a joke."

It took Jerry a long time to speak. "I don't remember taking them."

"Then who did? Beetlejuice?"

Jerry looked baffled, and Jessica remembered he'd probably already been dead when that movie came out. "I keep slipping," he said. "Like parts of me are pulling away. I hear things."

"What kind of things?"

Jerry shuddered. "Voices. I…I remember now. I started hearing them around the time when she…when I…" He shook his head, then looked at her. "What were we talking about again?"

Jessica hesitated. Was this all some act, or was Jerry genuinely confused?

A flare of pain shot through her, giving her a start. Yesterday had been a good day, all things considered—she hadn't needed Tylenol at all, and she'd thought she'd gotten over the aches that had tormented her for more than a week. What had she done to make herself sore again?

Jessica breathed in slowly, then exhaled. She couldn't waste her whole day scrolling through WebMD, trying to diagnose herself. Her channel had been doing so much better with her posting new videos every day, and she needed more content since discussing Jerry's murder with her followers was out of the question.

"What do you want to do today?" she asked him.

He looked surprised. "What do *I* want to do?"

"That's what I just asked. We could go somewhere. Get you out of the house."

He rubbed his chin. "Let me think about it."

"Cool. While you do that, I'm going to get dressed and eat."

Ten minutes later, they convened in the living room. Jerry sat in Wayne's recliner expectantly.

"Have you thought of anything?" Jessica asked.

"I'd like to see my old house," Jerry said.

"I'm not driving to Cleveland."

He smiled thinly. "Not my childhood home. The one where I lived in Clarkville. The one they kidnapped me from. I haven't seen it since that night."

It seemed a good sign Jerry was seeking out some closure, as small as it might have been. "We can do that," she said. "But just to warn you, it probably isn't going to look the same after twenty-four years."

"I understand that. But still…I'd like to see."

Forty-five minutes later, Jessica pulled up outside the address Jerry had given her.

The house was a quaint brick two-story, with large shade trees in the front. The houses on this street were on well-kept half-acre lots, so the neighboring homes were close, but not overwhelmingly so. Jessica thought about what a feat it would have been for a mob of angry people to wrestle Jerry out of the house without any witnesses.

Unless the mob had been comprised of Jerry's own neighbors.

Jerry appeared in the passenger seat, staring out the window at the house. His face grew long with wistfulness, and she imagined he was thinking about much more than just a building.

"We can't stay long," Jessica said. "Someone will think we're loitering."

"It's not that different," Jerry said at length. "The new owners have maintained it well."

"That's good to hear, I guess. Are you going in?"

"I'd better not." Jerry rubbed his eyes. "It won't be the same inside. Everything that was *me* will have been long gone."

"This place meant a lot to you, didn't it?" Jessica thought of her own lost apartment, which could potentially have a new occupant already.

Jerry nodded. "I bought it about a year after my divorce. I thought it would be a good place to start over. Ironic, right?"

"You were married?"

"Only for a few years."

"Were you too different from each other?"

Jerry seemed to weigh this for a moment. "I think we were too much alike."

"Who wanted the divorce?"

He pressed his lips together. "It was a mutual agreement."

"Jerry...please don't take this the wrong way, but do you think that your divorce had anything to do with your murder?"

"Why would you think that?"

"They both seem to be pretty significant events in your life. I just wondered if there might be a connection."

"My wife was not part of the group that killed me. I never saw her again after the divorce was finalized. I died about six years after that."

"What was her name?"

"Abigail." He spat out the syllables as if they tasted bad. "The worst mistake of my life. If I ever see her again...I think I would try to kill her."

After that, Jessica drove back into Ohio, to the Rowe Woods branch of the Cincinnati Nature Center, which Jerry claimed to have enjoyed visiting alone from time to time since Abigail was not fond of the outdoors. Jessica had never been there before and had to pay a small fee to get in, then snatched a free trail map from the visitor center and plotted out a course that didn't look overly difficult.

Though not exactly what she'd call "in shape," Jessica hiked out to one of the more remote trails, where she wouldn't run into as many hikers, and planted herself on a bench, panting hard. She unscrewed the top off a Gatorade she'd picked up on the way there and chugged heartily.

"I'll have to come here more often," Jessica said once she'd caught her breath. "It's beautiful."

"The trees are bigger." Jerry stood on the path in front of her, peering up at the towering treetops.

"I bet."

"Do you know the history of this place?" he asked.

"Not really. My class went on a field trip here once, but I caught the stomach bug and couldn't go."

Jerry closed his eyes. "There was a man, long ago, named Carl Krippendorf. He got sick as a child and was sent here to recover, and when he grew up, he bought the property so it wouldn't be turned into farmland. And now it's been preserved forever so that people will always come here and enjoy it."

"What are you getting at?" Jessica asked.

"That man left behind a great legacy. Generations of people can appreciate what he did here. Decades from now, locals will still remember his name."

"And?"

Jerry's shoulders slumped. "I left behind a very different legacy, Jessica."

"It would be boring if we all had the same legacy, right? I mean, we're all different."

Jerry didn't answer her. He seemed to be lost in thought.

Jessica sipped at her Gatorade. "Can I ask you something?"

"Of course."

"What do you miss the most about life?"

Jerry sat on the bench beside her and draped his left arm across the back of it. "Nearly everything. I miss sensation—warmth, touch, comfort. I miss the potential of each new day. I suppose I even miss sex, but *not* Abigail, which is an important distinction." He lapsed into silence for a short time. "But most of all, I miss hope. It's a terrible thing to lose."

Jessica tried to put herself in Jerry's place. What would it be like to have no Wayne, no Sidney, no hot breakfast or steaming coffee, no YouTube channel, no hobbies, no anything?

What would it be like to simply *be*?

Without thinking, Jessica leaned her head against Jerry's shoulder. It didn't feel cold at all this time and seemed more solid than it ever had.

"What are you doing?" Jerry asked her.

Jessica tried not to let her unshed tears show in her voice. "I'm sharing a little comfort. It might not be hope, but it's the only thing I've got to give."

Wayne spent the entire morning struggling to keep his thoughts on the tasks at hand. Cindy, the firm's secretary, had asked him if he was feeling okay at least three times, and he only heard half of what was said during the staff meeting at nine thirty.

Charlie Korman rapped on the doorframe of Wayne's corner office just after 11:00 a.m. "Wayne? Care if I come in?"

Wayne swiveled his chair around to face his boss. Today, Charlie wore a black tie with a pumpkin pattern printed on it.

"No, what is it?"

The older man took a few steps into the room and sat in a spare seat Wayne had pushed up against the wall. "You've been distracted today."

"Yeah, well, I couldn't find my leg braces. My cousin found them and dropped them off for me a while ago."

"Is something else eating at you?"

Too much. "I didn't sleep much last night. I'll be fine, though."

They stared at each other for a few long moments. "If you say so," Charlie finally said, rising. "But really, Wayne. We're like family here. If something's wrong, don't hesitate to tell me about it."

Wayne gave him a solemn nod. "Understood."

Charlie left the office and closed the door behind him. Good riddance. Charlie meant well, but Wayne was not about to go to the man with tales of restless spirits playing havoc with him in his own home.

The office emptied out around lunchtime. Instead of joining the majority of his coworkers at the café across the street, Wayne ordered a chicken wrap to-go and took it back to the office with him, claiming he needed to go over a client's financial statements one final time.

He sank into his swivel chair with the chicken wrap in one hand and gazed at the icons on the computer screen, thinking.

Fact: Jerry had tried to attack him, sent his emotions reeling, and stolen his ankle-foot orthotics for no apparent reason.

Conclusion: Jerry had to go.

Why had Jerry taken such a liking to Jessica in the first place? The cemetery at that church had to receive lots of visitors, and Jerry hadn't followed any of *them* home.

A pang of jealousy flared briefly inside him. *Don't be stupid*, he told himself. The dead did not seek romantic relationships with the living. Romance would be the least of Jerry's worries.

Taking a bite of the chicken wrap, Wayne clicked the web browser and typed "Jerry Madison" into the search bar on Google's home page. The search returned numerous links to social media sites like Facebook and LinkedIn, neither of which would help him learn more about his house's newest resident, since Jerry had evidently died more than twenty years ago.

He redid the search, adding the word "obituary" to the end of the keywords. More results came up, but none of the deceased Jerry Madisons were from Kentucky or anywhere else in the tri-state.

Several minutes ticked by while Wayne finished the wrap and washed it down with a bottle of Dasani. He returned his attention to the screen, fingers hovering over the keyboard. Billions of web pages floated around in cyberspace. Something about Jerry had to be out there.

A search for "Gerald Madison obituary" revealed nothing standing out in importance. He deleted "Gerald" and typed "Jeremiah" and then "Gerard." Still nothing. Wayne banged his hand on the desk in frustration. He supposed Jerry's obituary had yet to be digitized from old newspaper archives.

A new idea came to him then, and Wayne typed "Jerry Madison missing person Clarkville Kentucky."

He hit Enter.

The first several search results just coincidentally contained combinations of those terms, but the fifth link down said, "What Happened to Uncle Jerry?"

"Huh." Wayne clicked the link. The page loaded, and a blog with a purple background appeared.

He began to read:

What Happened to Uncle Jerry?

It's a question that my family and I have been asking for more than two decades. My name is Casey Madison Green, and I've set up this blog in the hope that someone out there will be able to tell us something.

My father Daniel's younger brother, Jerry Benjamin Madison, was last seen on June 29, 1986 at a Walgreens near Clarkville, Kentucky, which is the town where he lived at 640 Elderberry Drive. He was thirty-three years old, Caucasian, with a thin build, dark brown hair, and bright blue eyes.

I was twelve years old when he went missing. He and I weren't particularly close since we lived several hours apart from each other, but we did see each other at all the major family holiday gatherings. He wasn't very chatty unless he found the subject matter of interest, in which case he would (according to my other uncle, Alan Madison) be incapable of shutting up. He usually had his nose in a book. My family says that Jerry's sarcasm was legendary.

Jerry had been through an ugly divorce six years earlier, and according to my father, he sank into such a deep depression that he often spoke of suicide. My father—a therapist—counseled Jerry for free over the phone in the hope that it would help him.

My father tried to call Jerry on July 1, 1986 to check in with him but got no answer. He tried ringing again the next day, and the next. On July 4, he and my Uncle Alan drove down to Jerry's house in Clarkville and found that he was gone. Jerry's wallet and luggage were not missing from the house, and his car remained in the driveway.

The local police did not take Jerry's disappearance seriously despite my father's insistence that Jerry had been in an erratic mental state and may have been a danger to himself. They wouldn't even send out search teams to check the nearby rivers and forests to see if Jerry had chosen to commit suicide in the open air.

Increasingly frustrated at the police's blatant unwillingness to help, my family hired a private investigator, who unfortunately was unable to find any new leads. To this day, we don't know if Jerry committed suicide, had a terrible accident, was murdered, or ran off to start a new life somewhere else.

If someone is out there reading this and knows something, please send me an email through the contact form at the bottom of this page. My family has been waiting for many long years for the closure we deserve. And Jerry—if you're alive and reading this, please know that we love and miss you. You may not want to come home, but at least let us know you're okay.

Casey Madison Green had attached about a dozen different photos of a slender, dark-haired man ranging in age from his mid-twenties to his early thirties. He wore all black in most of them. Jessica hadn't been kidding; this guy looked like someone who hung out with talking ravens in his free time.

Wayne pasted the website text and photos into a Word document and printed them. He wondered if he should reach out to Casey with an anonymous tip that her dear uncle had been massacred by an angry mob.

But then he had a better idea.

17

Jessica had just finished recording and posting that day's video when Wayne called her cell phone. "What's up?" she asked, her tone guarded. The news clipping from his bedroom closet kept flashing through her mind, making her feel almost dizzy. She wanted to talk with him about it eventually—but now wasn't the time.

"I'm clocking out early today," Wayne said. "Can you come pick me up?"

"Is everything okay?"

"You know it's not. Is You-Know-Who there?"

"I don't think so. We went on a little trip today, and he seemed to fizzle out after a while. I haven't seen him since."

Wayne paused before speaking. "Maybe don't encourage him to come with you."

"Look at this," Wayne said, spreading out four sheets of paper across a table at the Eleanor Public Library, which is where Wayne asked Jessica to take him after picking him up from work.

Jessica leaned in closer and frowned. Three of the pages showed various photos of Jerry as he'd appeared in life, and the fourth was a blog post by someone named Casey Madison Green, talking about her missing uncle.

"Should we email Casey?" Jessica asked when she finished reading. She tried not to think about Wayne's mother beating him with a fireplace poker. Did he still have scars? She didn't think she'd ever seen him shirtless.

"Not yet." Wayne shoved his glasses farther up his nose. "I've been thinking. You hear all sorts of ghost stories. Apparently, some ghosts get stuck here because they don't have closure. You told me that Jerry was buried in an unmarked grave."

"Yeah, probably right where he was killed. They wouldn't have wanted to move the body."

"Too risky for them," Wayne agreed. "But what if you and I tried to find the body? We dig it up, call the police, and email Casey. Jerry's case gets reopened—"

"You mean 'opened.'"

"Right. They open Jerry's case, the bad guys get caught, Jerry gets a new grave with a nice headstone, and he finally has closure so he can leave us alone."

"Except for the fact that he thinks he'll go to hell."

"I'd forgotten about that. Hmm."

"I wonder if a priest or a pastor or someone would know what to do about that," Jessica said. "I have Al Tumler's number saved in my phone."

"Who?"

"He's the one who told me about the haunted graveyard in the first place. It's his church."

"I don't know how good of an idea it is to bring outside parties into this, in case things get too ugly. And if Jerry does go to hell, it's not our problem."

"That's awful!"

Wayne shrugged. "It would be of his own making. But anyway…

what do you think about my idea?"

Jessica chewed her lip. Find Jerry's body? Sounded like a plan. "When do you want to do it?" she asked.

"I'm not sure. We'll need to be prepared, and it might take a while to find him, so this afternoon isn't good. I don't want to go digging around out there after dark."

"We'd need permission to be there too," Jessica said. "I could tell Al that my equipment malfunctioned last week so I need to redo my investigation."

"It would be kind of hard to explain how we just so happened to dig a large hole and find human remains, though."

"That's true." Jessica thought about it. She would definitely need a convincing cover story to avoid suspicion and possible arrest for trespassing. "Do you still have your old metal detector?"

"Yeah, why?"

"I can ask Al Tumler if we're allowed to go metal detecting on his church's property. Then once we're there, we can ask Jerry to show us where they put him. We can pretend that we found the body while digging up a piece of metal."

"What if his body is six feet deep?"

"We could say it was a *big* piece of metal."

Wayne seemed to think about it, then nodded. "It's not great, but it does work. I can use another one of my sick days and take tomorrow off. We could head out early in the morning and call it a date."

"I can't tomorrow. Rachel and Eric are flying in, and I know they'll want to spend the day with me."

"Friday, then. I'm not waiting any longer than that to get that ghost out of my house."

Jessica dipped her head in agreement. "Friday morning it is."

Jessica's cell phone rang at seven thirty Thursday morning. She rolled over in bed and answered it. "Hi, Rachel," she slurred.

"Oh, did I wake you up? I'm sorry." A loud chatter of voices nearly drowned out her sister's words.

"Where are you?" Jessica asked, standing up and stretching. Her body was still aching. No surprise there.

"We're standing at the baggage claim," Rachel said. "We're getting a rental car and heading over to Uncle Esteban's to unload our stuff, if and when our suitcase appears. After that, we can meet up for lunch. If you're not busy, of course."

"I'm free all day. Did you have anywhere in mind?"

"Is Tim's Taco Barn still in business? I've been craving it like crazy. Damn pregnancy hormones."

Jessica laughed. "It's still there. What time?"

"Be there at a quarter to twelve. If you beat us there, get us a table. Hang on—Eric, our bag has the blue piping. No, not that one!" Rachel groaned. "Sorry, I've got to go before we end up stealing someone else's luggage. See you soon!"

Jessica didn't have to wait long for her sister and brother-in-law to arrive at the restaurant. She'd barely had a chance to look at the menu when a gray Nissan Altima glided into a space right outside the window. Rachel climbed out of the passenger seat wearing a copper-colored maxi dress, shouldered her Vera Bradley purse, and sashayed inside with Eric in tow.

Jessica stood and waved at them. "Over here!"

She and Rachel rushed toward each other and hugged. Then Jessica stepped back to take a good look at her sister. Rachel's hair was done in a light brown pixie cut, and she'd put on a few pounds around her middle. "You look great," Jessica said, and meant it.

"*Please* don't tell me I'm glowing," Rachel replied with a wink. "I just know I won't hear the end of it at the reunion on Saturday."

Jessica turned to Eric. "And how have you been?"

"Better than ever." Eric's dishwater-blond hair was cropped in a buzz cut, and he wore an Izod polo and khaki slacks. He gave her a tired smile. "I could definitely do with a nap, though. Kids were screaming the whole flight, and it was a *red-eye*."

"He's afraid that's what we have to look forward to," Rachel said.

Jessica grinned. "Isn't it?"

They took seats at the table and browsed their menus. After the server came and took their order, Jessica said, "Did you ever talk to Mom and Dad about your big news?"

Rachel and Eric exchanged dark glances. "Yeah." Rachel rolled her eyes. "Mom asked me if I thought it was wise to bring another child into the world, with the way it is."

"She has such a knack for making people feel good, doesn't she?"

"I gave up trying to psychoanalyze our mother a long time ago. She made it clear to me and you what was the most important to her, and I have to just accept that. Eric's parents are thrilled, though."

"Because they actually have souls," Eric commented.

Jessica's mood had begun to darken at the thought of Maria Roman-Dell coldly accepting impending grandparenthood. In all honesty, everything about Maria was cold. She was like a living ice sculpture: get her too close to human warmth, and it would destroy her.

"Dad did take it better than Mom," Rachel went on. "He wants us to keep him posted about any 'developments,' whatever that means."

"That sounds so clinical." Jessica could feel her mind slipping away from the restaurant and into the past, when she'd been small and vulnerable and just wanted a mother who would hold her and listen.

At least you had her and not Wayne's mother, whispered a voice. *Because let's face it: Maria never laid a hand on you.*

Maria had never done much of anything else either. Yay, Maria.

The food arrived, and the three of them dug in.

"So, Jessica," Rachel said after finishing her second bite of Burrito Supremo, "I'm dying to know what's inspired this new direction your YouTube channel is taking."

Jessica nearly inhaled a tortilla chip mid-swallow. "You follow me?"

"We both do," Eric said. "I've been sharing all your videos on my Facebook profile. Some of my friends are major paranormal buffs."

A grin spread across Jessica's face. "Wow, thanks. They're good, then?"

Eric nodded. "I have to say, they're captivating. How did you make that 'They must die' voice? I watched that one at my buddy's place, and the voice upset his dog."

"I didn't 'make' it," Jessica said, trying not to sound too irritated. She'd be skeptical too, if she were in Eric's place. "That was an actual recording. Everything I've been talking about in my videos is completely true."

Rachel's eyes went round. "You mean…?"

"I *mean*, Jerry Madison isn't a figment of my imagination. Wayne has felt him too. We've been trying to figure out how to get Jerry to move on so we don't have a ghost as a roommate for the rest of our lives."

"I don't know whether to be horrified or delighted for you," Rachel said, looking somewhat impressed.

"Be delighted," Jessica replied. "I checked my channel before I drove up here. I have three hundred and seven followers now."

"What's the threshold for getting monetized?" Eric asked.

"A thousand, I think. But people have to keep watching my videos too. Then YouTube will start putting ads in them—"

Eric groaned at this.

"—and then I'll get paid a percentage of the ad revenue. It's going to take a while to get there, but I really feel like I'm heading in the right direction with this whole thing. Honestly, meeting Jerry has been the best thing to happen to me in a long time."

"You mean moving in with your boy toy isn't?" Rachel asked, one eyebrow suggestively raised.

"Wayne and I aren't dating," Jessica said, a little too forcefully. She remembered how nice and warm it had been being under the covers with him and felt the heat rising in her cheeks.

"You really care about him, though, don't you?"

"I do. He's given me some tips for my channel too. He's the one who suggested that I include some local color, so I went to Promont House and Bobby Mackey's. I didn't meet any ghosts there, though. Which is fine; I'm learning it can be a little scary."

"I had a haunted dorm my first year at NYU," Eric said. "None of the guys believed me. Stuff was constantly getting moved. Doors would open and close for no reason. I'd hear whispering in the corners whenever I was alone..." He shivered at the memories. "I never saw any apparitions, but let me tell you, it sure made it hard to sleep when you didn't know if something was in there watching you."

"I can imagine."

"Jessica, did I ever tell you about the creepy stuff you did when you were little?" Rachel asked.

Jessica felt a chill pass over her. "What kind of creepy stuff?"

"You had an imaginary friend named Sarah. It all started one night when I got up to pee and heard you chattering away at someone in your room. I stood in the doorway, listening, because I thought it was funny that you were talking in your sleep, but then it started getting weird. 'Why are you red all over?' you asked. 'I don't like you floating on the ceiling like that.' You kept pausing like you were listening to someone. Then it got to where you'd be playing during the day and you'd get upset because I'd accidentally come along and sit on Sarah or walk on Sarah or who-the-hell-knew with Sarah. It made Mom really upset."

"I literally have no memory of any of that."

"Well, you were only three or four, and it stopped after a year or so.

Your ghost friend must have moved on to somewhere else."

The coldness settled deep into Jessica's bones, as if it planned to stay. "Do you think our house was haunted?"

"No idea. But let's say it was and that you can really see ghosts. How amazing is that?"

Jessica wasn't sure why, but her stomach began to churn. She pushed her half-eaten meal away from her and dabbed her lips with a napkin. Was Jerry not the first ghost she'd met, but the second? Had this mysterious "Sarah" planted the seed of an idea into Jessica's toddler-mind? A seed that had grown into a desire so intense, Jessica had dedicated her life to finding others like Sarah?

What things had Sarah said to her?

"Are you okay?" Rachel asked. "You don't look so good all of a sudden."

"I'm just trying to process this." Jessica swallowed. "If I can see ghosts...*all* ghosts...how many others have I seen and not had a clue?"

Her phone chimed. Forcing herself to breathe deeply to loosen the tightness in her chest, Jessica dug it out of her purse and checked her messages.

She had one, from Sidney: *Get back here NOW.*

18

Thursdays were generally Sidney's day off. She'd spent the morning tidying her half of the bedroom while Jessica lurked down below, working on the next installment in her online ghost saga. Once Jessica had gone off to meet her sister for lunch, Sidney had curled up on the living room couch with a crochet pattern book, a basket of yarn, and a steaming mug of coffee.

Neither Jessica nor Wayne knew this, but Sidney had been talking to a therapist named Jenna, who volunteered at Holy Trinity Church. Sidney really wasn't sure what sort of things she believed in these days, but it was her mother's old church, and the therapy was free, so she couldn't complain.

Jenna had encouraged Sidney to find joy in the small things, and Sidney really was *trying*. She'd searched for crochet books at the nearest Goodwill in an attempt to improve her mood and found one dedicated to cutesy Halloween decorations, but today, she kept reading the same step of Crocheted Cthulhu (Tentacle #4, Row 2) over and over without registering any of it.

She couldn't stop thinking about the Ghost Problem. Or was it the Jessica Problem? Perhaps they were one and the same.

At twelve fifteen, Sidney slapped the book shut and said, "Ugh!"

She'd found the papers about Jerry Madison Wayne had brought home from work and stuck on the kitchen counter. He seemed just as caught up in this whole thing as Jessica was, which made Sidney nervous. Wayne was a level-headed guy. If *he* believed in this ghost, then the ghost was probably real.

Sidney felt her teeth begin to chatter. Was the ghost there this very moment?

Damn, did she need a smoke.

Her purse lay on the kitchen counter next to the printouts of the Jerry Madison photos. Sidney hurried to it and grabbed out her pack of Camel Menthols and a lighter. She would take a quick smoke break outside, come back in, and finish Cthulhu's damned tentacle once she'd settled her nerves a bit.

As she started toward the mudroom behind the kitchen, the half-empty pack of cigarettes flew out of her hand and landed on the floor six feet in front of her.

She stared at it for a long moment, then carefully stooped and picked it up. Had she been so jittery she'd unintentionally flung it? Yes. Of course, that's what had happened.

A strong breeze whipped her hair around when she stepped out onto the deck. Now the area had finally received rain, Sidney no longer had to worry about torching the yard with a smoldering cigarette butt. She sank into a patio chair, slid one cigarette from the box, and lit it, inhaling deeply.

"Ghosts aren't real," she said out loud. Sometimes speaking things made them feel truer. "They're just stories, like vampires and Bigfoot and Mothman."

The nicotine was already making Sidney feel a little better. The drone of a lawn mower several houses down, combined with the balmy warmth of the autumn day, made her eyelids grow heavy. Maybe she should rest for a little while…

Sidney's head shot up. The cigarette had slipped through her fingers and gone out on the deck boards. The lawn mower that had lulled her into semiconsciousness still hummed as its owner made circuits around his yard.

The back of Sidney's neck prickled the way it did whenever she'd walk into a room and just *knew* there was a giant spider hiding in it somewhere. She slowly stood and turned in a complete circle, trying to pinpoint the source of her unease, half expecting to see undead faces peering out at her through the windows.

"Ghosts aren't real," she said, less certainly this time. Jessica and Wayne's delusions were getting to her bad, weren't they? Why else would she feel like invisible eyeballs had latched onto her?

Squaring her shoulders with a stoicism she didn't feel, Sidney went back into the house. Her feet rooted themselves to the mudroom floor, and her heart beat as frantically as a trapped bird.

What if she wasn't safe here? Could ghosts hurt people? Wayne and Jessica were certain a ghost had taken the leg braces as a mean prank. If a ghost could do that, what else could it do?

Sidney grabbed a Swiffer mop propped against the wall and aimed the handle in front of her, like a spear. She stepped into the kitchen. "Hello? Jerry?"

One of the printouts had wafted off the counter and onto the white tile floor. The breeze from the backdoor opening and closing had done that, right?

Right?

"I can't believe I've sunk to this level." Sidney scoped out the exercise room and living room, seeing nothing out of place in either location. Yet the sense of being watched burned even stronger, to the point of utmost certainty.

Someone *was* here, in this house. Sidney *knew* it.

She tiptoed up the stairs and investigated the two bedrooms on the second floor, then returned to the kitchen, still sure someone or something was keeping an eye on her every move.

One of the other printouts had fallen off the counter and onto the floor. Sidney picked up the two pieces of paper and stacked them with the others. The faded image of a thin man with dark hair and hauntingly blue eyes stared back at her. Sidney took the opportunity to study the picture in greater detail. Jerry wore jeans and a dark T-shirt and was leaning against a wall, holding a plastic party cup and giving the photographer a wry smile that did anything but convey happiness.

And someone had allegedly murdered him just a few years after the picture had been taken.

Why? Had the man whose "sarcasm was legendary," as the printout put it, taken it a step too far and pissed off the wrong person?

Not quite believing what she was about to do, Sidney hurried back up to her bedroom, dug a voice recorder out of Jessica's bulging bag of ghost hunting equipment, and then sat down at the kitchen table with a fresh track going.

"Hi," Sidney said uncertainly. "Um, this is really weird for me, so bear with me, okay?"

She paused like she knew Jessica did during sessions like these.

"I don't even really believe in this kind of thing, but I can feel that something is seriously wrong in this house. I've lived here with Wayne for over a year now, ever since I turned eighteen. I thought he'd like having me here to help since he has a hard time doing certain things on his own. I'm rambling now, aren't I? But I guess what I'm saying is, nothing here was weird until Jessica dragged you home with her."

Sidney strained to hear if any ghostly voices were replying to her.

The temperature in the kitchen began to drop.

"Oh, hello," she said, a fearful sweat breaking out across her body. "Are you trying to make contact?"

The air felt so cold now, she could see her breath curling into wisps, like a dissipating mist.

"Um, it's getting extremely cold in here. Why do ghosts do that, exactly? Is it for the ambiance?" Sidney's spidey senses went into overdrive. "You can show yourself, you know!" she all but shouted, rising from the chair. "You don't have to scare me!"

Sidney heard a soft sound. She turned and saw…

Her mind blanked, unable to comprehend the *thing* pulsating by the short hallway leading to the mudroom. At once she felt a blackness, as if poisoned tendrils were reaching out to claim her and draw her into a fathomless maw from which she could never escape.

What a cute little bitch, she thought, but the thought was not her own. *I like to watch you squirm.*

She fled.

Tires squealed as Jessica whipped her car into the driveway, followed closely by Rachel and Eric in their airport rental.

Sidney sat on the edge of the concrete slab in front of the house, staring at her feet. Jessica heaved a relieved sigh at the sight of her friend. Her urgent text had made Jessica fear the worst.

Jessica moved from the car to the porch as quickly as her cramping muscles would allow. "Sidney?" she asked. "What's going on?"

Sidney didn't lift her head. Rachel and Eric came up beside them, faces awash with concern.

Jessica knelt beside Sidney. Tears streaked down Sidney's cheeks, smudging her mascara.

"Talk to me. What happened here?"

Sidney licked her lips. "I…It…" She extended one arm, offering Jessica her own voice recorder. "Listen."

Jessica took the device and thumbed it to the newest track.

"The time draws near," rasped the same horrid voice that had hijacked Jessica's own recording the other day. *"The time draws near. The time draws near."*

"What the fuck?" Rachel blurted. "Turn that thing off!"

Jessica did, not wanting to hear the voice any longer than she had to. "Sidney," she said as delicately as possible, "can you tell me exactly what happened?"

Sidney's complexion, normally bone-white due to a large percentage of Irish ancestry, had become a death mask. "I felt like I was being watched. I wanted to…to talk to it. Him. It got so cold. And then…" Her breath hitched. "I saw something. Not a man. A thing."

"What kind of thing?" Eric asked, looking almost excited.

Sidney opened her mouth and closed it. "I can't wrap my mind around it. It *hated* me. It hated everything about me and wanted me to die. I think that's what it looked like."

Jessica frowned. "It looked like hate?"

"I don't know how else to put it." Sidney wiped her eyes on her sleeve. "I can see it perfectly clearly in my mind, but there aren't human words that can describe it, except for that."

"So, it didn't look like the photos of Jerry that Wayne found online."

"It wasn't *human*, Jessica."

"Okay. Um." Jessica's mind raced. Had Jerry manifested himself to Sidney in some other form Jessica hadn't seen yet? Instead of his physical shape, had he shown her his soul?

One thing was certain: this would make an *amazing* video for her channel. She even had another spooky voice to add to it now.

Then Jessica remembered something. "Did you feel an angry, red aura?" she asked Sidney.

"What the hell is that supposed to mean?"

"You'd know it if you'd felt it, so I'm guessing no."

Sidney's jaw clenched suddenly, and she stood. "I can't stay here," she said, more to herself than to Jessica. "I'll have to stay at Dad's until that thing is gone."

"Maybe we should go inside and have a look around?" Eric suggested.

Sidney crossed her arms. "You can go inside, but I'm staying right here until one of you brings me my purse and car keys. Then I'm out of here."

Once Sidney had driven away, Jessica, Rachel, and Eric assembled in the living room.

"How does it feel in here to you?" Eric asked.

"Normal," Jessica admitted. "I haven't seen Jerry today, so I don't know where he is."

"It sounds like he's busy scaring the daylights out of your friend." Rachel gave the room an appraising look. "Cute place, by the way."

"Thanks," Jessica said in a flat tone. "But I don't understand why he would have done that to Sidney. When he went after Wayne, it's because Wayne had pissed him off. And why didn't he look human?"

"Maybe whatever Sidney saw wasn't Jerry," Eric said.

Jessica stared at her brother-in-law. "Who else would it have been?"

Eric hesitated a moment. "I don't want to freak you out, but ghosts aren't the only things lurking around out there."

"What are you getting at?" Rachel asked.

"I hate to say it, but…" Eric drew in a deep breath and plowed forward. "It sounds like Sidney saw a demon."

It was all Jessica could do not to laugh out loud. "You're kidding, right? Are Sam and Dean pulling up in their Impala to come save the day?"

Eric didn't smile. "I'm not sure what you're referencing, but I wouldn't be flippant about that kind of thing. My friends who are into the paranormal have a lot of stories to tell. Not all of them good ones."

"How would a demon have gotten into our house?"

Eric shrugged. "The same way the ghost did. Presumably, the front door."

Jessica really wasn't sure she was buying Eric's theory. The odds of having both a ghost and a demon getting cozy in Wayne's house at the exact same time were so abysmally low, they were next to zero. And weren't demons supposed to go around possessing people, or something?

"Supposing there *is* a demon in this house," Jessica said, "how the hell do I get rid of it?"

"Easy," Eric said. "You call an exorcist."

"I think you've been watching too many horror movie marathons these past few weeks," Rachel said.

Eric's jaw clenched. "I'm serious about this. Something obviously spooked Jessica's friend badly enough that she isn't coming back."

"Well, it's gone now." Jessica put her hands on her hips. "Right?"

Eric shuffled his feet. Rachel gave the corners of the room wary glances.

"Yeah," Rachel said. "I think it's gone."

19

Dinner that evening was an extremely quiet affair, save for the clinking of forks on plates as Jessica and Wayne finished their chicken cordon bleu. Unspoken thoughts, heavier than rainclouds, hung above them. Jessica wasn't sure whose silence would crack first, nor did she know how ugly the ensuing conversation would be.

Wayne cleared his plate and wiped his mouth with a napkin. "So," he said, staring at her over the tops of his glasses.

"Um," Jessica said. *Very eloquent,* she thought. *I simply excel at communication during times of crisis.*

"I heard from Sidney."

"Yeah?"

Wayne's expression hardened. "Have you talked to Jerry today?"

She shook her head. "I think he might still be recharging after we went out yesterday."

"Recharging *how*? By giving my cousin a coronary?"

"I don't know!"

Wayne breathed in deeply, then slowly exhaled. "I'm not angry at you, you know. You didn't ask for any of this to happen. But your little buddy can't keep doing this to people."

"I know. That's why we're digging him up tomorrow, remember?"

Wayne nodded. "I'll be honest; I'm not looking forward to that.

You did get permission from that pastor, right?"

"I called him this morning after breakfast. He says we can use the metal detector anywhere we want, except for in the graveyard, and we have to put the dirt back into any holes we dig."

"Good. Do you think Jerry will lead us to his body?"

"I don't see why not. I know it really bothers him that he wasn't properly laid to rest."

They both fell silent, thinking. *Talk to him about the other thing,* whispered a voice inside Jessica's head. *Get it off your chest before it eats you to the core.*

Jessica looked down at the tabletop. "There's something else I need to talk to you about."

She could sense Wayne's gaze on her.

"Is this regarding the conversation we had the other night?"

"No. It's...something different. After Sidney took you to work yesterday, I kept looking for your leg braces. I opened your bedroom closet and accidentally knocked over a box full of old news clippings. They went all over the place, and I had to pick them up."

She lifted her head to see his reaction. At first, Wayne's expression was blank, but then his eyes widened.

"Oh."

"I read that article," she said. "I couldn't help it; it was right there."

"I'm sorry you had to see it," he replied softly.

"Do you want to tell me about it?"

Wayne kneaded his eyelids. "You realize that this is the point where my ex-girlfriends decided they were done with me, right?"

"I'm not your ex-girlfriends. You can tell me more."

"Fine." He stared at his plate, seeming to steel his emotions so they wouldn't pour out in a rush. "My mother had an addiction to alcohol. Vodka was her preferred poison. She wasn't the mother of the year when sober, and her moods would always get worse whenever she'd been drinking. She would have killed me eventually."

"So, you killed her."

The color rose in his cheeks, and his eyes watered. "She was beating me with a fireplace poker. I yanked it away from her and fought back. I'm not proud of it. I wish it could have ended differently, with her in prison. But it didn't."

"The article mentioned other adults in the house. Your dad and someone else?"

"My useless grandparents," Wayne corrected her. Anger rose behind his eyes. "They were in denial about far too many things. They're both still alive, the last I heard. I haven't seen them since 1994."

"They just *let* your mom beat you?"

Wayne's nostrils flared. "I don't know if 'let' is the right word. They'd be in the next room, pretending it wasn't happening. They were out of the house, getting groceries, on that last day. And the rest is history." He put his face in his hands. "God, I never imagined talking to you about this. When... When Beth Hornsby left me, she said that she'd never be able to think of me again without thinking of *that*." He paused, remembering. "It took a long time to get over the sting of that one. I'd thought she was the one."

"I'm really sorry." Tears welled in Jessica's eyes. "You deserved so much better than all of that."

Wayne perked up a bit. "And I got so much better, as a kid. Marjorie and Drew Miller were deemed the fittest relatives to take me in. The first few years were hard because I'd never been loved before. I think I went to therapy just about every day for a while. Physical therapy too. Better mobility let me do more for myself, and Marjorie and Drew taught me that I was just as worthy of love as their own children." Wayne looked at Jessica long and hard. "If you're not comfortable with any of this and want to go, I won't stop you."

"Wayne, I would never!"

"I killed my own mother, Jessica. Some people would call me a murderer."

"But it was an accident. She was hurting you."

He shrugged. "Semantics."

"Why did you keep that article?"

"It's my history. I can't pretend it never happened. I acknowledge the past, and I let it go."

Jessica knew then Wayne was a far braver person than she'd ever imagined. "Does that mean you forgive your mother for what she did?"

Wayne gave a hollow laugh. "I'll never forgive her. But I did forgive myself, and I think that makes all the difference."

At two minutes to midnight, Sidney turned a key in Wayne's front doorknob and crept on tiptoes into the house.

After a few hours at her dad's that evening, Sidney had begun to wonder if she'd imagined the *thing* that had sent her fleeing. She'd been drowsy after her nap on the deck; perhaps she'd still been half asleep when she went inside…? Because stuff like this was *fiction*, dammit. She shouldn't believe in hallucinations.

Sidney did, however, believe in taking precautions. Just in case.

Her sixteen-year-old brother Kyle followed her into Wayne's house, yawning. "So, where's the monster?" he asked.

"I don't know," she hissed. "You just stay here and keep watch while I grab my things."

"Sure." He plopped into one of the kitchen chairs and laid his head on the table.

"Kyle! You're supposed to stand guard!"

"I said I'm too tired. Maybe monsters need sleep too."

"Ugh." Sidney set her purse down and ascended the staircase as lightly as she could. In her haste to leave earlier, she'd forgotten to grab her favorite pillow and her bottle of melatonin tablets, two things that would ensure a decent night's sleep. She'd tried to sleep on borrowed pillows in her old bedroom at home but couldn't get comfortable, and the lack of melatonin had left her wide awake, questioning her own sanity.

Sidney reached the landing and pushed her bedroom door open, using a penlight to see. Jessica was curled into a big wad with her comforter on her side of the room, breathing softly. Good.

Sidney went to her own bed and reached for her pillow, when the wall behind her headboard creaked loudly. She gritted her teeth. *It's just because the temperature is dropping outside*, she told herself. Not every spooky sound had to be a ghost.

She eyed the bottle of melatonin sitting atop her nightstand and plucked it up with care so the contents wouldn't rattle.

"The time draws near," Jessica mumbled.

Sidney's breath caught in her throat.

Across the hall, Wayne let out one of his dream-yelps.

Jessica rolled over. "Make them stop looking at me. Don't like their eyes…Monsters…"

The wall creaked again, in a different place this time.

"Gotta kill them, make them go away…"

Sidney felt frozen in place while Jessica continued talking in her sleep. She must have been dreaming about Sidney's monster. Should she wake her, or…?

"The time draws near. They must die."

"Sidney?" Kyle called up the stairs. "You coming?"

She took her pillow and melatonin and hurried from the room, part of her wondering if she was making a terrible mistake and the other chiding her for overreacting.

Jessica was viewing the world once again through a man's eyes.

She—he—sat at a table in an unfamiliar kitchen, staring out the window at a bright green lawn. A woman at a neighboring house was hanging laundry on a line. Her baby sat on a blanket laid out beneath a broad maple tree, and an older child of six or seven rode her bicycle in circles through the grass, making *vrooming* noises as she went.

He couldn't stand to look at them, so he turned away. Abigail had just called. Said she'd been to the women's clinic that morning. At first, he couldn't understand why she'd gone; she'd already started putting together a nursery, for Christ's sake! But the deed was done, she'd said. There wasn't any going back. She'd written the check from their joint account, which had yet to be dissolved following their recent divorce.

Served him right, she had said. He'd helped make the thing.

But why? he had asked. *I would have taken full custody, if that's what you wanted.*

She'd laughed. He demanded to know where she was. The line went dead.

A pain greater than any he'd ever known filled him then. This was Abigail's final weapon against him—and it had struck him right in his core. The news of his impending fatherhood had been the only thing keeping him going these past few months. Single fatherhood and shared custody wouldn't have been easy, but he would have made it work, dammit.

He would have moved the entire universe to make it work.

The man rose and staggered to the bathroom and started retching over the toilet. Stomach acid burned his throat.

He had to do something. Go somewhere. Anything to get his mind off what had just happened.

He threw open the front door and ran down the sidewalk, out onto Main, past the churches, then down the Pike. His calves and lungs were on fire, like his throat. Spots swam before his eyes. He felt like he was about to die out here in the muggy heat of midspring.

And what did it matter if he lived or died? The only thing he'd been living for was gone.

His legs carried him all the way down to the community park. Many young couples were there, playing with their children, tossing horseshoes, swinging, and the like. Heads turned as he rushed down the nature trail encircling a pond coated in patches of lily pads. The man didn't want anyone to look at him. He wished he could just disappear and never be seen again.

Sinking into the grass by the pond's northern bank, he wept. A female mallard paddled by on the pond's glassy surface between the lily pads, four ducklings trailing in her wake. Two children played tag a short distance away from him, squealing with joy. Another mother sat on a bench, nursing her infant.

A sudden rage replaced his sadness. There were children everywhere! What was so special about them? What had they done to deserve life?

He thought about the two other children he and Abigail had lost—the ones who'd died of natural causes early in pregnancy. Both he and Abigail had been heartbroken then. They'd wanted a family so badly, in spite of the arguments and fighting. Or had Abigail only been pretending…?

Jessica was flung from the dream so suddenly, the breath left her lungs. It took her a moment to reorient herself to the fact she lay in bed, and then she heard a cry from Wayne's bedroom.

"Stop it! Stop it, please!"

"Shit." Jessica untangled herself from her covers and scrambled out to the hall. She threw open Wayne's door and flipped on the overhead light, fully expecting to see Jerry attacking him, but the only visible soul was Wayne himself, tossing and turning as if fending off a phantom in a dream.

Wayne grew still, blinked, and sat up. He wasn't wearing a shirt—a fact that made Jessica feel very warm. She made a point of not looking for scars.

"What's going on?" he asked.

"You were shouting. I thought that Jerry…"

"It was just a bad dream." Wayne switched on his bedside lamp. "Turn that light off. I feel half blind."

Jessica did. The bedside lamp sent a soft, yellow glow over the room. "I'm sorry I woke you up. I guess I'll go back to bed."

She turned to go, but Wayne said, "Wait."

Jessica paused. "What is it?"

"You can stay in here, if you want."

Her pulse sped up by a few beats per minute. She *did* want but also didn't want to seem needy. Spending the night beside him the other night had felt so normal, and safe.

She sat beside him on the bed. "So, what was your dream about?"

"I'm not sure. It's gone already."

"Lucky. I had a bad dream too."

"Oh yeah?"

Jessica concentrated, trying to dredge up the fading details. "I think Jerry was showing me something again. It's like I was inside his head."

"Should I be disturbed by that?"

"It wasn't anything X-rated, if that's what you're worried about."

Wayne seemed to relax a bit. "Well, what did he show you?"

"He told me he went through an ugly divorce. In my dream, his ex-wife had just called him and told him she'd had an abortion. He was devastated."

"Makes sense, if they weren't on the same page about that. I'm guessing it was his?"

"Yeah. And I get the feeling it was late-term. He thought she was using it as a weapon against him. I mean, she probably had her reasons, but who *does* that?"

"I don't know, Jessica. People are complicated."

"Jerry told me that if he ever sees his ex-wife again, he would try to kill her."

"What a great guy. All the more reason to try to get this whole ordeal over with. Between that and what's been going on here, I'm really worried that someone is going to get hurt." Wayne shook his head. "Jerry shared his pain with me the other night—he must have gotten inside my head somehow too. It was the loneliest, most awful feeling I've ever had, and that's saying something."

"Why didn't you tell me that before?"

Wayne gave a halfhearted shrug. "I didn't want to scare you. I'd wondered if he was trying to torment me for fun, but if he's sharing stuff with you, maybe he was just trying to get me to understand him a little better. I mean, damn. If that's what he's been feeling like for all these years, it's no wonder he's so unstable."

"Yeah." Jessica closed her eyes and breathed in deeply. "Maybe we should talk about this more in the morning."

"I'm fine with that."

They both grew quiet, and neither of them budged.

What next? Jessica wondered. It was twelve thirty in the morning, and Wayne wouldn't be getting up early for work. That left plenty of time for…whatever.

"I'm nine years older than you…and disabled," Wayne said suddenly.

"What does that have to do with anything?" She eyed him coyly, taking in his sculpted abs. Wayne really did make an effort to work out every day, partly to compensate for his disability. She'd just never had the chance to admire the fruits of his labors.

"I'm just making sure that you're okay with that," he said.

"I don't have a problem with it if you don't."

"Good; we're on the same page. So, what would you like for me to do to you?"

Jessica opened and closed her mouth a few times—apparently, she'd forgotten how to speak. "You mean *right now*?"

"Unless there's something else you'd rather be doing, now that we're both awake."

A tremble passed through Jessica's body. "Um. Maybe let's just lie down first."

Wayne's brown eyes sparkled with amusement. "Sure."

They rearranged themselves so Wayne lay on the side closest to the bedroom doorway and Jessica nearer to the closet. As they moved, Jessica did catch sight of countless old scars twisting their way across Wayne's back. She tried not to feel angry about it—now was not the time.

"You know," Jessica said, "we're not exactly dating."

"It's the twenty-first century."

"I'm old-fashioned. Ask me out first."

Wayne snorted. "Old-fashioned, my ass. But if you insist, I hear that exhuming unmarked graves is an incredibly romantic first date. So let's say, ten, eleven in the morning, behind the old Methodist graveyard? Does that work for you? I can bring roses and chocolates."

She smiled, but only briefly. "Let's call it a date. But let's not talk about any of *that* right now, okay?"

"Good idea. Death tends to kill the mood. Do you think we're alone?"

Jessica looked from one end of the room to the other. "We're alone." She regarded his eyes, which were slightly out of focus since he wasn't wearing his glasses. "You know I'm very new to this, right?"

"I gathered that from our conversation the other day."

"I don't really know where to begin."

"Just let your instincts take over." He winked at her. "And if you don't feel comfortable with what we're doing, just let me know, and we can stop."

"Okay." Jessica's heart raced faster. Without thinking, she leaned forward and kissed Wayne on the lips. He pulled her against him, and she could feel herself melting, their tongues exploring each other's mouths. She ran her hands over his toned shoulders and wrapped her legs around his waist.

Time blurred. Jessica realized, at some point in the proceedings, she'd misplaced her clothes and he his boxers.

"Are you ready?" Wayne murmured in her ear.

She let out an excited breath. "Yes."

A minute later, Wayne said, "I'm still pretty tight right now." He nodded at his legs. "So tell me what you want me to do to you, and I'll let you know if I can do it."

Jessica told him.

He gave her a tender smile. "I think I can manage that one."

"But I don't want to get pregnant."

"Top nightstand drawer."

"Ah. You were already prepared."

"I'm practically an honorary Boy Scout."

And as the night progressed, Jessica forgot about death and murder and demons and ghosts.

20

Jessica woke up early and couldn't help but smile at the sleeping man beside her. Wayne's gorgeous dark hair was plastered to his head, and a line of drool rolled down his face and onto his pillow—two facts that would have scandalized him if he'd known there were any witnesses.

Opting to let him sleep in, Jessica showered and dressed in the downstairs bathroom and set to recording her video of the day out in the living room.

"Good morning, folks!" she beamed at the camera. "It's me, your Friendly Neighborhood Ghost Hunter, and I've got some interesting news for all of you.

"If you're new here, I'll summarize what's been going on: a ghost named Jerry Madison followed me home from an investigation and won't leave. He was tortured and killed by an angry mob in 1986, and he doesn't think his killers have ever been caught. Understandably, he's a very moody spirit.

"My good friend Wayne thinks I should be careful talking about all of this. If Jerry's killers really are still out there, that might put me in danger. But should I really shy away from doing the right thing? Jerry's soul needs to be at rest, and that won't happen until justice has been served. So, if you're watching this, and you're responsible for what happened to Jerry, just turn yourself in, okay? Jerry still has family out there. They deserve closure just as much as Jerry does.

"Oh, and we're going to go find Jerry's body today. Crazy, right? So, wish us luck. We're going to need it."

Jessica ended the recording and spent the next fifteen or so minutes uploading it to her channel, then checking her notifications. She was up to 351 followers now and had even more comments to check over.

@CreepyCrowley92 "They must die" has got to be the creepiest EVP I've ever heard. Well done!

@ghostwiththemost666 Wow, your ghost said THAT? Proceed with caution. I'm serious. You're messing with some dangerous stuff.

@OatmealTheDestroyer If you can't show us the ghost, I will gladly accept spooky voices. Boo!

@mindyjohnson1975 My dogs literally started howling when they heard me playing this video. Time for you to get the holy water and rock salt.

Jessica typed up replies to each comment on that video and was in the middle of replying to one on another when the erratic pain that had been plaguing her off and on for days sliced through her body, leaving her gasping. She stood to get more medicine but had to immediately sit when a wave of vertigo sent her reeling.

It occurred to her, as she struggled for breath, that moving furniture from her apartment to Wayne's house should not have caused her this much pain, and for so many days afterward.

It's cancer, she thought wildly. *Just like Sidney's mom.* How would she even survive something like that, with no money and no health insurance?

Her muscles contorted tighter than she thought possible. She was sure ligaments and sinews would start separating from her bones, and—

The next thing she knew, she was no longer in the living room. Wherever she was was shrouded in mist, and she felt somewhat detached from herself, though the pains were still sharp and raw.

It sounded like footsteps were coming toward her. "Hello?" Jessica croaked. "Is anybody here?"

You're inside your own head, stupid, she told herself. *You've blacked out, or something. The only person in here is going to be you.*

A figure emerged through the mist. At first, it seemed blurry, but then it resolved itself into a young man with platinum blond hair and lanky limbs.

"Hello, Jessica," he said. He must have been a manifestation of her consciousness.

Jessica doubled over on herself, pain shooting through every nerve in her body. She sobbed, unable to speak. Was she dying this very moment?

"You've been going through a little bit of trouble," the man commented idly, as if remarking on the weather. "Strange pains, right?"

Jessica managed to nod. It made her feel ill.

"I can make them go away."

"How?" she rasped. "You're a figment of my imagination."

The man smiled. "I happen to know a thing or two about pain and saw that you've been suffering terribly."

Jessica spoke through clenched teeth. "What could you even do about it?"

The man flickered a moment, like an image on a glitchy screen. "If you want to feel as good as new, all you have to do is let me in, and I'll make you better."

"What do you mean by that?"

"I mean, I can't help you unless you let me get close to you."

"Isn't being inside my head close enough?"

"Oh, Jessica. I'm merely on the doorstep." He tilted his head, giving her a pitying look. "I'll leave you for now and let you think it over."

Jessica was back in Wayne's living room then, sprawled across the couch in a daze. Wayne thumped down the stairs and drew short when he arrived in the open archway to the living room. "Jessica? Are you all right?"

"No," she said, trying to sit up. "I—I must have blacked out again. I'm not really sure what just happened. Had another little dream, I think. I'm so sore…"

Wayne's face went grave. "Do you want to skip our 'date' this morning so you can rest?"

"No, no, we have to go out there. I just…" She winced. "I don't understand why I've been hurting so bad. Sometimes, it just hits out of nowhere…" Jessica thought about the blond man in her dream. He'd said he could help. Wishful thinking on her part? Was her mind conjuring phantom physicians to heal her? Would she really be healing *herself*?

All you have to do is let me in, the man had said.

Then come on in and fix me, Jessica thought. *Because I can't handle this for much longer.*

At once, the pain stopped, flooding her with such a deep relief she could hardly describe it. Startled, Jessica sat up straighter. She flexed her arms and her legs and smiled. "*And* it's gone again."

Wayne took a seat beside her on the couch. "I can take you to the hospital for testing. If it's neurological, it could be a sign of something serious."

"I honestly feel fine." Jessica stood up and turned in a circle to demonstrate. "See?"

Wayne folded his arms. "Thirty seconds ago, you looked half dead."

"Well, I'm better now." Jessica's veins were practically buzzing with verve. It was all she could do not to race out the door and down the street to test her newfound bliss.

"If you say so." Wayne pursed his lips. "Now I'm going to cook a hearty breakfast and take about half a bottle of muscle relaxant so I can help you dig, but at the first sign of trouble, we're calling it off.

Okay?"

Jessica shrugged, and her stomach started growling at the thought of food. "Sounds good to me."

"Talk about isolated," Wayne said.

They were heading down Hill Road in Wayne's pickup truck, coming up on the entrance to the church. They hadn't passed another car for at least ten minutes.

Jessica had started feeling jittery the moment they'd crossed the Combs-Hehl Bridge into Kentucky. "Yeah," she said. "Like something out of a horror film."

"The happy couple takes a wrong turn and ends up in a castle full of bisexual aliens?"

"Not that horror film."

Despite their banter, a grim pallor had settled over the two of them. Wayne knew as well as she did the morbid implications of what they were about to do.

"Turn here," she said.

Wayne swung the pickup truck onto the lane leading back to the church. Jessica was on the verge of gnawing her nails down to nubs. What had she been thinking, coming here to dig up a body? They should have left this to the authorities!

Wayne pulled into a parking space right in front of the graveyard, just down from where Jessica had parked last week. Like before, no other cars occupied the lot.

"My nerves are feeling pretty rocky," Wayne said. "We could have meatloaf for dinner tonight."

"If you don't stop making terrible jokes, I'm leaving."

"If I stop making terrible jokes, I'm going to get too freaked out to get the job done."

"Fair point." Jessica stared at the countless headstones standing before them like a concrete army. She spotted the bench where she'd first met Jerry, half expecting to see him there again.

Where was Jerry, anyway? She hadn't seen him since Wednesday, but she knew he wasn't *gone*. Somehow, she could feel him lurking at the edges of her awareness, like a lost thought. He just seemed to be…waiting.

"You ready?" Wayne asked.

Jessica unbuckled her seatbelt. "No."

"Me neither. So let's get it over with."

Jessica climbed out of the truck and let down the tailgate, grabbing the metal detector, two shovels, a trowel, a five-gallon bucket, and a backpack full of snacks and bottled water. She had the crazy urge to laugh. *Introducing Jessica Roman-Dell, Friendly Neighborhood Ghost Hunter and Body Snatcher!* Or something like that.

"You're not going to take a video of any of this, are you?" Wayne slipped on the backpack and held the metal detector over his shoulder.

"It might get me even more views. Internet people love horrible things."

"It *might* get you into serious trouble, depending on how this turns out. Now which way are we going?"

"Jerry said he was killed in a clearing past the final row of headstones, so let's go that way."

They set off down the gravel path together, Jessica walking slowly to match Wayne's pace.

"See that bench?" Jessica asked.

"Uh-huh."

"That's where I first saw Jerry."

"Sitting right there?"

"Yep."

The path curved to the left, but Jessica kept walking straight on toward the trees. The headstones in this part of the graveyard were newer, most of them from the nineties and early 2000s. Some of them were adorned with arrangements of artificial flowers.

A dismal thought struck Jessica then. What would her own headstone look like someday? Who would come to her funeral and leave flowers for her? What bitter end was she not suspecting? Cancer, like Sidney's mom? An accident? Murder?

How blessed people were to not know.

They entered the woods, their feet crunching in the curled leaves carpeting the ground. Jessica kept her eyes peeled for a clearing, but the trunks and brambles obstructed any view she might have had of it.

"What if it's not a clearing anymore?" Wayne asked a few minutes later. "Twenty-four years is a long time."

"I'll find out." Jessica halted and set the shovels and bucket down, and Wayne shifted the metal detector from one shoulder to the other. "Jerry? Can you show us where you're buried?"

The spirit did not appear.

Jessica pursed her lips in frustration. "Jerry, I want you to be properly laid to rest. Your family can finally have a funeral for you. You'll get your own headstone, and people can visit you. Or you can be cremated, if you want."

"God, this is depressing," Wayne muttered.

Jessica ignored him. "Your niece, Casey, has been looking for you, Jerry. Help us find where they put you so she can move on with her life."

"Is that a building over there?" Wayne asked.

Jessica turned in the direction he was looking. "Where?"

"There, behind that thicket." He pointed.

Sure enough, a small structure mostly concealed by vines and undergrowth sat about fifty yards to the north of them. "It looks like an old shed. Want to go look?"

"Sure, why not? Maybe there's a hermit in there who can point us in the right direction."

"Nah, probably just some riffraff."

Wayne's eyebrows shot upward. "Who's making terrible jokes now?"

They reached the shed, which turned out to be more of a cabin, probably about ten feet by twenty. Jessica itched to explore it, knowing it would cut into their body-hunting time but not particularly caring. This cabin was an anomaly: no road or path led to it, and it could potentially contain clues of some sort.

Jessica found the door on the cabin's narrower side, swiped away some Virginia creeper, and tried the knob. "It's unlocked."

"And probably full of spiders the size of minivans," Wayne said. "You go first."

Jessica pushed the door inward. Light from a grimy side window illuminated most of the single-room structure. A couple of chairs and an overturned table sat around in disarray. Dust and cobwebs coated it all in gray shrouds.

"Wish I'd brought a flashlight," Jessica said, stepping inside. Large, dark stains that made her breath catch covered the floor. "Uh, Wayne?"

He poked his head inside. "What?"

"I need a second opinion here."

Sighing, he joined her inside the cabin, pulling the collar of his T-shirt over his nose so he wouldn't inhale any dust. His eyes came to rest on the stained floor. "Holy shit."

"Maybe it's some kid's idea of a joke," Jessica said, not entirely convinced of her own theory. "They could have found this cabin and painted stains on the floor to make it look…like that."

"Riiight." Wayne adjusted his glasses again. "I think we should just keep looking for Jerry. Avoid distractions. Okay?"

"Good idea."

Wayne left the cabin first. Jessica started to follow but paused in her tracks when the floorboards creaked beneath her feet. What if there were bodies *under* the cabin? Not Jerry's, but someone else's? Because those stains looked an awful lot like…

The red aura slammed into her without warning, turning the

whole world crimson.

"Wayne!" she cried. Jessica could feel herself sinking, like the victim of a shipwreck, but instead of some cold, dark sea, she was drowning in a hatred so deep, so *primal*, she was sure she would feel nothing else ever again.

¡Mataste a mi nieta! echoed the voices in her head. *¡Vete a la verga!*

Her vision cleared faster this time. She came to, lying on the ground outside the cabin. Wayne's arms were folded tightly across his chest, and his eyes blazed.

"I'm pretty sure this qualifies as a sign of trouble. Let's go home."

"Can't we even *try* first? We just got here!"

He gave her a hard look. "Fine. But we're getting this over with *now*."

Wayne picked up the metal detector and traipsed away from her. Jessica gathered up the rest of their supplies and hurried after him.

"Wayne, wait! Couldn't you feel it?"

"I felt something. Not enough to make me black out, though."

"It's the same thing that happened my first time here, and then in the bathroom at home. It's some kind of replaying of emotions, I think."

"If that's so, why would you have felt it in my bathroom?"

That gave Jessica pause. Why, indeed? "Maybe the psychic energy latched onto me somehow. But there were voices too."

"What did they say?"

"Well, it was in Spanish, but I remember this time. They said…" Jessica shivered a little. "They said, 'You killed my granddaughter. Go to hell.'"

"Lovely."

"That old blood in the cabin…you don't think?"

"I don't know what to think anymore. I just want to get this over with so we don't have to deal with any creepy shit ever again. Okay?"

Jessica let out a huff. "Okay."

The trees thinned a minute or so later in an area sixty or seventy feet across, the sun beating down overhead. Three immense oak trees grew here and there in the open clearing. But was it *the* clearing? They would soon find out.

"This is a lot of area to cover." Wayne slid the backpack from his shoulders and set it on the ground, then switched on the metal detector. It emitted a series of warm-up beeps. "Bones don't set this thing off, you know."

"I know," Jessica said, "but think about it. Jerry was tortured out here. The people who did it wouldn't have wanted to take their weapons home with them. They probably buried all of it with him."

"Well, I hope they didn't bury any of it too deep. This is a decent model, and it's got a maximum range of eighteen inches. Want to try talking to Jerry again?"

Jessica cleared her throat. "Jerry, I know you're with me. You might not have enough energy right now to talk or show yourself, but can you give me some sign of where to dig? It'll save us a lot of trouble."

She waited, then felt a slight nudging inside her. Jessica walked about twenty paces to the west and stopped.

"Let's try here."

Wayne approached the spot and swept the metal detector over the ground in a four-foot arc. It let out a low beep. "Iron," Wayne said, examining the screen. "Just a few inches down."

Jessica stabbed the shovel into the dirt, pulling up a clump of earth. She picked up the clump and held it in her hands. Wayne swept the metal detector over it, and it beeped again.

Jessica hurriedly broke the clump apart, finding only a rusty nail inside it. She tossed the nail into the bucket and brushed her hands together. "Well, that was disappointing."

Wayne was already moving on to another spot. "Why do you think I've had this thing in my closet for so long? All I ever found was a few coins and a bent spoon."

The metal detector beeped once more. A bit of digging revealed a greenish circle the size of Jessica's thumbnail. "A 1978 penny," Jessica said. "We're rich."

They continued in the same fashion for the next half hour, unearthing another nail, a crushed soda can, and a warped scrap of metal that might have melted in a fire. In some places, tree roots made the digging more difficult. Jessica could already feel blisters forming on her palms, and she wished she'd brought work gloves with them.

"So, about last night," Wayne said, adding the scrap to their growing collection in the bucket.

Jessica could feel her cheeks flushing. "What about it?"

"Was it good?"

"It was amazing."

"I'm glad to hear it."

"And the view?" Jessica asked, feigning coyness.

"Ten out of ten. Would view it again." Wayne continued to sweep the ground. "You know what attracted me to you when we first met?"

"What?"

"You never pitied me. You saw me for who I am, and you accepted it, brain damage and all."

Jessica put her hands on her hips. "What else would I have done?"

"Plenty of people offer me their condolences when I tell them that the reason I walk like I do is because I have cerebral palsy and that it isn't ever going away. I've had people argue with me because they think I can just 'get better' if I do enough physical therapy, or use the right oils, because they refuse to understand that it's literally a problem in my brain. You? You asked questions. You wanted to learn more, and you listened."

"That's what friends do, Wayne."

He smiled at her. "We've moved beyond friends now, remember? This is officially our first date."

"I know. It's so romantic. There isn't anyone else I'd rather be digging up a body with."

They slowly progressed across the clearing, waving the metal detector back and forth in slow, wide arcs. At noon, they took a short break in the shade of the oak trees to munch on the granola bars and beef jerky they'd brought in the backpack.

"We've covered just about this whole area," Wayne said, screwing the cap back onto his water bottle.

Jessica peered at their collection of dirty, metallic bric-a-brac piled in the bottom of the five-gallon bucket. "We're just not able to go deep enough," she mused. "If the killers had this whole thing planned out ahead of time, they could have dug a deep grave, and we'll never be able to find it without Jerry's help."

Wayne put his head in his hands.

"But we can keep trying," Jessica quickly added.

"We've been out here over an hour."

"We have plenty of time left, then." Jessica thought hard. *Jerry, you've got to talk to me. If this is the wrong clearing, let us know.*

A cracking sound above made them both look up in time to see an overhanging oak limb snap off and crash to the ground close to where they'd started.

It seemed as good a sign as any.

Jessica stood, brushed off her jeans, and trudged to the tree limb. Wayne joined her with the metal detector and turned it back on, and Jessica dragged the limb out of the way.

"We already checked here," Wayne said, giving the ground another sweep.

"Then we'll just have to go deeper."

"You mean…"

"We have to remove a layer of soil and scan it again."

The sun progressed past its zenith. They each dug and piled the loose soil in a heap close by. Once they'd removed a foot of soil in a circle roughly eight feet in diameter, Jessica said, "Let's check again."

"I hope this doesn't take much longer," Wayne said wearily. He switched on the metal detector with the zeal of a third-shift motel clerk and scanned the ground anew.

The detector let out a high-pitched beep.

Wayne's eyebrows furrowed. "It's aluminum, about a foot down." He waved the detector back and forth, and it kept beeping. "A *lot* of aluminum."

Jessica's heart stuttered. "Jerry told me his killers tied him to a chair before they started on him. Maybe it was an aluminum lawn chair."

"Let's find out."

Even though they were both tiring, they began to dig more frantically. Jessica's shovel soon scraped something hard, and she used the trowel to remove more of the dirt from around it.

"It's definitely a pipe of some sort," she said, her stomach squirming. She could see a ragged, shining gleam where the shovel had raked across it.

More digging revealed the rest of what was clearly the skeletal remains of a lawn chair with green plastic webbing. Once they'd extracted it from the earth, Wayne checked the ground with the detector again.

It beeped in several different pitches, as if confused by what it had found. Wayne scratched his head. "Um. There's a lot of stuff down here."

This time, Wayne rested while Jessica dug alone. Her shovel struck another hard object just a few inches down, and when she pulled it from the earth, her stomach clenched.

It was a pair of pliers.

She kept digging and found a pair of scissors, a Zippo lighter, a flathead screwdriver, a short length of chain, three butcher knives, and a dagger, brown with soil and age. Jessica quietly placed each one into the bucket, then sat back as tears welled in her eyes.

Wayne took a seat beside her. "We can stop now. Call this in and let the authorities take care of the rest of it."

"But we haven't found anything criminal yet. If the cops see this, they'll just think someone dumped out their toolbox a long time ago."

"True. I'll check again."

The metal detector emitted a high-pitched beep for half a second when Wayne waved it over the pit. He frowned. "Huh. It must be something small."

"Could it have been a glitch?"

"I don't know." He tried in vain to find the signal again. "It might not be anything important."

But Jessica was already digging.

21

Jessica's shovel brought up a chunk of dirt. A shred of thin, black plastic, like a piece of garbage bag, protruded from it.

A bead of sweat trickled down her scalp. She tossed the dirt aside and dug in again, more plastic ripping from the earth with the next scoop. Jessica set the shovel aside and began to scrape as much dirt away from the plastic as she could with her bare hands. Wayne knelt beside her and worked at the dirt in a different spot with the trowel, presumably so he wouldn't ruin his glossy manicure.

Within minutes, they'd uncovered the rest of the ancient bag, which remained intact save for the rips her shovel had torn into it. Jessica peered over at Wayne, her pale face reflected in the lenses of his glasses.

"Together?" Jessica whispered.

Wayne nodded. "Let's do it."

They each grabbed the biggest rip and pulled the bag the rest of the way open.

A yellowed skull stared back at them, with empty eye sockets. The mouth was open slightly, as if uttering a silent plea that had gone unanswered.

Spots danced in Jessica's vision, and she had to turn away from the skull.

"Are you all right?" Wayne asked.

"Sorry, this just got very real for me." Jessica drew in as deep a breath as she could, then turned back to the remains. She reached down to touch the skull but hesitated. "What do you think set off the detector?"

Wayne frowned in thought. "See if you can open his mouth a little wider."

Gingerly, Jessica placed her hand on the jawbone and tugged it downward. Dark spots showed on three of Jerry's molars.

"Dental fillings," Wayne said.

Jessica bit her lip and forced herself to examine the other contents of the bag. Loose dirt had sifted through the bones of Jerry's collapsed ribcage. Some of the ribs were chipped in places, more so over Jerry's long-vanished heart.

She thought about the knives she'd set in the bucket and wished she hadn't.

The arms, somewhat visible through the ribs, were pinned beneath the body. The bony hands were clenched tightly into fists that had never been given the chance to relax, and the wrists were tied together with strips of a grayish, fraying substance which could only be deteriorating duct tape.

She had difficulty grasping the fact the bones at her feet had once been part of a living, breathing person. Jerry's face had been painted in flesh over this very skull. A heart had once beaten inside the now-broken chest, and two bright blue eyes had watched the world from those gaping, sightless sockets.

The body ended at the pelvis, which was draped with scraps of yellow fabric. "His legs are gone," Jessica said in disbelief.

"Maybe..." Wayne swallowed. "Maybe they wouldn't fit in the bag."

A black rage erupted inside Jessica. "What kind of monster would *do* this to a person?" she cried, her own hands balling into fists so hard her fingernails cut into her palms. "They strangled him and mutilated him until he died, and then they cut off his legs and turned him into *garbage*!"

"Jessica, can you please try to ca—"

"I am *not* going to calm down!" Tears streaked down her face. "The people who did this should be executed. Let them feel what he felt. Oh God, he must have been so scared…"

Wayne grabbed her and pulled her against his chest. "We're going to call the police now," he said into her hair. "They'll open an investigation into all of this. Jerry *will* get justice."

Jessica tugged herself away from him. "No."

His face grew stony. "No, what?"

"We're not calling the cops."

"Then why did we just spend half a fucking day looking for Jerry's body?" Wayne's complexion was deepening to an angry scarlet.

A shudder pulsed through Jessica's body. "The time isn't right. We have to be ready. They have to *see*."

"What are you talking about? Who has to see what?"

Jessica felt odd then, like her words weren't exactly her own. "The murderers. The murderer. The one who dealt the killing blow. They have to *see* what they did. They have to drink it in and suffer for their sins."

Wayne took one step in reverse. "You're scaring me."

"Let's put Jerry in that cabin. The bag with his legs is probably underneath this one. It won't take long to dig it up."

Wayne stared at her hard, his face still red. "We are *going*," he said, "to call the police."

"Sunday," Jessica said, unsure why that word had just burst forth from her mouth. "We'll call the police Sunday. Everything should be ready by then." She felt herself growing calmer, and she smiled at Wayne. "Are you okay with that?"

It took Wayne several moments to speak. He was staring at her like he'd never seen her before. "Fine," he said. "We'll put Jerry in the cabin. We'll wait two fucking days to call the cops, and we'll probably both get arrested for mishandling a human corpse if the cops find out it's us who gave them the tip. Oh, and our fingerprints are all over the scene. Am I missing anything else?"

"I don't think so."

"God, and now we have to put all this dirt back in the hole."

"Shouldn't we leave it as it is so the cops can do their forensic stuff to it?"

Wayne's gaze had grown as sharp as the knives in the bucket. "You know, you're probably right. Why keep your promise to the minister, after all, on top of everything else?"

Jessica's phone rang. She answered it while Wayne continued to seethe and said, "Hi, Sidney."

"Where are you?" Sidney gasped, her voice quavering with panic. Jessica could hear another voice in the background that sounded like one of Sidney's brothers talking on another phone.

"Kentucky," Jessica replied. "Wayne and I…went out. Why?"

"I came back to the house with Kyle after work so I could pick up more of my things to take to Dad's place."

"I thought you were too afraid to come back."

"I was! I mean, I am. I thought maybe I imagined the whole thing? You've been freaking me out about this ghost stuff, after all…"

"Sidney's *what's happened*?"

Sidney hesitated. "We couldn't get the door open."

"Why not?"

"There was a bunch of furniture piled behind it. We had to come in the back. Jessica…there's stuff flung *everywhere*. Books. Papers. I tried to turn on the lights, but all the breakers had been tripped."

It took a moment for Jessica to fully absorb Sidney's words. She licked her lips and said, "Has anything been stolen?"

"I can't tell. It's just such a mess…The TV is still here, though, and our computers. So probably not."

To Jessica, this meant only one thing. "It sounds like Jerry went poltergeist. He must have tapped into the electricity to power himself and overloaded the circuits, or something."

Wayne folded his arms. "I thought Jerry was here, in your head."

"That's what I thought too." Jessica began to pace. "But if Jerry was at home, who guided us to this spot? Who broke the branch out of the tree?"

"Jessica?" Sidney was saying in her ear.

"Hold tight," Jessica said to her. "Wayne and I will be there as soon as we can."

Sidney was leaning against her car in the driveway when Jessica and Wayne arrived home. Lengthening shadows gathered as the sun prepared to set.

It had been an extraordinarily long day—Jessica could feel it in her bones.

She and Wayne hadn't spoken much to each other during the drive home. Wayne was still upset Jessica didn't want to involve the police yet—which was understandable—but she knew in the deepest part of her gut she was making the right decision.

No, it didn't make sense. But did it have to?

"Where's Kyle?" Jessica asked, hopping out of the truck.

Sidney straightened. "I took him home so he could get some dinner. I came back here to wait for you two."

"Were you able to clean up at all?" Wayne asked, walking to the front door with his key in hand.

"Um, no," Sidney said. "The furniture is still blocking the door. You'll have to go through the back, like we did."

Wayne sighed. "Hooray. More work for me."

The three of them filed into the mudroom at the back of the house,

Sidney coming in last and hesitating by the door. "You two are a mess," she said, looking them up and down. "Want to share?"

Jessica exchanged a dark look with Wayne, then looked back to Sidney. "Can you let us shower first?" she asked.

"You're not leaving me alone in here."

"Then wait outside," Wayne said, his tone short. "After that, the three of us are going to have a very long talk."

Wayne disappeared into his room, and Jessica could hear his shower come on while she stood at her dresser, picking out a clean pair of pajamas. Nothing in Sidney's bedroom seemed to have been disturbed—the mess had been contained to the first floor.

"You found it, didn't you?"

Jessica's heart flew into her throat, and she whirled. Jerry sat on the edge of her bed, his face long.

"Where have you *been*?" she hissed. "I haven't seen you in two days."

"You don't understand," Jerry replied. "None of this has been easy for me. The traveling, the moving…I'm not used to it. I need to be stronger. And I am stronger now, I think."

"Because you tripped our breakers feeding off the electricity?"

"Did I?" He said it almost absentmindedly. "Interesting."

Jessica put her hands on her hips. "Why is Wayne's recliner shoved up against the front door? Why is stuff flung all over the house?"

"I didn't mean to. I finally felt strong enough after resting for two days. I came to, and nobody was here. And then I saw papers on the counter. Papers about *me*." Tears—or the memory of tears, rather—glistened in Jerry's eyes. "Little Casey is looking for me. Oh, God. If she knew…"

"Look, Jerry, I know it's hard. But you can't go poltergeist when you get upset. We did find your body today. All of this is going to be over soon."

Jerry's eyes grew round. "Are you sure?"

Jessica shivered, and once again, she felt as if her words trickled into her mouth from somewhere else. "We put you in the cabin to wait. You don't just want to hurt Abigail. You want to hurt the people who killed you too. Don't you?"

He worked his jaw. "It's only fair."

"It's what you've been wanting for twenty-four years. You pretend to struggle, even now, but you know the truth." Jessica sucked in a breath and shook her head. What had she been talking about? It had been such a long day; she must have lost her train of thought. "Do you know anything about that cabin in the woods?" she asked.

Jerry was giving her a peculiar look. "Not at first," he said, relaxing a bit. "I only came across it later, after I...well, you know. Some fine, upstanding officers of the law sometimes brought people there to have their way with them. Beatings, mostly. They liked to take things into their own hands."

"Did you know them?"

He nodded. "The officers were part of the group who killed me."

"I take it they stopped using the cabin? It was pretty filthy inside, like no one had been there in years."

"They did. One time, they brought a boy to the cabin. He might have been ten years old."

Jessica's throat tightened. "What were they doing with him?"

"I was under the impression that one of the officers had caught him stealing. They tied him to a chair and cut off one of his fingers, promising that if he stole again, they'd cut off more than that."

Jessica realized she'd put a hand over her mouth.

A wicked smile spread across Jerry's face. "The next time they came to the cabin with some poor soul they wanted to torment, I drew every ounce of power from the environment that I could to manifest myself as I appeared at the moment of my death, and I drove them out. I did it the next time, and the time after that too. Eventually, they stopped showing up. Even monsters don't like being inside a haunted house."

"Do you think...?" Jessica paused, trying to organize her thoughts. "If those cops were part of the group that killed you...they knew that was an isolated place back there. They would have told the others about it."

"I suppose so. I had no connection to the Methodist Church or the property surrounding it. I think it was just a convenient location for everyone involved. Everyone but *me*, of course."

"Not a lot of houses nearby, are there?"

"Not that I've seen, no."

Jessica thought about that. Then she heard the water shut off in Wayne's bathroom and knew it was her turn to shower.

Jerry stayed behind in the bedroom while Jessica went off to clean herself, struggling against the temptation seizing him like a snare.

Jessica should have suspected him. How could she *not*? She might have been young, but she was bright, no doubt about that. The fact she hadn't figured it out days ago meant only one thing:

She didn't know.

The thought both amused and sickened him. What kind of person wouldn't...? But of course, that's how it would be. Bury the past along with his bones; call it a day.

He really shouldn't involve himself with her anymore. Jerry could go away somewhere to silently wait for an angel to drag him to hell. Jessica would go on with her life, making silly little videos for her YouTube. She would grow old and die blissfully ignorant of the things that transpired during that muggy summer, when the world still reeled from the Chernobyl disaster and glam metal had been all the rage.

The voices nudged at his conscience like a bratty kid poking a dying animal with a stick. *Where's the beauty in leaving her alone?* they asked him. *She's the only one who can help you.*

They made a good point. Justice had never been served. He could have forgiven those terrible people for killing him, but did they deserve it? Of course not! They deserved to be dismembered alive and left out as carrion.

The thing was, they would never have killed him if he hadn't—

Don't think that way. They didn't have to retaliate. You could have been sentenced to the electric chair instead. It would have been more merciful.

True…

They must die, Jerry. They've walked free for far too long, and they should pay for what they did.

But he didn't even know all their names.

You know some of them, and you know the most important one. Use the knowledge you already have and stop stalling.

Suddenly, all the faces swam into his mind's eye. The laughing, giggling faces that mocked him with every glance—the faces the same age his own child would have been, if born.

Countless phantom voices filled his head in an echoing playground chant. *We're more special than* your *kid, we're more special than* your *kid, we're more special than* your *kid…*

Echoing, echoing…

The residents of Clarkville had consisted of many young professionals whose children practically ran amok all summer while their parents worked. Jerry often watched through his back window, knowing *he* never would have abandoned his children for a career. If he'd had to, he would have at least put his own child in a daycare facility, far from the view of neighbors like Jerry himself.

One summer day, amid the sound of kids on another street setting off cherry bombs and bottle rockets every thirty seconds, Jerry paced back and forth in his living room, his heart racing and his hands trembling. He couldn't stop thinking about what day it was, what he would be doing right this very moment if his life had gone according to plan. There would have been presents. Birthday cake. A wish and blown-out candles.

Then he heard a sound in the lull between explosions: the laughter of children.

He stopped pacing to look out the back window again and saw them.

His vision narrowed to a point, and a blackness darker than his soul flooded his core. He could change this. Make it stop. Forever.

Jerry remembered stepping out his back door and approaching the four of them gathered at a neighboring picnic table. He remembered lifting the revolver. Drawing back the trigger. Delight had filled him at the sight of the stunned look on the first one's face when the bullet tore a hole through its skull. The others were in too much shock to move, like a trio of fawns caught in a high-wattage beam of light. He cut them down in rapid succession, studied the four corpses a moment, and then calmly went back inside.

Jerry remembered the lightness in his chest. The immense feeling of relief, knowing he would never have to see their faces again.

It felt good, didn't it?

Had it? He'd never wanted to…had never *conceived* of doing…

Yes, you did, Jerry. It's what you were made to do.

But the voices, they had told him…

You felt amazing once it was done. Your murderers took that away from you, Jerry. They tortured you. Do you remember how it felt when they cut you open? Do you remember how frightened you were? How you cried?

Yes. All too well.

You're dead, Jerry. You're nothing but memory and bone. It isn't your fault that they chose to do what they did.

But...

Stop resisting! Justice, Jerry. Serve it well.

22

After Jessica and Wayne had showered, and after Sidney had helped them put the furniture back where it was supposed to be and organized the books scattered all over the living room floor, Wayne fixed a giant bowl of popcorn. The three of them ate it together out on the couch.

It was almost 10:00 p.m.

Jerry leaned against the front wall with his arms folded over his chest, observing them with an unreadable expression. Jessica didn't feel it would be prudent to mention that fact to anyone, but if her friends were paying any kind of attention, they'd probably already noticed an unnatural chill in the air.

While they snacked, Jessica and Wayne took turns telling Sidney about what they'd been up to all day, Sidney's eyes widening with every word.

"And you just left him there?" Sidney asked. "Why didn't you call the cops?"

"The timing is wrong," Jessica said, feeling a little guilty. "I have a family reunion to go to tomorrow. Once that's over with…" She let the sentence hang.

"I thought you didn't want anything to do with your family," Sidney said with a frown.

"My sister will be there. I'd rather spend time with her than sit in a police station, answering questions."

"But you could have done that today and been free tomorrow."

"I don't have any idea how long it would have taken," Jessica said. "I just thought it would be better to wait."

She flicked her gaze to Jerry, who said, "I've been waiting for more than two decades. An extra couple of days won't hurt me."

Sidney followed Jessica's line of sight and narrowed her eyes in suspicion. "What are you looking at?"

Jessica sighed. "The man of the hour. Don't worry. He isn't going to hurt you."

Sidney scrambled to her feet as if to run for it. "But that thing I saw in the kitchen…"

"I don't know what you think you saw, but it wasn't Jerry. And the reason he made a mess earlier is because he found the stuff his niece posted online and got upset about it."

Sidney's eyes had grown wide behind the lenses of her purple-framed glasses. "Um…can I talk to him?"

Jessica looked back to Jerry, who dipped his head.

"He's okay with that."

"Where is he, exactly?"

"Just to the left of the TV."

Sidney took four strides forward and stopped. Her voice trembled when she said, "Mr. Madison? Jerry?"

Jerry rolled his eyes. "How can I help you?"

"He wants to know what you want," Jessica said.

Sidney gulped. "What *did* I see in the kitchen yesterday? If it wasn't you, and I wasn't hallucinating?"

"What's she talking about?" Jerry asked Jessica.

"She saw some kind of creature or something while I was out at lunch with my sister," Jessica said. "A creature made of hate."

His brows knitted together. "But that sounds like…never mind. I'm not an expert on these things."

"He isn't sure," Jessica said to Sidney.

"Great." Sidney drew her arms closer to her body, as if making herself a smaller target. "Can it hurt us?"

Jerry thought about it for a moment or two. "No," he said at length. "It won't hurt you."

"He says no."

Wayne cleared his throat. His face had turned a shade of gray. "I'd like to ask Jerry something too."

Jerry turned to him, expression turning colder. "Go ahead."

"We're going to notify the authorities about the location of your remains," Wayne said, as if he'd heard him. "We can let your family know what your wishes are for them once your case is closed."

"I think they would have a hard time believing where you received your source of information," Jerry said, "seeing as I've been dead for quite some time. I never made a will."

Jessica relayed that to Wayne, who responded, "They can believe whatever they want, and I can't promise that they'd listen to us, but what *do* you want done with them?"

Jerry's eyes grew sad. "Let me think about it."

He walked through a wall and disappeared.

"He's gone," Jessica said, her shoulders slumping. "But I think he'll let us know once he's made a decision."

"This is weird as hell," Sidney moaned.

No kidding. "Are you going back to your dad's now?"

"You bet I am. If Jerry didn't even know what I saw, that's bad news. Now I'm going to go load up a suitcase and get the hell out of here."

Sidney left the room and went upstairs.

Jessica looked to Wayne and said, "Not to change the subject, but about the family reunion tomorrow—"

"What about it?" Wayne's tone was curt. His half-closed eyes and lined face made him look unimaginably tired.

"Well, would you want to come with me? It's supposed to be Halloween-themed; you can wear a costume if you want."

Wayne smirked. "Whose idea was it to have a family reunion so late in the year? I thought they were a summer thing."

"Uncle Esteban, probably. He loves Halloween. I mean, he's practically Stephen King."

"I'll go," Wayne said, "but I'll probably skip the costume. I'm scary enough already."

Jessica just shook her head.

"It'll be interesting seeing your parents again, now that you and I—"

"Do *not* tell them about that, Wayne. And I really don't feel like talking to them."

"I can talk for both of us, then. I've known your mom for longer than I've known you. She doesn't scare me."

"Good. I'll keep my distance."

"Jessica, they're your *parents*."

"I wouldn't want to upset them by reminding them that I exist."

Wayne made a derisive eye roll. "I may not understand the entire history you have with them, but try to be civil tomorrow, okay?"

"To be honest, I don't even know what we'd talk about."

"Tell them about your YouTube channel."

"I don't think they believe in ghosts." Jessica sighed. Suddenly, the prospect of seeing her mother and father was more unpleasant than digging up Jerry's body. She and her parents had nothing in common, save for some DNA and a last name, and if they did manage to strike up a conversation with her, they'd probably end up berating her for losing her job, being evicted, and hanging out in spooky houses half the night, talking to nobody.

"I'll just stick with Rachel and Eric as much as I can," she added.

"Are we supposed to bring something to eat?"

"No idea, but we could bring potato salad or something."

Wayne raised an eyebrow. "Who's going to make it?"

Preparing food that didn't involve a microwave required rocket science Jessica wasn't quite familiar with. "We can just buy some down at Eleanor Market on the way there."

"Way to make an impression on your family," Sidney said, coming down the stairs with a smirk and a bulging suitcase.

"I've never made potato salad in my life."

"If it's going to be this much of an issue," Wayne said, "I can make it myself. I'm sure I've got all the ingredients already."

"How about this—you can show me what to do, and we can collaborate on it," Jessica said. "We could bring some drinks too, like that Mike's Hard Lemonade you're always drinking."

"I don't share my Mike's."

"I can buy one pack. I have exactly $20.47 left in my bank account."

Sidney set her suitcase down in the archway between the living room and the entryway. "You're *that* broke?"

"You know I haven't had a job in more than four months."

"But how will you be able to pay your rent here?"

Jessica quickly looked to Wayne, who was giving his head a slight shake.

Sidney's face hardened. "You're living here for free?"

"Just until Jessica gets back on her feet," Wayne said in a warning tone.

"But she hasn't even been trying! All she does is hang out with Jerry, hoping to go viral!"

"Sidney—"

"And you *just* increased my own rent, Wayne. Is that why? You wanted me to pay Jessica's portion too?"

"Sidney!" Wayne pinched the bridge of his nose. "It has been an incredibly long day. I'm exhausted. How about we all get a decent night's sleep and talk about it when we're in better moods?"

Sidney pursed her lips at her cousin. "Fine."

"Good. I'm going to bed." Wayne rose and left them.

Sidney folded her arms and stared at Jessica long and hard. "Are you just going to mooch off of my cousin for the rest of your life?"

"I'm not mooching!" Jessica's blood simmered. "You think I like being unemployed?"

"You must not hate it too much."

"Nobody's hiring. Believe me, I've checked. And besides…" She shook her head. "You know I'd wanted to go to college. And maybe I will someday, once I get things back in order."

"Thank God for that."

"You're acting like someone's eighty-year-old grandpa. You ought to go find a cane to shake at me."

That made Sidney smile. "Maybe Wayne is right."

"About?"

"Getting a decent night's sleep." Sidney picked up her suitcase and carried it toward the front door. "But *don't* think this argument is over. Have fun at your family reunion."

"I'm sure I will."

Despite the lingering animosity between them, they hugged each other goodbye, and Sidney slipped out into the night. Jessica filled a glass of water at the sink, sipped at it, and took it upstairs, pausing on the landing between the two open bedroom doorways.

"Not sure where to sleep?" Wayne asked from the darkness in his bedroom.

"I didn't want to presume anything."

His bedside lamp flicked on. Wayne lay on his back, shirt and glasses off. "It's your decision," he said, his voice sterner than usual. "But don't think I'll be able to do anything tonight. I've never done so much digging in my life."

"You and me both." Jessica stepped into the room, set her glass atop the nightstand, and walked around to the empty half of the bed. She flopped onto her back and then rolled onto her side to face him.

"You don't think I'm a freeloader, do you?"

He gave her a long look. "No. Good night, Jessica."

"Good night."

He turned the light off. Jessica wriggled around to get comfortable, and while Wayne's soft breathing soon filled the air, Jessica couldn't shut her own mind off long enough to even consider sleep.

The minutes flashed by one by one on Wayne's alarm clock. At ten after twelve, a voice spoke beside her head. "Jessica?"

It was Jerry.

"What is it?" she whispered, sitting up.

"Can we talk?"

"It's the middle of the night."

"You aren't asleep. What does it matter?"

She sighed. "Let's go out to the deck. I need some fresh air, anyway."

Jessica went into Sidney's room and swiped a pair of Sidney's fuzzy pink slippers that lay on the floor beside her bed, then tiptoed down the stairs and out the back door.

The porch light clicked on as soon as she stepped onto the deck. The outside temperature was cooler than she'd anticipated, or perhaps the contrast with the temperature in the house made the air seem colder than it actually was. Her breath formed fleeting clouds of mist each time she exhaled.

"Where are you?" she asked, hugging her arms close to her chest to warm them.

A vague haze materialized between her and the door and slowly came into focus. "Sorry," Jerry said. He faded away for a moment, then appeared again as he usually did. Black clothes. No blood. That funny scar with the stitches on the back of his hand. "Sometimes this is difficult." He wrung his hands together and kept glancing around him, as if keeping an eye out for someone or something he didn't want to see. "I'm so sorry."

His evident agitation unnerved her. "What are you sorry about?"

she asked.

Jerry seemed to struggle to find the words. "Have you ever wanted something so badly...You know it's wrong, but you have to do it anyway or you'll die?"

Jessica took a step backward. "I'm not sure what you mean."

The light above the back door gleamed through him, as if his apparition wasn't entirely complete. He looked her right in the eye. "Do you know anyone named Sarah?"

The question took her aback. "What?"

"It's a fairly simple question."

Jessica frowned. Sarah? The name meant something, but right now, she couldn't remember its significance. It was late, and she felt so tired. "I don't know," she said. "I don't think so."

The light shining through him made his eyes glow. "Are you sure?"

"Why are you asking me this?"

He smiled. "I would like to kill the people who killed me. And once I've done that, I would like to kill Abigail. But I can't do it alone."

Jessica's heart beat faster. A few days ago, she would have been appalled at Jerry's words, but now, they only made sense. Why shouldn't he want them all to die? An eye for an eye made the whole world even. "Is Sarah one of the people who killed you?"

"No." He let out a dark chuckle. "There's so much you don't know."

"Then tell me!"

"I don't want to hurt you." Genuine sadness glistened in his eyes. "You've been extremely kind to me, talking to me and offering me comfort. But if you help me with this, you'll never be the same."

Jessica shrugged. "If you give me their names, I might be able to find their addresses online. It's better than a phonebook. You can find anything on the internet."

Jerry winced suddenly. "I can't kill anyone. It's not right. Stooping to their level like a blind idiot...do unto others...but she *deserves* it. I want to put my hands around her neck and snap her bones one by one by one."

"Why did you marry her in the first place?"

"What? Not *her.*" He laughed. "But Abigail? She was beautiful, with the most golden hair I've ever seen, and I was a young man driven by hormones. We met at the high school where I worked. I was the new English teacher, and she was the new secretary. We were both twenty-two. It was 1975—you should have seen us."

"Pointy collars and tight pants?"

"Please don't remind me." His eyes sparkled with a brief mirth. "I thought I'd found God's gift to mankind in her. We couldn't get enough of each other at first, but then the novelty began to wear off. She had two miscarriages and developed a cruel temper, which I suppose was her own form of grief. She'd throw dishes at me on our better days, and knives on our worse ones." He rubbed the stitches on the back of his hand. "She found out she was pregnant again right after we'd agreed to divorce. She'd planned on keeping it. My mother and hers helped her work on the nursery." He swallowed. "And then she changed her mind. She told me…She told me she couldn't raise a child who'd have my temper. *My* temper! Not hers! She didn't even give me the chance to talk it over with her. She just…did it." Jerry tilted his head up toward the sky. "Look at all those stars."

She followed his gaze. Clouds were rolling in from the west, but several twinkling constellations were still visible in the blackness directly overhead. "What about them?" she asked.

"Some nights, at the graveyard, I would look up and think of my three children. I wondered if they were like me somewhere, or if they'd gone on to some paradise I'd never see, or if they even had souls at all since they died before birth. I've had my doubts before. It's so easy to look at what's out there and think we must be afterthoughts in God's mind. We're smaller than dust, Jessica."

"I'd like to think we're so much bigger." She sat down in one of the patio chairs. Jerry's ramblings were far from linear, and she had the feeling he'd keep on going until he ran out of steam.

"Do we really have meaning in our lives?" he asked her.

"I don't see why not."

"What meaning did my children have, when they were never born? What meaning did my cousin have, who died in a car accident on a snowy highway at the age of sixteen? What meaning do any of us have?"

Jessica opened her mouth to offer some saccharine answer, but Jerry didn't give her the chance. "I used to write poetry when I was young," he said. "When my cousin Christopher died, I wrote one for his funeral. Would you like to hear it?"

"Are you going to give me a choice?" Jessica asked with a kindly smirk.

He began to recite:

In those days I knew no sorrow.
Sun did shine on endless day.
Only now, and no tomorrow.
Not a thought of life's decay.
Death came like a thief at nighttime.
Sly, unwanted phantoms took
Your hand and led you far away
To places where we cannot look.
Eyes stare from a frame that sits in
Silence on a dusty shelf.
Your frozen smile cannot deceive
That force which seeks to claim myself.
From the picture frame you grin in
Blissful innocence of youth.
But in those days, did you know sorrow?
Or could you see the grimmer truth?

He remained silent for a time. Jessica thought of Marjorie Miller, gone from the world far too soon. Jerry had died even younger than she, his children far younger than that. And what had any of them left behind? Memories as frail as smoke, and pain.

"I never wrote another poem after that," Jerry finally said. "I couldn't bring myself to." He looked at the sky again. "I miss my cousin so much. I miss my parents and my brothers. Little Casey too. I love them, and they don't even know where I am."

"I can contact Casey, if you'd like. There's a form on her website."

"And tell her what wonderful shape I'm in? No, thank you."

Jessica mulled over this increasingly erratic conversation. "You seem to be in two minds about this situation," she said.

"My eternal struggle. Should I, or shouldn't I?"

"Well, which one is it going to be?"

"If lives have no meaning," Jerry said quietly, "then it shouldn't be so difficult to take them."

"But if they do?"

"Then you and I can burn in hell together. Deal?"

He held out a hand to her, and she shook it. "Deal."

Something murky slithered into Jessica's dreams once again. The pathetic child was too stupid to realize what was going on. This amused the voices, whose name was Vindictam, to no end.

Her ignorance and spite would be her downfall, much as Jerry's weaknesses had led to his.

The voices spoke inside Jessica's mind in tones sweeter than the finest honey. *Kill them,* they said. *Kill them…*

And in the silence of the night, the voices could hear Jerry repeat the words, like echoes in a void.

The young woman giggled softly in her sleep. Her gentleman friend next to her in the bed sat up and stared at Jessica with wide eyes, which also amused Vindictam. Wayne Thompson was just as damaged as Jerry had been. An easy mark.

Vindictam would turn its attention to Wayne once Jessica was gone, and it would be so much fun seeing what sort of delicious things it could make Wayne do. Perhaps he could do something about his annoying cousin…

Wayne muttered something—a prayer?—and Vindictam felt a fraction of its strength leave. *Fucking bastard.*

Remember what they did to you, Vindictam said to Jessica, choosing to ignore Wayne for now. *Remember how they made you hurt.*

Her lips moved to form words. "I remember…"

23

"The high today is only going to be fifty-five." Wayne switched off the television in the living room. "I hope your relatives rented a place with walls."

"There's a lodge at Campbell Community Park," Jessica said. "We'll be fine."

Still wearing her pajamas, she stood at the kitchen counter, peeling potatoes, a job proving far more tedious than she'd hoped. Her hands were already cramping, and more bits of peel were landing on the floor than in the scrap bowl.

Wayne joined her in the kitchen but kept his distance. Jessica could tell he was still silently fuming about their argument yesterday afternoon, but she knew he would come around eventually.

"How are you feeling today?" Wayne asked. "Any more weird pains?"

"No." Jessica felt surprised by the question. "I'm not even sore from all that digging yesterday. Maybe I'm finally getting buff like you."

"Maybe so." He paused, thinking. "You said the family reunion is Halloween-themed, but what about *Día de Muertos*? Isn't that coming up soon?"

"That's the beginning of November, and none of us is actually from Mexico, you know. My *abuelo* has been gone for years. Uncle Esteban might put up an *ofrenda* in his and Grandma's honor, though." She continued peeling, peeling, peeling. Would it never end? They should have just gone down to Eleanor Market.

Jessica giggled suddenly and slapped a hand over her mouth when a thought occurred to her.

"What?" Wayne asked, eyebrows rising. "Is there something on my face?"

"No, no. I just remembered something from last night after you went to bed. Jerry and I were talking again. He wants me to help him kill his murderers and his wife." Mirthful tears sprang into her eyes, and she gripped her stomach, laughter racking her body. "Can you imagine? Me! Killing people!"

She didn't know why it seemed so funny in the light of day. Jessica imagined herself lifting a gun to someone's head and pulling the trigger, *pew pew pew*. It would be so messy!

Wayne's expression turned glacial.

Jessica wiped at her eyes and managed to say, "What?"

It took him a moment to speak. "And how did you respond to that rather alarming suggestion?"

"You know me, Wayne. I'd make a terrible assassin."

His jaw clenched. "Who is his wife? If Jerry can come here, he can find her and go there. We might have to warn her."

"Someone named Abigail." Jessica peeled her final potato and massaged her hands. "But she could have remarried by now, or moved out of state, so it might be hard to find her."

"Abigail, huh?" Wayne's lips twisted downward. "Did he give you any details about her?"

"Let me think." She reviewed the long chat she and Jerry had had on the deck while Wayne slumbered upstairs. "He and Abigail were the same age, so she'd be about fifty-seven by now. She had golden hair and was a secretary at Lyle Mercer High School. That's where they met."

"Interesting."

"And he asked me about someone named Sarah, but I don't understand why." Then it came to her: "Rachel told me I had an imaginary friend named Sarah when I was little. Must be a coincidence."

"Are you not the least bit concerned that Jerry asked for your help with *murder*?"

Jessica shrugged. "It's not like I could do much, anyway. I could take out every Patrick Smith in the phonebook and still not bag the right one. Jerry needs to give me something more specific to go on, you know?"

She was fully aware of Wayne's gaze boring into her as she placed a skinned potato on the glass cutting board and began dicing it into uneven cubes that would have had Chef Gordon Ramsay in hysterics. "Is there a problem?" she asked him.

"Have you been listening to yourself?"

"What, about the *ofrenda*?" Jessica studied him, feeling slightly baffled, like her mind were a train that had briefly jumped to the wrong set of tracks. "It's like an altar honoring the dead. You place offerings and stuff on it. Photos, flowers, etcetera."

Wayne put a hand to his forehead. "You have got to be fucking kidding me."

"Wayne, what is *wrong*?"

He made a wordless gesture she couldn't interpret, then said, "Let's just finish the goddamn potato salad and get the hell out of here."

They departed for Campbell Community Park at 11:30 a.m. Jessica balanced the bowl of potato salad on her lap and buckled her seatbelt, unable to figure out why Wayne wasn't speaking to her. All she'd been talking about was Day of the Dead stuff, and then he'd gotten all weird. Had she missed something?

"Do we have everything?" he said at last.

"I think so."

"Good." Wayne climbed behind the wheel and slammed the door shut with unnecessary force, then pulled a white plastic bottle emblazoned with a gold cross out of his pocket and stuffed it into the center cupholder.

She would have been less surprised if he'd produced a grenade. "Is that holy water?"

"Yep."

"Why haven't I seen it before?"

His cheeks flushed. "I forgot I had it until this morning when... Never mind. I keep it in my bottom nightstand drawer. Marjorie gave it to me years ago."

"Are you expecting some kind of trouble?"

"I have no fucking clue what I should be expecting right now." He backed the truck out of the driveway in a squeal of tires.

"My mother isn't a demon, you know," she said as he brought the truck up to speed. "Holy water won't have any effect on her."

"Sorry, I was all out of sharpened stakes."

Jessica started to laugh, but the emotion died within her. She would see her mother and father within the hour.

She should just ignore them. They never had anything good to say. She *knew* they would disapprove of her living arrangements since she was twenty-one and Wayne was thirty and they weren't married and *what would people think*? Not to mention she'd lost her job, but it wasn't her fault the truck stop wasn't making money anymore.

Then again, her parents might not speak a single word to her. Somehow, that would be the most hurtful thing of all.

Wayne switched on the radio. Jessica closed her eyes to wait for the inevitable.

They arrived in Kentucky less than thirty minutes later. Traffic on U.S. 27 was backed up due to an accident up ahead, Lady Gaga was belting her lungs out from the truck's speakers, and Jessica's pulse had nearly doubled in anticipation.

"You'll have to direct me from here," Wayne said.

"Get into this lane and turn right at the next light. Then make a left."

"Got it."

Campbell Community Park consisted of a ballfield, a large play area for children, two picnic pavilions, and the three-story Kemper House, which had formerly been a home but was now rented out for family gatherings, like the one today. Jessica had often wondered if the place had its own ghosts since it was so old. She'd have to call the park office sometime and get permission to investigate some night soon. It would make another nice video for her channel.

Wayne pulled into a handicapped parking space just to the right of a familiar gold Lexus bearing an Indiana license plate.

Jessica swallowed a knot of apprehension. Her parents were already here.

Remember what they did to you. Remember how they made you hurt.

"Maybe I should just stay in the truck while you mingle with *Los Reyes*," Jessica said with some uncertainty, eyeing the white brick building where Maria and Stephen lay in wait.

Wayne killed the engine. "I think you need to grow up."

Jessica grudgingly stepped out into the shade of the massive alder tree looming between Kemper House and the faded pavement. She clutched the bowl of potato salad to her chest, just now noticing she was hungry.

Wayne led the way up a handicapped ramp onto a white, wooden porch where her mother's brother Esteban Reyes and one of his cousins were having a smoke. Uncle Esteban had donned a black bodysuit printed with bones so he'd look like an animated skeleton in the dark, and his cousin—Enrique? Ernesto? She couldn't remember—wore brown Jedi robes and had a collapsible lightsaber tucked into his belt.

"I'm feeling underdressed," Wayne commented, peering down at his pastel-pink polo shirt.

"Jessica!" Uncle Esteban exclaimed when he saw her. "Where is your costume?"

"I'm an unemployed ghost hunter," Jessica said. She'd put on a plain gray hooded sweatshirt and a pair of blue jeans that had a rip in one knee. "We look like everyone else, but poorer."

"Nice, nice," said her uncle. "And who is this?"

"I'm Wayne, her plus one." Wayne leaned in to shake Uncle Esteban's hand. "I'm a disabled accountant."

"Ah, you would get along well with my sister."

"If your sister is Maria Roman-Dell, then we're already acquainted. You must be Esteban."

"That's right! I'm Jessica's favorite uncle, and this Jedi knight here is Ernesto. His dad and my dad were brothers, both from Juárez."

Ernesto dipped his head at Wayne. "Greetings, Padawan."

"Are you really disabled, Wayne?" Esteban asked, cocking his head to one side, assessing him.

"I wouldn't fake a walk this ridiculous." Wayne hitched up one khaki pant leg to display a leg brace. "I have cerebral palsy. I wear these to help me get around."

Uncle Esteban gave a nod of approval. "Blue flames? Nice."

Wayne lowered his pant leg and brushed out a wrinkle. "I had them custom-printed. They make me feel like a badass."

"Like the pink shirt?" Uncle Esteban winked.

"You bet."

Jessica sighed and smiled. If Wayne was going to be a social butterfly with her relatives today, she might not have to do much talking after all.

Ernesto drifted back into the building while Uncle Esteban proceeded to educate Wayne in Reyes family history. "My father was Andrés Reyes

Pizano, who came to America with his siblings and later married my mother, Karen Greenwald. They dropped the Latino surname tradition and stuck with Reyes, and here we are."

Jessica's attention began to waver. She needed something to eat.

"—it on the table inside."

"Sorry, what?" Jessica looked up.

Wayne and Uncle Esteban were staring at her, no longer smiling.

"That bowl you're carrying," her uncle said. "You can set it on the table with all of the other food inside."

"Oh. Okay." She took a deep breath and walked past them into the big room, where numerous round tables had been set up and covered in orange and black plastic tablecloths, befitting the season. The ceiling and walls had been festooned with streamers dangling paper bats and pumpkins, and a variety of dishes covered a long buffet table: deviled eggs, veggie and meat trays, tiny sandwiches, and more. There were even bowls of candy and a platter of sugar skulls decorated with icing.

Jessica set the bowl of potato salad next to the deviled eggs, pried off the lid, and jabbed a spoon into it. Her work here was done.

Wayne remained outside, trapped there by Uncle Esteban's infatuation with genealogy, and Rachel and Eric hadn't shown up yet, so Jessica drifted aimlessly across the room, nodding at some older Reyes women she didn't know very well. They'd dressed up as a trio of witches, complete with capes and pointy hats. Maybe she and Wayne should have made more of an effort, but of course, they'd been preoccupied with other matters.

A peal of laughter echoed in from an adjoining room. It belonged to Marco Reyes, her mother's thirtyish cousin who performed magic shows in drag down at the Levee on the weekends.

"Oh, Maria," she heard him say, "you remember that time when…"

Marco and Maria walked into the banquet room, still chatting. Neither of them looked Jessica's way.

Marco had donned a glittering, floor-length dress and a cinnamon-colored wig. Maria, on the other hand, wore a dark gray skirt with a matching blazer, a cream-colored top, and black pumps, as if it were any old day at the office. Her glossy black hair was piled on top of her head and pinned in place with a silver clip shaped like a blossom.

Her regular clothes, Jessica thought. *Just like me.*

Maria was fifty-two and didn't look a day over forty. Her ability to age gracefully was the only thing Jessica had ever desired to inherit from her.

Jessica's temper began to rise at the sight of her mother. Maria's outfit had probably cost more than the rent at Jessica's old apartment, and here Jessica was, wearing holey jeans, a sweatshirt with fraying cuffs, and sneakers that had been old three years ago.

Maria must have sensed Jessica's gaze, for she turned and said, "Oh. Hi, Jessica." She smiled, but the look in her eyes was distant.

Hi, Jessica. No "I've missed you." No warm embrace. No sign that she cared.

"Where's Dad?" Jessica asked in a weak voice. Her pulse pounded in her ears.

"He hitched a ride with David—they're out getting more beer, if you can believe it. They should be back soon."

David was yet another Reyes cousin. Jessica wondered if Wayne would have a hard time keeping everyone straight.

"I'll leave you two alone," Marco said. "Esteban might need help with something." He glided away in his high heels, far more elegantly than Jessica would have managed.

Jessica and her mother regarded each other. "Rachel tells me you're living with Wayne now," Maria said.

"Yeah." Jessica shuffled her feet.

"Is that a permanent arrangement?"

"I don't know."

"Are you sharing a room?"

Jessica ground her teeth together. Of course, it would take the conversation five seconds to end up here. "That's my business," she said.

Maria pursed her lips. "Wayne is a decent man, but I hope you'll exercise good judgment."

Jessica's temper refused to remain at bay. "I'll do whatever the hell I want."

The banquet room grew as quiet as a tomb. The three witches gaped like beached fish. Maria's eyes blazed, but Jessica didn't care.

"Do you *want* to humiliate me in front of my family?" her mother hissed.

Did she? "You may have forgotten, *Mother*," Jessica said, "but I'm an adult and can make my own decisions."

"I just want you to be responsible."

"Why? Are you afraid I'll get knocked up and bring another child into this cruel world, or some bullshit?"

"Jessica!"

"For your information," Jessica said, "we did sleep together. And I *liked* it."

"I have the feeling I've come in at the wrong end of this conversation," Wayne said, sidling up next to her with a can of Pepsi in one hand. He gave Jessica a warning glance.

The women dressed as witches resumed their own conversation but still threw Jessica and Maria snooping glances every few seconds.

Maria's gaze flicked from Jessica to Wayne. "Hello, Wayne," she said in a politer tone. "Have you been well?"

"Even better now that your daughter lives with me." Wayne winked. He'd been right; Maria *didn't* scare him. "I still put up with Charlie five days a week. He misses you. He doesn't understand how your replacement ever passed the CPA exam."

Maria actually smiled at him. "It's nice to hear I made an impression on him. Tell everyone I said hi." Then, to Jessica, she said, "If you see your sister, could you tell her to come talk to me? I got a little something for her."

"What, is it for the baby you don't want her to have?"

Her mother's mouth fell open in shock. "What has gotten *into* you?"

Jessica felt a tug on her arm.

"Sorry, she's had a stressful week or two," Wayne said, leading her away from Maria. "Don't take it personally."

They went back out to the porch, which was now vacant. "What do you think you're doing?" Wayne whispered, setting his Pepsi down on a railing.

Tears brimmed in Jessica's eyes. The brief encounter with her mother had made her feel like curling into a ball and crying until the sun burned out. "Every time I look at her, I want to make her hurt like she made me hurt."

Wayne put his hands on her shoulders. "You have to learn to put it behind you, or it's just going to eat you all up. Take it from an expert."

"She never cared about me. She only ever cared about her stupid *job*."

"I'm not saying you have to be her friend. I'm saying you have to let it go."

Jessica stared into Wayne's coffee-brown eyes, which were giving her a piercing stare. "I can't just stop calling myself Jessica and get over it. That's why you go by your middle name, right? You couldn't stand for anyone to call you Robert like *she* did."

He dropped his hands. "Jessica..."

Jessica brushed him off. She'd made a mistake in coming here, and not even the promise of a free meal could convince her to stay. "Let's go home."

He shook his head. "You need to learn to get along with people, even if you don't like them."

Why couldn't Wayne understand this one simple thing? "She deserves to be hurt. She needs to know what it's like."

He gave her a cold look. “You’re starting to sound like Jerry.”

“Maybe he’s on to something.”

A car slid into a parking space and belched out more of Jessica’s relatives: Elena the dinner theater actress, her husband, and children. Elena gave Jessica and Wayne polite nods hello and strode past them into Kemper House without saying a word to them. Jessica wondered if Elena even remembered Jessica’s name.

“How many Reyeses are there?” Wayne asked as three more cars pulled in, including one familiar Nissan Altima.

“An ungodly quantity.”

“Maybe don’t make a fool of yourself in front of all of them?”

“You don’t know what it’s like.” It felt as if a carefully built dam inside her had sprung a leak, and a vast lake of buried emotions was gushing out from the hole. “Never giving me hugs or kisses or a shoulder to cry on…”

“Rachel and Eric are here,” Wayne said, scanning the parking lot. “I suggest you act happy to see them.”

24

"You never answered the text I sent you earlier," Rachel said while they ate. She wore a knee-length black dress, a hot pink feather boa, shades, and a tiara.

She, Eric, Jessica, and Wayne had selected a table close to the rear of the room because Maria and Stephen were sitting toward the front. This arrangement had given Jessica's mood a slight boost.

"I didn't know you sent one." Jessica picked up her purse and slid her phone out of its compartment. "Well, that explains it. Dead battery. What did you want?"

"Nothing important." Rachel stabbed a piece of broccoli onto her fork and dipped it into a glob of ranch dressing. "I've been craving the jalapeno ranch sauce they sell at Tim's Taco Barn, and I wondered if you could pick up a bottle of it on the way here."

Jessica wrinkled her nose. "Are you trying to burn the kid?"

"Just toughening him up. Or her." She popped the broccoli into her mouth and chewed. "Normal ranch is still pretty darn good too."

Wayne and Eric started telling each other stories about their respective places of employment. While they talked, Jessica's gaze drifted over to her parents' table. Stephen Roman-Dell—a tall man with sandy hair and a strong jawline—sipped at a bottle of Corona, saying something to Marco and emphasizing a point with his free hand like he usually did. Maria sat between them, smiling in amusement.

Why had her parents bothered having children in the first place? They clearly had more fun without them.

She returned her attention to their own table. "What did Mom give you?" she asked Rachel. She'd seen the two of them mingling by the buffet table shortly after Rachel and Eric arrived. Maria had passed Rachel a tiny gift bag.

"Oh!" Rachel's face brightened. She reached into her purse and pulled out a pastel green baby onesie. "She told me she was sorry about the way she reacted when I told her about the baby."

"Do you believe her?"

Rachel rolled her eyes. "Mom isn't some kind of evil villain, Jessica. She just has terrible mom-skills."

"Hmph."

Jessica looked over at the Roman-Dells' table again. Marco Reyes caught sight of her, left his seat, and strutted to the empty chair at their table, taking it for himself.

"Hello, kiddos."

"Hi, Marco," Rachel said. "Your makeup looks fantastic."

Marco beamed. "Thank you! Need any tips?"

"Maybe later." Rachel turned to Wayne. "Have you met Marco yet?"

"Not as such." Wayne leaned across the table and shook Marco's hand. "I'm Wayne, Jessica's plus one."

"It's lovely to meet you." Marco then turned to Jessica. "I wanted you to know that I *love* what you're doing with your YouTube channel. I've watched every single video."

Jessica felt herself perk up, as if his words were fertilizer. "You really like them?"

"Would I lie? They're amazing. You've captured just the right eerie vibes. I'm Oatmeal the Destroyer, by the way. I've commented on some of your videos."

"You're the one who wanted me to 'show you the ghost,'" Jessica said, remembering.

"Yep, that's me! So, is it all true? Or are you entertaining us with clever lies?"

Jessica flicked her gaze to Wayne, then back to Marco. "It's all true," she said. "And it gets even weirder. I haven't told the whole story on my channel."

"Drawing out the suspense for your eager viewers?"

"Something like that."

Jessica's teenage second-cousin Allie slid into an empty chair next to Marco. Skinnier than a twig, she'd dressed in a pink leotard and tutu. "Did I hear you talking about your YouTube channel?" Allie asked, eyes wide with fascination.

"You did. Are you one of my subscribers too?"

"I am! I'm Spooky Baybee 1994. Did you really meet a ghost?"

"I really did."

"Were you scared?"

Jessica noticed more sets of eyes latching onto her from across the room. She drew in a breath and said, "At first, yes. But Jerry and I have gotten to know each other a little better. He's a very interesting person."

"Is he here now?"

"I don't think so."

Allie looked almost disappointed. "Oh."

"So, Jerry was murdered?" Marco asked her in a quieter tone.

"That's all true too."

"Poor guy."

"Yeah."

"If he's a ghost, how can you see him?" Allie asked as another cousin wandered over to listen in on the conversation.

It was starting to feel a little overwhelming, having so much attention focused on her. Attention on the internet was one thing, but in person, it made Jessica feel claustrophobic.

"I think I have some kind of special ability," Jessica said. "Apparently, I see dead people."

"Yeah," Rachel butted in. "When she was little, she had an imaginary friend named Sarah. Only *I* think Sarah was a ghost."

"So apparently, I've been seeing dead people all my life," Jessica said. "Sarah and Jerry are just the only two I know of."

A utensil clattered to the floor. One of Jessica's great-aunts had dropped a fork and was leaning to pick it up with a trembling, arthritic hand. The old woman's face had turned paler than milk. A few other snooping Reyeses had become white-faced, too, and quickly turned away when they saw Jessica watching.

What the hell was that all about?

"Anyway," Jessica said, "it's been really weird lately. Um, if you'll excuse me."

She pushed her chair back and hurried out of the banquet room, into a short hallway leading to a set of restrooms. Jessica slipped into the women's room and stood with her hands braced on the edge of the sink, trying to catch her breath. So many people had been watching her, listening…

She took slow breaths to try to regulate her pulse. Maybe then she would stop feeling so dizzy.

Don't get distracted, a voice said inside of her. *The time draws near.*

"I know," she said, though she wasn't completely sure what the voice meant.

You must be prepared.

"Like an honorary Boy Scout?"

The voice didn't reply. Jessica splashed some water onto her face to cool herself off, then dabbed it dry with a paper towel, wadded it into a ball, and tossed it into the wastebasket.

She returned to the banquet room. Both Marco and Allie had left her table, finding more relatives to mingle with.

Conversation at her table had moved on to other matters. Throughout the room, people chattered and laughed. Jessica forced herself to continue eating, her appetite having abandoned her. How could everyone act so cheerful when a monster sat only a few tables away from them? She wanted to stand on her chair and shout, "Look at her! She may have the body of an angel, but inside, she's a devil!"

Wayne had known what to do about his devil of a mother. *He'd* bludgeoned Mother Dearest to death with a fireplace poker.

Jessica swayed a little in her chair. It grew difficult to think clearly. She hadn't slept well, had she?

All sound in the room grew fainter and eventually ceased. Her mind drifted, like a ship lost at sea. Where was she? Not at home, though home was where the heart was, and her heart was in her chest, so she must have been home because home was anywhere…

Her vision cleared. She saw her mother sitting in a recliner, reading a book, turning the pages one by one.

"Mommy, read me a story!"

Ignored. Another page turning.

"Please, Mommy?"

A glance. "They'll teach you to read when you're in school. Then you can read stories whenever you like."

"But I want you to read me a story. Mommy, please!"

The image changed. Her mother, scrubbing a kitchen counter.

"Mommy! I cut my finger!" Blood. Pain.

A pause. "What did you cut your finger on?"

"There—there was a piece of glass in the yard, and I picked it up, and…and…"

Leading her into the bathroom. Washing the cut, wrapping it in a bandage.

No kisses. No more blood, but pain…

Her mother. Doing paperwork by the window in the living room.

"Mom, do you care if I go hang out at the library?"

A distracted glance. "Hmm?"

"The library. Do you care if I go?"

"No, go ahead. Why would I care about that kind of thing? Why would I care? Why would I care? Why would I—"

Laughter. Jessica twitched. She was sitting at a round table covered in a black tablecloth at the Kemper House, and her brother-in-law, Eric, was chuckling at something Wayne had just said.

"Good one, man!"

Jessica rubbed her eyes and blinked. She must have dozed off for a moment or two. Good thing she hadn't slumped over and fallen out of her seat. Maria would have died of embarrassment. But would that have been a problem?

A Reyes walked past the table, carrying an unopened bottle of tequila. Rachel nudged her husband in the side. "Look, I told you they'd have the harder stuff here. Go knock yourself out."

Eric's eyes lit up. "Don't mind if I do!" He rose and followed the tequila-bearer over to the buffet table.

"Jess, you look tired," Rachel said.

"Do I?" Jessica blinked. "I cut my finger."

Rachel frowned. "On what?"

Jessica wobbled in the chair again and gripped the edge of the table to steady herself. "There was a piece of glass in the yard. It cut me when I picked it up. She never kissed it to make it better."

"What are you talking about?"

Why couldn't Rachel understand? "No kisses. She never let herself get too close, to make things easier if something happened to us. It was just a pretense of motherhood. She did the bare minimum because she had to."

"Are you feeling all right?"

A hand placed itself on Jessica's forehead. "She feels a little warm. She might be running a fever."

"And that's going to make her act like this? What's in her cup?"

The cup she'd poured herself rose into the air. "It tastes like Coke."

Her vision doubled. She blinked again to bring everything back into focus. Two people were sitting at the table with her—a man and a woman. Other people were in the room too, talking and eating.

"Jessica, can you hear me?" the man asked. He had glasses and dark brown hair styled with gel.

Of course, Jessica could hear; she wasn't deaf. Who did these people think she was?

"I think she's having a seizure," the woman said, her tone dark with worry.

"Then why is she still sitting up?"

"It could be an absence seizure. Jessica, honey, snap out of this!"

Jessica shivered. Someone must have left a door open because the air in the room was turning to ice.

Another man came and sat at the table, with a plastic cup half filled with tequila. "What's going on?"

Eric! His name was Eric. And with him were Rachel and Wayne, and she was Jessica, and they were at a miserable family reunion somewhere in northern Kentucky.

Jessica shook her head. She'd zoned out again. Half her food remained on her plate. "Sorry. Did I miss something?"

Her three companions were giving her uncomfortable stares.

"What day is it?" Rachel asked. She'd shoved her Hollywood starlet shades onto the top of her head to study her better.

"Um, October 23, I think."

"What's seventeen times three?"

"Fifty-one."

"What's this building we're in?"

"Kemper House. Why are you asking me all these questions?"

Rachel let out a terse breath. "I think you just had an absence seizure."

"You're not a doctor."

Rachel did not seem to be in the mood for humor. "That may be true, but when we're talking to you and you're not responding, that's kind of a flashing sign saying something's wrong."

"Huh." A few tendrils of fog wove in and out of her thoughts, derailing any line of thinking before it could come to fruition in her head.

"Should I take her to the hospital?" Wayne asked Rachel.

Wayne was squeezing her hand, hard. She almost couldn't feel her fingers.

His words cleared Jessica's head in about two seconds. "I'm fine," she said. "I didn't get a lot of sleep last night. Maybe I need more caffeine." She picked up her Coke and chugged the rest of it down in one gulp. Then, frowning, she said, "I wonder if this is what happened to Jerry."

Wayne dropped his voice so low, she almost couldn't hear it over the hubbub. "What do you mean by that?"

But Jessica didn't know what she'd meant. She shrugged and said, "Can we talk about something else for a while?"

"What about that monster your friend saw on Thursday?" Eric asked. "Did you ever figure out what it was?"

"Nope. Maybe it was just a fluke."

Jessica bit into a baby carrot and glanced over at her parents' table again. Her father, having finished his beer, yawned and checked his watch. He said something to her mother, who shook her head.

"So," Jessica said, "are Mom and Dad driving straight back to Indy tonight?"

"No, they're staying with us at Uncle Esteban's. Aunt Sharon's giving them the guest bedroom down the hall from us. Why?"

"Just wondered." She stood up. Her drink had gone to her bladder awfully fast. "I'm going to the bathroom again. Be right back."

Jessica wove her way around tables full of gossiping Reyeses and went back out to the restrooms. She pushed open the first stall and latched it behind her.

She felt fine. She felt great. She felt wonderful. She felt—

Fog overtook her unexpectedly, and before it could occur to her that she was not as fine as she had thought, she was gone.

"Hey, Maria. Can I talk to you a second?"

Maria Roman-Dell looked up at her brother, trying not to laugh at the silly skeleton costume he'd worn today. Esteban would always be the eternal child. "What is it?"

Esteban's expression was tense. "It's about Jessica."

Jessica had left for the restroom a few minutes earlier. Maria turned toward the table of drinks, where Stephen was selecting another beer.

"Should Stephen hear this too?"

"Nah, best not worry him. Come outside with me."

"Tell Stephen I'll be back," Maria said to Marco, then followed Esteban out the door. She thought they would linger on the wraparound porch, but Esteban walked all the way out to the nearest picnic pavilion, easily fifty yards from the back of Kemper House.

Tension knotted Maria's stomach as they stood regarding each other. Esteban was always the jolly one. To see him like this was *wrong.*

"Did you know that Jessica has a channel on YouTube?" Esteban asked.

"I know that she hunts ghosts and shares videos about it." Maria tried to keep the derision out of her voice. "I wish she wouldn't waste her time and money, but when has she ever listened to me?"

"Have you watched any of the videos she's uploaded?"

"A few. It seems like she mostly sits in dark cellars, moping out loud about how awful of a mother I am and hoping some ghost will answer her." Her heart ached as she thought about it. "It's been so hard being a mother to her and Rachel. If things could have been different…"

"Look, I know you and I have had disagreements on proper parenting technique," Esteban said. "That's not what I want you to know about." His breath hitched. "I don't even want to bring this up, but I'm afraid it's going to get out of hand and blow up or something."

"Will you just get to the point?"

Esteban closed his eyes. "Aunt Jean heard Marco and Allie talking to Jessica a little bit ago. Apparently, they both follow her channel. Aunt Jean heard some names mentioned and told me, and I swiped Sharon's iPhone to see for myself. I took it out to the car and found Jessica's channel. She's been posting more often and getting a lot more views."

"I suppose that's good for her," Maria said. "But what does this have to do with me?"

Esteban opened his eyes, and stared straight into Maria's. "Last week, Jessica did an investigation at the graveyard behind the Iron Springs United Methodist Church."

Maria clapped a hand over her mouth to stifle a gasp.

Esteban continued without pause. "Apparently, she met a man there. A *dead* man. He came home with her. They've been hanging out a lot the past few days, getting to know each other better."

That's impossible, Maria thought, but she said, "Who is this man?"

Esteban waited a beat. "I think you already know who it is."

"Just say it!"

"Maybe it's better if I just show you." He slid an iPhone out of his skeleton costume, tinkered with the screen for a minute or two, and then handed it to Maria as a video began to play.

Jessica's smiling face was centered in the video. "Good morning, folks! It's me, your Friendly Neighborhood Ghost Hunter, and I've got some interesting news for all of you. If you're new here, I'll summarize what's been going on: a ghost named Jerry Madison followed me home from an investigation and won't leave. He was tortured and killed by an angry mob in 1986, and he doesn't think his killers have ever been caught."

Maria threw the phone. It landed in the dying grass beside the pavilion. Esteban bent, picked it up, silenced it, and watched her.

"Ghosts aren't real," she whispered. Her ears were ringing.

"If that's the case," Esteban said, "then how in the world does Jessica *know*?"

25

Sidney had been scheduled to work Saturday morning, but Travis called her twenty minutes before her shift was supposed to start and told her not to come in.

"It's just dead out here this morning," Travis had said. "Stay home and enjoy your day."

Instead of doing just that, Sidney had flopped onto her father's couch with her laptop to start searching for job openings within a ten-mile radius of Eleanor. She refused to end up as broke as Jessica—it went against her principles.

Lunchtime came and went. Sidney had whipped up a short resume and sent it off to three different places, keeping her fingers crossed. If the inevitable happened and the truck stop shuttered its doors, she could have a new job lined up and ready to go, no problem.

Just after one o'clock, Sidney went outside to enjoy the crisp, fall air. Her brothers, Kyle and Brian, had commandeered the living room to play *Mario Kart* on their Nintendo Wii, and she could hear them laughing and shouting at each other through the open window.

It made her smile to hear them happy. They were finding joy in the small things.

Sidney lit a cigarette and took delight in the sunny day as best she could.

Her dad's property was just over half an acre in size. From the back porch, she could see six other houses. A woman was raking leaves at one of them. A man sat in a lounge chair, reading a book, at another.

She reviewed what Jessica had told her about Jerry. The man had been kidnapped from his own home. If his neighborhood had been anything like this one, someone would have seen or heard something. And why wouldn't law enforcement have suspected murder? A person vanishes without taking their wallet or car with them? They have to be dead.

She remembered what the printout from Casey Madison Green's website had said. Casey's family sought help from the authorities after Jerry went missing, and nothing had come of it.

Maybe the whole thing was a coverup.

Sidney went back inside, retrieved her laptop, and returned to the back porch. She flipped it open, clicked on the web browser, and typed "Clarkville Kentucky Murder 1986" into the search bar.

She hit Enter.

The top link bore the headline: "No Suspects Linked to Clarkville Shooting."

Pulse quickening, Sidney clicked on the link, which took her to a reprinted article from a library archive. The article had been taken from a July 1986 edition of a smalltown newspaper she'd never heard of.

She began to read.

The investigation into the June 27 homicides of Megan Smith, age 13, Josie Smith, age 6, Lauren Scott, age 6, and Sarah Roman-Dell, age 6, has stalled due to lack of evidence.

The shooting occurred between 2:00 and 2:15 p.m. on Friday, June 27, at 712 Pine Street in Clarkville. Megan Smith was watching her sister and her sister's friends outside while her mother, Amy Smith, made a quick trip to the grocery store. The four girls had been reportedly sitting at a picnic table in the Smiths' backyard, playing Candy Land. When Smith arrived back at the house, all four girls lay dead on the ground with gunshot wounds to their heads.

The article continued for a few more paragraphs, but Sidney had stopped reading. Her pulse beat loudly in her ears. *Sarah* Roman-Dell? Who on Earth was that?

Opening a new tab, she quickly found Casey Madison Green's website and the lines she was looking for.

My father's younger brother, Jerry Benjamin Madison, was last seen on June 29, 1986, at a Walgreens near Clarkville, Kentucky, which is the town where he lived at 640 Elderberry Drive.

Sidney opened a third tab, pulled up Google Maps, and typed in "640 Elderberry Drive Clarkville."

A red pin appeared on the map.

She added 712 Pine Street as a destination and hit Enter.

A second red pin appeared on the map, practically on top of the first.

Sidney zoomed in, hardly daring to breathe.—640 Elderberry Drive and 712 Pine Street butted up against each other. Their backyards shared a property line.

Sidney said, "Holy shit."

And all of the pieces fell together.

26

1986

Like Christ on his way to Calvary, they forced Jerry along to his place of execution. Though fortunately, they'd not required him to carry anything. The effects of the drug they'd injected him with were slowly wearing off, but he hadn't regained enough strength to resist them and run. All he could do was stagger where they dragged him…and pray.

They were clearly in a forest now. Tree frogs chirped high above, and the earthy smell of decaying leaf matter filled the air. Voices murmured close by. Something crackled, and he caught a whiff of smoke. Maybe they were going to burn him alive.

"We got him," a man said so close to his ear, he jumped.

A hush fell over the forest. Rough hands shoved him into a sitting position and lashed his arms and legs to what felt like a lawn chair. Bark scratched the back of his head. The chair must have been secured to a tree. Any moment now and they'd douse him with gasoline, igniting him with the strike of a match.

Jerry's clock was rapidly winding down to zero. He knew it with as much certainty as he knew the sun would rise and set, and it occurred to him then he would never see another daybreak, nor the blue of the sky, nor the full moon's white orb traversing the heavens on a summer night.

Tears streamed down his cheeks. He couldn't die like this, blind to the world. "Please let me see!"

The bag was torn from his head. He blinked. A multitude of people stood before him in an unfamiliar forest clearing. A crackling bonfire raged behind them, turning each figure into a silhouette, not unlike the ones who had kidnapped him.

Someone among the throng was weeping bitterly, and a man shouted obscenities in Spanish.

Jerry licked some of the blood from his lips and struggled against his bindings. "Untie me!"

A man stepped directly in front of him. The firelight illuminated his police uniform. "Hello, Jerry."

"Officer Ridgeway?" Jerry spluttered.

The cop dipped his head in acknowledgment. "Do you know why you're here?"

Jerry's mind buzzed with adrenaline. He didn't feel like answering any questions. "Get me out of here and arrest these people!"

Officer Ridgeway let out a disappointed sigh. "I'm not going to do that, Jerry. I saw you out my back window two days ago. You murdered those little girls one by one and then went back inside, like all you'd done was take out the trash. And I thought, wow, I'm the only witness to this. I know it was you. I could have wasted my time arresting you and sending you to prison, and you would have sat in a cell, getting fat on prison food while your attorneys appealed your death sentence year after year. But I didn't think I should waste the taxpayers' money. Right, everyone?"

There came a murmur of assent. Jerry ground his teeth together so hard, he thought he might break them. "You can't do this."

"You're not in the best position to argue, Mr. Madison," said another uniformed cop coming to stand beside Officer Ridgeway. "Now, why did you do it? You owe the families that much before we kill you."

Somewhere behind Jerry, a gas-powered generator sputtered to life, and a floodlight winked on, revealing at least three dozen faces. Some were strangers to him, but others he knew well.

He had never seen so much hatred in anyone's eyes before. Somewhere deep inside Jerry's mind, he could hear something cackling in delight.

"I had to do it," Jerry stammered. "Don't you get it? They wouldn't stop looking at me. They were taunting me because they were allowed to live."

"Nobody was taunting you, Jerry," said Officer Ridgeway. "I saw the whole thing; I just wasn't fast enough to stop you. Those girls were outside, playing a board game. They never talked to you. Maybe the taunting you heard was just the voices in your goddamned head."

Voices? How did Officer Ridgeway know about the voices?

You're so fucking stupid, Jerry. You've known what's been happening. You just didn't want to admit it and get help.

But who would have helped him with *this*?

"I'm going to step aside now," Officer Ridgeway said. "I've given the families permission to do whatever they'd like to you without consequences."

"Someone will hear me," Jerry snarled.

"They won't." Both cops smiled. "The nearest house is too far away."

The cops moved out of the way. Patrick Smith, the father of two of the victims, broke away from the throng, holding a length of rope.

"Patrick, please," Jerry started to say, but his words were cut short when Patrick coiled the rope around Jerry's neck and jerked it tight.

Pain exploded in Jerry's head and throat, and his body cried for oxygen. He tried to rise by taking the chair with him, but it was stuck fast to the tree.

Please, God, let this be fast, oh please oh please oh please—

And just when Jerry felt sure death was upon him, Patrick let go, never saying a word. The man took the rope with him and stepped back toward the crowd, heartbroken tears streaking down his stubble.

Jerry sucked in a breath through his half-crushed throat just in time to see a middle-aged Latino man step forward with a knife. "You killed my beautiful little granddaughter," he sobbed. "She was only six years old. She had a whole lifetime ahead of her, and you took it all away. This is for *her*."

And the man raked the knife down Jerry's chest, not deep enough to kill, but deep enough to make Jerry scream.

They took turns torturing him. Some were men, some were women, and none showed any mercy as they made him bleed. His mindless cries of agony even elicited some laughter—a level of humiliation he hadn't thought possible.

It went on for so long, time lost all meaning. Jerry felt so lightheaded from pain and blood loss he could scarcely think.

"Stop!"

The man who'd just been carving at Jerry with a steak knife stepped aside. "He's almost gone," the man spat. "Let me finish this so we can all go home."

"I want to talk to him."

"Fine." The man stepped aside, and a woman in her late twenties approached Jerry.

She had long, dark hair, and her stomach bulged with late pregnancy. The woman didn't have any blood on her—she hadn't taken her turn yet. For that matter, neither had her husband. The tall man lurked off to the right, his face long with sorrow.

The woman's jaw was tight, and her eyes brimmed with tears. She didn't say anything, just regarded Jerry as if unsure what to do.

"Maria, please," Jerry rasped. His heartbeat was so uneven now, it might stop any moment. "Have mercy."

"I thought you were our *friend*," she said quietly. "We let you into our home. We laughed and cried with you. And then you did *this*."

For just a moment, the fog lifted in Jerry's head, and he understood, with a deepening horror, exactly what he'd done.

"I'm sorry," Jerry sobbed, the truth hitting him harder than the pain. "I never wanted anything to do with this. I don't know what came over me. Maria, *please*. Let me go. Get me to a hospital and then lock me away. I'll never hurt anyone again."

Maria stepped so close to him, he could have touched her if he wasn't restrained. "I know you won't."

Jerry felt a glimmer of hope. "Does that mean—"

He hadn't noticed the dagger in Maria's hand.

"This is for Sarah, you son of a bitch."

She raised her arm and plunged the blade between his ribs with a moist sound. The point met his stuttering heart, which shuddered and fell still.

Please forgive me, he thought, and then his head fell forward as he died.

27

2010

"Shit, shit, *shit.*" Sidney's hands shook when Jessica's phone went straight to voicemail for the sixth time. Why the hell would she have her phone off during a family reunion? Knowing Jessica, she would have welcomed a ringing phone as a distraction from all the chitchat endemic to events like that.

Wayne's phone, on the other hand, simply rang until the voicemail came on. He tended to keep it silent most of the time—which defeated the purpose of having a phone to begin with, in Sidney's opinion—and Sidney assumed that was still currently the case.

She'd left them each a voicemail saying, "Call me *now*! It's a matter of life and death!"

Because that's what it was, right? Jerry was a psychopathic murderer. He'd shot up four kids in the yard behind his and then went missing forever two days later. Somebody had obviously decided to save law enforcement a lot of trouble and took matters into their own hands.

But now Jerry was back. Sidney didn't want to believe in ghosts, but she had to for Jessica's sake. That girl, Sarah Roman-Dell? She had to be Jessica's sister. Jessica must not have known she'd ever existed. And when Jessica had met Jerry and blabbed her name to him, like it was nothing, Jerry would have made the connection since "Roman-Dell" was a far cry from "Jones" or "Brown" or even "Miller."

Sidney hit Jessica's number on her speed dial for the seventh time. Once again, it went to voicemail without ringing. "Turn your phone on, you nitwit!" she screamed.

Her brother Brian's head appeared in the open window. "What's the matter with you?"

"I'm having a bad day."

"Can I help?"

"You just keep throwing banana peels at Kyle."

Sidney took her laptop and her phone, marched into the house, grabbed her car keys, and departed with hardly a goodbye. She sped across town and turned onto Wayne's street. His truck was gone from the driveway, but Jessica's Taurus remained in its spot.

Sidney sprinted to the front door and turned the knob. Locked! She jammed her key into the knob and let herself inside. "Jessica! Where are you?"

The silence within the house nearly deafened her.

"Jessica?" She rushed up the stairs, checked both bedrooms, then investigated the mudroom, exercise room, and basement.

Okay, so Jessica was still with Wayne. That was a good sign, at least.

"Jerry, are you here?" Sidney called out. She knew it was stupid; she didn't have Jessica's psychic ghost powers and wouldn't be able to see or hear him.

But she'd seen that *thing*, whatever it was, so who knew?

Sidney clenched her fists in frustration. "Talk to me, Jerry!"

The house gave no sign the spirit was here. That meant he'd gone with Jessica to the family reunion.

Where, presumably, he'd have much easier access to Jessica's family.

It was very easy to do the math.

Sidney strode back to the front door and halted.

Where was the family reunion being held? She didn't think Jessica had ever told her.

Think, she urged herself. Sidney knew Jessica's uncle and most of her legion of extended cousins lived in northern Kentucky. There were so many Reyeses, they wouldn't all fit in someone's home. It was logical to conclude they'd rented out a place somewhere, which narrowed the location down from just about anywhere to any reception hall or park with a lodge in a twenty-mile radius.

God help me, Sidney prayed, even though she wasn't sure anyone was listening.

She turned and spotted the magnetic whiteboard stuck to the refrigerator. Wayne typically used it to mark down appointments, but at the very top, in Jessica's own writing, were the words: "Campbell Community Park 10/23 noon."

A quick Google search on her laptop showed Sidney the address. As she barreled across the bridge into Kentucky a short time later, she wondered if she might be overreacting. What could a ghost do to anyone? Jerry didn't have a body. Well, he *did*, but he wasn't attached to it anymore.

But Jerry had gone poltergeist and flung the furniture around as if it were paper when he'd found his niece's website printout. If he could get that upset knowing his family still loved and missed him and wanted him back, there was no telling what he might be capable of when facing his murderers.

She got stopped at a traffic light on U.S. 27 and banged on the steering wheel. "Come *on*!"

The light changed, and traffic inched forward. It was all Sidney could do not to jump out of the car and start running—she'd probably get there faster.

At last, she made the turnoff and whipped her car into the lot in front of a large, white brick house. She recognized the Roman-Dells' gold Lexus sitting a few spaces down from hers, but Wayne's pickup truck was nowhere to be seen.

"I don't believe it." She might have passed them on the highway going the other direction, but the fact they were no longer here didn't necessarily mean they'd gone straight home.

Some of Jessica's relatives milled around outside. Jessica's father leaned against the porch railing, holding a bottle of Corona while he talked to a bronze-skinned man in brown Jedi robes.

Sidney got out of the car and ran up to them. "Stephen!" she panted. "How long ago did Jessica and Wayne leave?"

Stephen Roman-Dell stood about six two and had sand-colored hair graying at the temples. Neatly-trimmed sideburns stretched down to his jawline. He didn't look like a liar, but she knew he and Maria had lied to Jessica for her entire life.

All of Jessica's family had lied to her—Reyeses and Roman-Dells alike. The younger ones wouldn't have known, of course, but anyone who'd been alive in 1986 certainly did.

Stephen's eyebrows knitted together when he saw Sidney. "Almost twenty minutes ago. Why?"

The Jedi next to Stephen was giving Sidney a skeptical look. She supposed she must look like a crazy person, swooping in out of the blue with hardly a greeting.

"I need to talk to them, and they're not answering their phones," Sidney said. "Did they say where they were going?"

Sadness filled Stephen's eyes, and he shook his head. "Jess didn't say a word to me today. I know she got into an argument with Maria—what's new?—but that's it."

Sidney felt a flash of annoyance at her friend for being such a jerk to her own family, even if they *were* a bunch of liars who might or might not have murdered a man in the woods. Of course, said man had *deserved* it...

"Is Rachel still here?"

Stephen shook his head. "She and Eric left around the same time that Jessica and Wayne did."

"Damn."

"Has something happened?"

Not yet. "No. I just really need to get hold of them. I—I guess I'll try them at home again. Bye, Stephen."

She started back toward her car, but Stephen said, "Wait."

Sidney turned.

Stephen said, "You're Wayne's cousin, right?"

"That's me."

"He and Jessica barely left each other's sides this afternoon. Have they finally started seeing each other?"

"That's a good question."

Stephen smiled. "Well, if that's the case, tell Jess I'm happy for her. Maria's always said Wayne was a good coworker. He'll make a fine boyfriend, I'm sure."

Sidney tried not to snort. This family *really* needed to work on communication. "Why don't you tell her yourself?"

She hurried back to her car and made it back to Eleanor around four o'clock. Wayne's truck had returned to his driveway. Sidney could hear its engine ticking when she got out of the car.

"Jessica!" she exclaimed, bursting through the door with her laptop. "I've got awful news!"

"She's not here," Wayne said, lounging in his recliner with his leg braces off. He picked up the remote and muted the television. Three empty Mike's Hard Lemonade bottles sat on the end table beside him.

Sidney set the laptop on the coffee table and put her hands on her hips. "Then where the hell is she?"

"She and Rachel decided to have a girls' day out. I didn't think it was a great idea, based on the way Jessica has been acting all day, but at least she's not alone."

Sidney sat down on the couch, a lead weight settling in her

stomach. "How has Jessica been acting?"

"Like a complete head case." Worry lined his face. "She was saying some troubling stuff this morning, and then she kept zoning out during lunch and jabbering a lot of nonsense. Rachel promised me she'd take Jessica to the hospital the moment she starts acting up again."

Sidney pondered that a moment, then caught a whiff of cigarettes. "Have you been *smoking*?"

Wayne leveled a glare at her. "It works for you, doesn't it?"

"You hate cigarettes! What's going on with you?"

"Look, it's been a day, okay?" He folded his arms. "I came back here to try to sort some things out."

"How is that working out for you?" Sidney nodded at the empty bottles.

Wayne's expression grew hollow. "Not very well. I'm wondering... did I make a mistake, letting Jessica stay here? I thought I was *helping* her, and now it's like she's not even the same person."

Sidney wasn't sure how to respond to that. "Is your phone on silent?" she asked.

"Probably. Why?"

"Goddammit, Wayne! I've been trying to get hold of you. I found out some bad stuff today. Jessica and her family might be in danger."

Wayne closed his eyes and exhaled deeply, then opened them again. "Tell me."

Sidney let out a huff and flipped the laptop open. She'd left the article on the screen before she left her dad's house, so all she had to do was hand the computer over to him. "Read this."

Wayne leaned over the screen, frowning. A pallor washed over him as he read. It was all Sidney could do not to gnaw off her fingernails while she waited for him to finish.

Two minutes later, Wayne leaned back in the chair and rubbed at his five o'clock shadow. His eyes swam with unspoken despair.

"Well? What do you think?" Sidney asked.

He stared dolefully at the screen. "Those murders happened two days before Jerry's disappearance."

"It's kind of hard to miss."

"You think Jerry did it."

"It's the only thing that makes sense. I looked up Jerry's old address from Casey's website. His house and the murder scene literally share a property line."

Wayne took off his glasses and started rubbing his eyes. "That's why the angry mob got him, isn't it?"

"You've got to admit, the fucker had it coming."

Wayne flinched.

"Pardon my French," Sidney added. "But Jerry knows Jessica is related to Stephen and Maria. If they're any way responsible for Jerry's death, he might try to go after them."

"If that's true, wouldn't they *have it coming*?" Wayne asked.

"Jerry doesn't have a body. He might try to use Jessica to do the deed."

Wayne immediately straightened, and the remaining color left his face. "Oh, God. Jessica said...She said...I never should have let her go with Rachel. I'm so *stupid*."

"Do you have Rachel's number?"

"No. And I don't know where they were going. *Dammit.*" Wayne put his face in his hands. "Sidney, this isn't good."

"We'll figure it out," Sidney said with an optimism she didn't feel. "We won't let Jessica get caught up in all of this."

"She already is. You should have heard her today. It's like it wasn't even her talking to me."

They lapsed into the silence of deep thought. Sidney said, "You came back here to sort things out?"

"Yeah, there were some things Jessica said that really got me thinking." Wayne wiped at his eyes. "It's actually worse than what you've told me."

"What could possibly be worse?"

Wayne looked her straight in the eye and repeated everything Jessica had said to him that morning. It took several minutes.

And he'd been right.

It *was* worse.

28

"Where do you think we should go?" Wayne asked, fastening his braces. His tone was flat, as if he were afraid of betraying any more emotions.

Sidney's nerves were stretched so thin, the slightest touch would have made them snap. "I don't know."

"Rachel and Eric are staying with Esteban. Maria and Stephen too. It's somewhere to start."

"Do you know where Esteban lives?"

"No, but I can find out." Wayne crossed the room, dug a fraying phonebook out of the bookshelf, and started paging through it. "And there's no sense in going there unless we know for certain that's where they are. Raleigh, Raymond, Remington, here we go. Reyes." He ran a finger down the page. "Esteban isn't listed."

"Jessica's got twenty thousand other relatives we can talk to."

"Right. Here's Marco Reyes. I wonder if it's the same one I met today."

"Well, call him and see!" Sidney rushed to the kitchen, plucked the cordless phone off the counter, and thrust it into Wayne's hand.

Wayne dialed Marco's number, waited, and then let out a curse. "He's not answering."

"Then try someone else!"

Wayne glanced at the book again. "I met an Ernesto Reyes today, and he's listed here, assuming it's the same guy." He punched in Ernesto's number, and his face lit up a few seconds later. "Hi, is this Ernesto Reyes?...This is Wayne Thompson. I believe I met you at the family reunion earlier today?...Yes, I was with Jessica...Uh-huh...I wondered if you might have Rachel's cell phone number—she and Jessica went out, and Jessica's phone is dead." His shoulders dropped. "I see. Well, do you have Esteban's number?" Wayne held the phone away from his mouth for a moment and hissed, "Get me a pen."

Sidney yanked the magnetic whiteboard off the fridge and shoved it into Wayne's free hand. He popped the dry erase marker out of its attached holder.

"Okay, go ahead." He jotted down a ten-digit number. "Thank you. I really appreciate this."

Wayne immediately ended the call and dialed Esteban's number.

"Keep your fingers crossed," he said to Sidney while he waited for Jessica's uncle to pick up.

Sidney crossed all her fingers, and even her toes. A healthy dose of superstition couldn't hurt.

Wayne straightened. "Hello, Esteban?...This is Wayne Thompson—we met at the family reunion today. Do you by chance know where Jessica and Rachel were headed off to?" He swore again. "I really need to talk to Jessica, and her phone is dead. Do you have Rachel's number? Dammit—sorry."

"Get Maria's number from him," Sidney whispered. "I know she'll have Rachel's number."

Wayne relayed that request to Esteban, then scribbled another phone number onto the whiteboard. "Thank you so much," he said. "It means a lot."

He ended the call, and he and Sidney stared at the second phone number as if it were a particularly terrifying tarantula.

"It's funny," he said. "I always got along well with Jessica's mom. She never gossiped or tried to nose her way into anyone else's business. I *thought* I knew her."

"You'd think that someone would have mentioned that Sarah existed. Or even if they hadn't wanted to mention it, there would have been photographs. Drawings. Stuff kids make. It's like they buried her memories right along with her."

Wayne nodded. "Maybe it was less painful that way. I guess I'd better go ahead and make this call."

He dialed Maria's phone number and waited. When Jessica's mother answered, Wayne set the phone to speaker.

"Wayne?" Maria asked by way of greeting.

"I'm still in your contact list, I see."

"What's going on? Why are you calling?"

Sidney raised her eyebrows at Wayne. The woman sounded nearly frantic.

"Um…Jessica's phone is dead. Is everything okay with you?"

"I'm fine," Maria said too quickly. "I'm assuming you'd like Rachel's number, if you can't get through to Jessica? I know they left together."

"That would be ideal."

Maria recited Rachel's phone number with no hesitation. Wayne copied it onto the whiteboard.

"I heard Rachel say they were going shopping in Kenwood this afternoon," Maria said. "'Girls' Day Out,' is what Rachel called it. It's funny, they'd never think to invite me."

"Thank you for letting me know." Wayne paused. "Maria, why didn't you and your family ever tell your children about Sarah?"

There came a click and a dial tone.

"I don't believe it," Sidney said. "She hung up on you."

Eric had dropped Jessica and Rachel off at the Kenwood Towne Center on the northeast side of Cincinnati and then left to go browse the Barnes and Noble across the street. Jessica knew he'd left them alone so he wouldn't have to suffer looking at women's clothing with them all afternoon.

"How can anyone afford this stuff?" Jessica asked while they wandered through Nordstrom. She felt like a hobo in her tatty clothes. If her channel ever got to be monetized, she might be able to afford something a little nicer—which in turn might make her look a little more visually appealing to her viewers.

"I don't know, but it's fun to look at." Rachel pulled a slinky red dress off a rack and held it up in front of her, striking what was probably supposed to be a seductive pose. "What do you think?"

"I think Eric would have that off of you in about five seconds."

"Yeah." Rachel gazed lovingly at the dress, then put it back on the rack. "It would be stupid to buy new clothes now, anyway, since I'll be gaining half a ton in the next six months. But I can dream."

Rachel wandered off to another part of the women's section. Jessica fell in step behind her, barely glancing at the other clothes since there really wasn't any point. *It's all going to be over soon, anyway,* Jessica thought, then frowned. Why had she just thought that?

Rachel was saying something.

"What?" Jessica asked, snapping back to attention.

"I said, have you felt like zoning out again? But I think you already answered that question."

Jessica shivered. "I'm fine."

She hadn't told Rachel she'd zoned out big-time in the restroom at Kemper House. One minute, she'd been walking into the stall, and the next she was standing at the sink, washing her hands.

Jessica had left the restroom feeling resolute, though, as if she'd unknowingly come to some great decision and accepted it. But what had it been? She couldn't remember.

Rachel frowned at her. "*Swear* to me that you're fine, and I'll believe it."

Jessica felt a wave of defensiveness wash through her. "Look, I've been through a lot, okay? Give me some slack."

Her sister's expression softened a bit. "I know losing your job and your apartment must have been hard. But if the stress of it is causing these weird episodes, you might want to get checked out."

"It's more than just that," Jessica said. "I was *murdered*. And there's no getting past that."

Rachel's eyebrows shot toward her hairline. "What did you just say?"

Jessica's fists clenched of their own accord. "They tortured me until I died, cut me into pieces, and buried me in *garbage bags*, and I've had to live with that every single day for the past twenty-four years."

"This isn't funny, Jessica." Rachel's eyes grew watery, as if unsure whether or not to cry.

"So, we're in agreement about that," Jessica said. "Excellent."

"Stop it."

"Stop what?"

"You don't even sound like yourself right now! I think this whole thing has gone way too far. You got so obsessed with your ghost that you don't even know who you are anymore."

A laugh burst from Jessica's mouth. "I know exactly who I am."

"I'm taking you to the hospital." Rachel made an about-face and strode toward the exit.

Jessica jogged after her, nearly colliding with a display of neckties. "I'm not sick."

"You could have fooled me."

They stepped out into the crowded parking lot, where afternoon sunlight glinted off thousands of vehicles. Rachel cursed and retreated to the curb.

"Great. I forgot Eric has the car." She got out her phone and dialed. "Eric, meet us outside of Nordstrom. We need to take Jessica to the ER."

"You can't make me go." Jessica crossed her arms over her chest.

Did Rachel really expect to drag Jessica, kicking and screaming, through the emergency room doors? She was an adult and could make her own decisions.

Rachel ignored her. "Please hurry." She thrust her phone back into her bag and looked at Jessica. "When is your birthday?"

"I don't have amnesia."

"Answer me!"

Jessica rolled her eyes. "January 1, 1989."

"And my birthday?"

"September 3, 1986. Do I get an A?"

"Stop acting like this is a joke! You've been acting weird all day. The hospital can run tests to see why."

"I don't have any health insurance or money."

"You're more important than money, Jessica."

Jessica's heart fluttered. They couldn't do this to her! Not when she was so close to the end of things. "Please don't take me to the hospital. I'm just tired. Take me home, and I'll be fine."

Rachel didn't answer. Eric pulled up to the curb in their rental car, and Jessica and Rachel climbed in.

"Don't you dare take me to a hospital!" Jessica blurted before anyone else could get a word in.

Eric cocked his head and looked at her in the rearview mirror. "Ohhh-kay."

"Eric, she's acting like a complete basket case."

"I just want to go home and sleep."

Eric cast his bewildered gaze back and forth between them. "Um. What am I supposed to do?"

Rachel's phone rang. She grabbed it out, frowned at the screen, and answered it. "Hello? Oh, hi, Wayne. Uh-huh."

Jessica perked up, wondering how Wayne had gotten her sister's number.

Rachel was silent for a long time while Wayne talked, though

Jessica couldn't hear a word he said. "Oh," Rachel said at length. "Okay. We'll see you soon."

She ended the call and looked to Eric.

"Take us back to Wayne's house. He wants to talk to us."

"Will do." Eric put the car into gear and headed toward the exit.

Thank you, Wayne, Jessica thought.

Silence settled over them as they hopped onto the interstate. Jessica leaned her head against the window and watched the mile marker signs flash by.

She closed her eyes. Her consciousness wavered, and a face swam in her mind's eye. A woman. Blond, with dark brown eyes. Abigail. The one who had to die, though she would not be the first to perish. Abigail could be spared until the very end, her death being the grand finale of it all. It might take weeks to track her down, but the wait would be worth it.

A tear of joy rolled down Jessica's cheek, and through the fog, she smiled.

29

Wayne was more distraught than he would let on to Sidney. Now that his initial shock had worn off, an almost paralyzing anxiety had set in, tightening his chest so much he could scarcely breathe.

"They'll be back in forty minutes," he said when he got off the phone with Rachel. He wiped his forehead and drew in a shuddering breath.

"And Jessica's been acting up again?" Sidney asked.

Wayne's mouth felt dry. "Yeah. And now we know a hospital won't be able to help her."

He remembered the first time Sidney had invited Jessica over, not long after they'd started working together at the truck stop. Wayne and Jessica had laughed at each other's jokes and flirted the whole evening away, like they'd known each other for years. Where had that woman gone? Was there any way to get her back, or was it too late?

And even if they *did* get Jessica back, how could she and Wayne continue as they had, considering what Wayne now knew? It would forever be a stain on them both.

He and Sidney remained silent for a time. Sidney kept glancing at the door, even though it was far too soon for Jessica and the others to arrive.

"I have a question," Sidney said.

"Just one?"

"Yeah. How are we going to fix Jessica? If Jerry's inside her head, that is."

Wayne blinked. "I could call Father George up at Holy Trinity. He might know what to do."

"You think Jessica needs an *exorcism*?"

"Do you have any better ideas? Jerry's depressed, he's angry, and he's going to be extremely volatile. I don't know that sitting down and having a polite chat with him will help."

"I don't see how a priest flinging holy water at Jessica will help either."

"Holy water! I forgot. Be right back." Wayne went out to his truck, retrieved the bottle of holy water from the cupholder, brought it back inside, and set it on the table.

"You're kidding me." Sidney eyed the white plastic bottle as if it were a rubber chicken.

"Your mother always assured me this would work spiritual miracles in times of trouble."

"It's *water*."

"It's been blessed."

"It's a myth."

"So are ghosts."

Sidney opened her mouth and closed it a few times before saying, "What if Jessica can't be fixed? She can't live with us like that."

"I know."

"And what if…" Sidney trailed off. "*No*."

"What is it?"

"I'm sorry. I was just thinking. What if the only way to get Jerry out of Jessica's head is to…is if she dies?"

Wayne felt his eyes watering, begging the heavens that Sidney's fears would prove unfounded. "Let's focus on the now, okay?"

"Okay." Sidney gritted her teeth. "Jerry wants to kill his killers.

There might be dozens of them, and Jessica's parents are just the first ones he's had access to."

"I know. And if holy water can somehow eject Jerry from Jessica, then that's one less problem for us to deal with."

The clock on the wall ticked the seconds away, like a bomb counting down to detonation. Half an hour later, the sound of gravel crunching beneath tires outside lifted some of the apprehension squeezing Wayne's chest, and he took a welcoming breath of relief, knowing Jessica would soon be within his sight.

Babbling voices moved up onto the porch. Sidney threw the door open so hard, it bounced off the wall, leaving a small dent. "Come in!"

A yawning Jessica waddled in first, followed by Rachel, whose short hair stood up in odd little tufts from running her hands through it so many times. Eric brought up the rear with his hands jammed into his pockets, looking like he'd rather be anywhere else.

The five of them stood there awkwardly for a moment. Well, four of them did—Jessica had opened the fridge and was rummaging through it, like a raccoon in a dumpster.

"Uh. Jessica?" Wayne asked, heart thudding.

She emerged from the fridge with a packet of string cheese and a cup of yogurt. Jessica ripped the string cheese open and devoured it in three bites. "God, I'm hungry. I'd forgotten what that felt like." She grabbed a spoon from the silverware drawer and proceeded to dig in to the yogurt.

"Jessica, look at me."

She turned to Wayne and gazed at him blankly, with a glob of yogurt on her upper lip. Her pupils were dilated disks, like those of a sleepwalker. "What?"

"We have some important things to talk about," Wayne said in as delicate a tone as he could manage. "Can we maybe all sit out in the living room and make ourselves comfortable? It's going to take a while."

"This is about Jerry, isn't it?" Rachel asked.

"Yes, and a whole lot more. And—God, this isn't going to be easy for any of us. You have to understand that nothing is ever going to be the same again after you've heard what Sidney and I have to say."

They filed into the living room. Jessica brought up the rear and plopped onto the floor, looking bored while she finished her yogurt.

Sidney and Eric took seats on the couch, and Wayne sat in his recliner, but Rachel remained standing. "She's possessed, isn't she?" Rachel asked, flicking her gaze to her sister.

"We'll get to that part," Wayne said. "Rachel, what all do you know about Jerry?"

"Just what Jessica has told us: he followed her home from some spooky graveyard, and he was murdered."

Jessica twitched at Rachel's words but remained silent.

"Jerry was murdered by an angry mob," Wayne said.

"We know that too," Eric replied. "We watch her YouTube videos."

"Good," Wayne said. "I did some research online and learned that Jerry was last seen on June 29, 1986. And today, Sidney did some sleuthing of her own and found out that four kids were murdered in the yard behind Jerry's two days earlier."

Jessica stood suddenly. "Dammit, I left my purse in the car. Be back in a sec."

She hurried out the door. Once she'd gone, Rachel said, "Jerry killed them?"

"That's what it looks like. The families must have gone after him."

"And he's in my sister's *brain*?"

"I'm really sorry, Rachel. It gets worse."

Tears choked Rachel's voice. "How could anything be worse than that?"

A car's engine roared to life outside. The three able-bodied people in the room leapt up and looked out the window.

"She's driving away!" Sidney shouted.

Wayne stood, feeling the blood leave his face. He needed to go after Jessica, to save her and hold her tight and never let go, but Rachel also needed to *know*.

"We need to stop her!" Rachel cried, lunging toward the door.

"Wait," Wayne said. "I think I know where she's headed."

"Great—then let's go!"

"Rachel, I can't put this off any longer. You have to understand exactly what we're dealing with. Sidney, show her the article you found."

Sidney woke her laptop from hibernation and pulled the article up on the screen. "Don't shoot the messenger," she said weakly and handed it over to Rachel and Eric.

Rachel's brow creased while she read. Suddenly, every last bit of color left her face, and she put a hand over her mouth.

"Who's *Sarah* Roman-Dell?" Eric asked.

"I don't..." Rachel said, wonderingly. "I never..."

"Evidently," Wayne said as carefully as he could, "you aren't Stephen and Maria's first child."

"Of course, I am!" Spots of color appeared on Rachel's cheeks. "I mean, I know that my parents lived in Kentucky before they bought a house here in Eleanor, but..." She trailed off.

"What year did they move?"

She swallowed. "1986. Just a month before I was born."

"Did you ever wonder why they moved?"

"I thought...I thought they were finding a bigger place since I was coming along." Rachel started shaking her head. "This doesn't make any sense. I have a huge extended family. Why didn't anyone ever mention this Sarah? Wouldn't there be pictures and things?" She gasped. "Oh my God. Pictures!"

"What is it?" Eric asked, his eyes round.

Rachel sounded almost excited. "Years ago, I was digging around in some old boxes in my parents' basement. I forget what I was looking for, but I found an entire box of old photos. Stuff from birthdays and Christmas and whatnot. I thought they were pictures of Jessica because the girl in them had dark brown hair, but I couldn't tell where the pictures had been taken. And I wasn't in any of them."

"And you never suspected anything?" Sidney asked.

Rachel's expression soured. "What was I supposed to think? That my parents had another kid they conveniently forgot to tell me and Jessica about? One who obviously received far more attention than we ever did?"

"Rach, you're forgetting something," Eric said quietly. "The other day at lunch, you told Jessica that she had an imaginary friend named Sarah."

A pin drop would have been deafening in those next few moments. Wayne felt terrible for Rachel—he knew all too well how it felt to have your entire world turned upside down and inside out. But they *had* to hurry and finish this up so they could form a plan to save Jessica.

"Why would Jerry have killed those kids?" Rachel asked at last, her tone oddly flat.

Wayne drew in a deep breath. "I've been able to piece a lot of it together based on what Jessica has told me. Jerry's ex-wife had an abortion six years earlier. Jessica said he was devastated over it. I think it went to his head and festered inside him until he couldn't stand it anymore. He must have watched the other kids in his neighborhood growing up around him until he finally snapped. Three of those girls were six years old. His own child would have been six years old. The whole thing is sick, but it makes sense."

"Oh my God," Eric muttered.

"Who snaps like *that*?" Rachel retorted.

Wayne closed his eyes. "Anybody could, given the wrong kind of stimulus."

He couldn't tell Rachel or Eric he himself had been down a similar dark road seventeen years earlier because now wasn't the time—but he remembered the moment well.

He, Robert Wayne Thompson, had been trying to do his homework on a section of the sofa that wasn't buried under unwashed laundry and empty liquor bottles. His spastic legs were practically useless—his mother would punish him if he didn't wear his ankle-foot orthotics even though he'd outgrown them ages ago, and they hurt too badly to wear for long. Better to endure the pain of those braces than the pain of her beatings.

"Robbie," she had called from the bedroom.

He stiffened, having thought she was asleep.

"Robbie?"

He tried to calm his frantic heart with deep breaths. "What?" he asked in a cracking voice that had just begun its adolescent deepening the week before.

"Bring me my vodka."

His mother always kept her favorite beverage on the counter beside the coffee maker. She could have easily retrieved it herself, but it always seemed to amuse her to watch him struggle.

"Okay." Wayne limped into the kitchen, leaning against the walls for support, and picked up the hateful drink. He started toward her room but halted. The stuff was killing her, and while he didn't particularly care if it finished the job, he knew that if she drank more, it would only make her more unpredictable. An angry drunk was a force of nature unto itself.

The woman rarely beat him when sober. Sometimes, she actually seemed friendly and begged for forgiveness for hurting him, but once more alcohol touched her tongue, the cycle would begin again.

He made a decision. Instead of bringing the vodka into his mother's room, he unscrewed the cap and poured it into the kitchen sink. The drain gurgled, and the vodka was gone.

Wayne heard movement at the other end of the house.

"What's taking so long?"

She appeared in the archway connecting the small kitchen and living room. Her bloodshot eyes widened, and she looked from the empty bottle in his hand to the sink, and then to his face. Her mouth opened in a wordless snarl of rage. She snatched a sooty fireplace poker from the rack beside the hearth and swung it at him with the strength of a major league hitter.

He ducked. The poker clipped him on the shoulder. Pain exploded in shock waves from the point of impact, and he staggered on his unsteady legs, just in time for her to strike him again.

And again.

He could hardly breathe. She was going to kill him this time! His grandparents had gone out for the day, so there would be no witnesses to his untimely demise.

At that moment, a switch seemed to flip somewhere inside his brain. Why should he be a victim? His upper body was strong to compensate for his weakness. Maybe he could fight back.

Young Wayne, who had been Robbie, lunged toward his mother instead of cowering. Her brief moment of surprise allowed him to jerk the poker out of her hands before she could hit him again.

The altercation could have ended there, and maybe it should have, but something had broken loose inside of him, and the next thing he knew, *he* was beating *her*. The poker smashed into the side of her head, and she crumpled to the floor, screaming, but he couldn't stop. The long years of torment and abuse had concentrated themselves into a physical energy he channeled into his weapon.

He pounded her in the face until the screams stopped.

Wayne felt something wet on his own face and noticed his entire front, as well as everything else in the immediate vicinity, was sticky and red. He blinked a few times, dropped the poker to the floor, and gaped at what he had done.

All because he had finally snapped.

Just like Jerry did.

It chilled Wayne to think they might be anything alike.

In the present, Wayne took a deep breath. "Rachel, I'm sorry to be the one to tell you this, but I'm almost certain your parents were involved in Jerry's death."

Rachel barked out a disbelieving laugh. "*My* parents."

"*Your* parents have lied to you and Jessica for your entire lives, so you have absolutely no idea what they might be capable of."

"What am I supposed to *do*?"

"Call them. Warn them. Because Jessica—and Jerry—are coming."

30

Maria Roman-Dell was helping her sister-in-law Sharon clean up the Kemper House banquet room after most of the other Reyeses had gone home. Thank goodness this alarming day was drawing to a close—returning to the peace of her office Monday morning couldn't come soon enough.

"Hey, congrats on the grandbaby," Sharon Reyes said, wadding up one of the disposable tablecloths and tossing it into the giant garbage can they'd been lugging around the room. "I meant to tell you earlier."

"Oh!" Maria forced a smile. "Thank you."

Sharon laughed. "You don't have to sound so grim about it."

"They're just so young. Maybe too young."

Sharon's expression softened. "You were younger than Rachel when you had Sarah."

Maria's heart felt like it was being crushed in a vise. "And look how that turned out."

"I know you don't want to hear it, but what happened to her wasn't your fault."

"I let her hang out with the Smiths that day. If she'd stayed home, she'd still be here."

Everything would have been so different if Sarah had lived. Sarah might be married and have children of her own by now. Maria imagined Sarah would look like an older version of Jessica—Jessica had been the spitting image of her lost sister as a child.

"Have you ever sat down with your girls and told them what happened?" Sharon asked.

"No."

"Why keep putting it off?"

"They would ask too many questions. And at this point, neither of them wants anything to do with me, anyway, so that's that."

Her sister-in-law frowned. "Did you ever act like you wanted anything to do with them?"

Maria felt the blood rise into her face. "Don't you start on that too."

She'd had Rachel so soon after Sarah's death. *Yes*, she'd been thrilled when Rachel was born, and Jessica too, but how could she ever have been a good mother to either of them after what she'd done that night in the woods? Her actions that night had awakened a coldness inside of her that still hadn't begun to thaw.

And now, impossibly, it was all coming to light despite so many years of secrets kept.

"Is something else bothering you?" Sharon asked.

"No," Maria said much too quickly. "I'm fine."

"Well, if you ever want to talk, don't forget I'm here."

Sharon wandered onward to clean up the next table. Maria was about to follow when her purse began emitting a tinny version of *Rondo Alla Turca*, the ringtone she'd assigned to Rachel's incoming calls.

Dear God, now what?

Praying that her carefully crafted illusion of reality wouldn't come crashing down around her like a flimsy house of cards, she hurried to where she'd left her purse, snatched up her phone, and accepted the call. "Hi, Rachel."

Her daughter's words burst out in a rush. "Mom! Wayne says you've got to stay away from Jessica. She's not right in the head, and she might hurt you and Dad, and she just drove off, and we don't know where she is right now. Wayne thinks she's looking for you, and we know about Sarah being killed, so don't try to deny it."

It was all Maria could do not to drop the phone from her shaking hands. "Honey, slow down. What is all this?"

She could hear her daughter take a deep breath. "Sidney Miller found an old article about a quadruple homicide that took place in 1986. One of the victims was Sarah Roman-Dell. Care to explain?"

Maria squeezed her eyes shut. This *wasn't* happening.

"Mom?"

"Yes," Maria said quietly. "That happened."

"No *shit*, Mom!"

"Don't you dare talk to me like that."

"I'll talk to you however I want to. You've spent more than two decades treating me and Jessica like shit because you were too stubborn to work through your own trauma. Well, I'm not taking it anymore. Oh, and Jerry Madison is back, by the way. I just thought you should know before he comes along and kills you."

Anger flared inside of her. "Don't you dare mention that name."

There was a scuffling noise, and Wayne Thompson's voice came on the line. "Maria?"

"Yes?" Her voice shook as much as her hands.

"If you see Jessica, let us know immediately, and we'll come get her. But *do not* let her get anywhere near you."

"I don't understand."

"She's possessed, Maria." There was an edge to Wayne's voice she had never heard before. "Jerry has gotten inside her somehow. He wants revenge on the people who killed him."

He let the sentence hang, like a corpse at the gallows. Horror and fear flooded Maria's veins. *Oh my God. He knows.*

"Promise me you'll call if you see her," Wayne said.

"I—I promise."

"Good. We'll be in touch."

The line went dead. Maria stared vacantly at the wall for a moment, then slipped her phone into the pocket of her blazer.

"What was all that about?" Sharon asked.

Maria wondered what all her sister-in-law had heard.

She forced herself to breathe. "Jerry Madison," she said, feeling as if part of her were detaching and floating away. "He's come back to kill me."

Wayne handed the phone to Rachel. He took a few moments to steel his nerves…and failed miserably. How could this possibly turn out all right in the end? Would defeating Jerry cause irreparable harm to Jessica? Was it even possible to save one, while banishing the other?

If only he had discouraged Jessica from ghost hunting in the first place…but what kind of friend would that have made him?

"Now what?" asked Sidney, who was practically bouncing on the balls of her feet to get moving.

Wayne tried to think as fast as he could. "Rachel, you and Eric go back to your uncle's house. If that's where your parents are staying too, it's possible Jessica might make an appearance there."

"What do we do if she shows up?" Eric asked.

"Tie her up and call me. Let's all swap numbers."

They each took turns typing their cell numbers into each other's contact lists. Once they'd finished, Sidney asked, "What do you want me to do?"

"Stay here in case Jessica needs to come back for something."

"Like what? A butcher knife?"

"Sidney…"

"Sorry. But you're right. I'll stay here." Sidney paused. "What will *you* be doing?"

Wayne thought about it. Logic indicated Jessica would go straight to her uncle's house to waylay her parents, but how logical would she be with a rabid ghost riding around inside her head? What if Jerry needed supplies of some sort? Would Jessica stop somewhere first to procure them?

"I'll stop at all the hardware stores between here and there to see if her car is parked there," Wayne said.

"Hardware stores?" Rachel asked. Then her eyes widened. "*Oh.* Eric, let's go."

"Good luck," Wayne said to them and watched the couple leave. Then he turned to Sidney and said, "Try to stay safe here, okay?"

"Safe. Sure. Got it."

Wayne started toward the door with his truck key in one hand and the bottle of holy water in the other, but Sidney said, "Wait."

He turned back to her, and she wrapped her arms around him in a tight squeeze.

"You stay safe too, okay?"

A hard lump formed in Wayne's throat. "I'll do my best."

Sidney waited around the house for about twenty minutes before she couldn't take the suspense anymore. Staying in this house alone would help no one—not the Roman-Dells, and especially not Jessica.

Since driving around the tri-state, searching for Jessica, was going to be about as easy as finding a particular droplet of water in a pond, Sidney's efforts might not help anyone either. But at least she would feel more useful.

She would have to take some precautions, however. If Jessica's brain had indeed become some kind of duplex housing Jerry's mind as well as her own, she might become violent, even to Sidney.

She stood at the bottom of the basement stairs, assessing what was available to her. A souvenir Reds baseball bat leaning against a storage cabinet caught her eye. She picked it up and tested its weight in her hands. It was solid but not too heavy for her. Perfect.

Bile rose in her throat without warning. Jessica was her friend. They'd spent hundreds of hours together, laughing at B-movie schlock on the couch while stuffing their faces with Doritos and cheese dip, and Jessica had been there when Sidney's mother got sick and died. Her old friends from high school certainly hadn't stuck around for that.

And now Sidney was considering bludgeoning Jessica if need be. What kind of person was Sidney turning into?

A prepared one, she thought.

She took the bat with her to the car. Maybe she wouldn't even find Jessica. Maybe she wouldn't have to use the bat after all.

31

It was dark.

Jessica sat in her car, eating a burrito. The wrapper had the Taco Bell logo printed all over it. When in the world had she stopped there?

She paused in her chewing and peered outside. Jessica was in a large parking lot beneath a streetlamp. A group of drab cement buildings loomed off to the left. Almost all the windows in the buildings were dark. A few young people laughing about something walked by on a sidewalk running perpendicular to her parking spot. None of them paid her any notice.

A police cruiser coasted by. The Northern Kentucky University name and logo were emblazoned on its side.

Jessica finished the burrito, wadded up the wrapper, and tossed it onto the floor. How had she even gotten here? She was clearly on campus, but why?

Jerry Madison sat in the passenger seat, eyeing the retreating cops with some distaste. "How are you feeling?"

"Extremely confused." She had been with Rachel at a mall, looking at expensive dresses. They'd been arguing about something, but the topic of their disagreement eluded her. "Why are we here? I'm not a student."

"It's just a place to rest for a while. Your friends won't think to look for us here."

Were her friends looking for her? She didn't know she was lost.

"We're very close to our goal," Jerry went on. "It's too early to leave right now. We're waiting for the right moment."

Just then, Jessica caught a whiff of woodsmoke on her clothes. Frowning, she turned the key in her ignition to light up the dashboard clock. It was 7:02 p.m.

Jessica flicked on the light overhead. Her nails were caked with dirt, and burrs clung to her jeans. "What the hell?"

"Don't worry about it," Jerry said, and she began to feel a little better.

This is perfectly normal, a voice murmured inside her. *You two are just resting before the fun begins. I'll keep both of you safe. The campus police won't even notice that you don't have a parking pass.*

Well, that was good. Jessica didn't have enough money to pay for a parking ticket in the first place.

"I have a confession to make," Jerry said.

"Oh?"

He turned to face her, wearing a grim smirk. "I knew your parents."

"You're kidding me."

"No. They lived two houses down from me in Clarkville, and we attended the same church. We were at each other's houses all the time, usually to play cards."

Jessica caught on to his error right away. "My parents are lapsed Catholics. They don't go to church."

Jerry shrugged. "Maybe they don't now, but they used to. They're just a little younger than me. It was a small town, and we young folk stuck together."

Strangely, his admission didn't feel all that shocking. "Why didn't you tell me any of this before?"

"You weren't ready to hear the truth."

"And now I am?"

"If you weren't, we wouldn't be here. Tell me—do you love your mother?"

Jessica thought about it. "I'm supposed to."

"But do you?"

She sighed. "Sometimes, people hurt you so much that you can't love them. And it's not like she *did* anything to me. It's what she didn't do."

"And what didn't she do?"

"God, I could write a book." Jessica blew a strand of hair out of her face. "She didn't hug me. She didn't come to any school programs we did. She didn't listen to my problems. Nothing's ever going to be right between us. She lives in her world, and I live in mine, and things are so much easier that way." She folded her arms. "I don't want to talk about her anymore."

"But I do."

Annoyance flared through her. "Why? Did you have a crush on her, or something?"

He glowered at her. "Not even close."

"Then why are you so fixated on her all of a sudden?"

"Because," he said, "Maria Roman-Dell, accountant extraordinaire and devout churchwoman, slaughtered me like a pig in the woods behind the Methodist church."

At first, Jessica stared at him, speechless. Then she smiled. Her mother, a killer? It would have been too much effort.

"You don't believe me," he said.

"Mom can't stand the sight of blood. It makes her puke."

"She didn't seem to mind so much then."

"You said it was a group of people who did it."

"She was part of that group. Your father too, but he only watched. Some local cops organized my murder. People took their turns with me, and after I'd been choked, beaten, and flayed beyond recognition, your mother plunged a knife straight into my heart."

They were both quiet for a few beats.

Jessica remembered Jerry's words the night she had met him in the graveyard. *You could come across severed limbs, bleeding torsos, entrails spread across the ground…*

And her own voice, as a child. *Mommy, read me a story!*

Suddenly, Jessica's mind felt very clear, and she wanted to run. She would flee the campus, race out to the highway, and cross the bridge back into Ohio. She would keep on running past Eleanor, until she collapsed and her bones turned into dust.

Jessica remained glued to the seat. "Why did she kill you?"

A manic look contorted his features. "You don't know what it's like. My child was gone, and suddenly, babies were everywhere. They'd smile and coo like they knew what had happened and didn't want me to forget it, even for a minute. They got older, and it killed me because I'd missed out on so much. No birthday parties. No little-league champs or first-place ballerinas. No scraped knees needing kisses. You don't know what it's like, being like that. Everything crashing down. I wanted to die. I tried to die. You know how that worked out.

"One day, I heard kids laughing outside. Four of them were playing a game in the yard behind mine."

Jessica didn't like where this was going.

"I didn't want to do it," Jerry said in a voice that was almost pleading. "I *hated* to do it. But I had to. If I let them live, it would never end. I shot the older Smith girl first. Then her sister. The Scott girl started to scream, and I took her down before she could run away. Stephen and Maria's girl watched it all happen. She was so numb, she didn't even cry. I put a bullet through her forehead."

Jessica felt very cold. "Stephen and Maria's girl?"

"Sarah looked a lot like you." Jerry tilted his head, studying her. "She had dark brown hair and blue-gray eyes, just like yours. They doted on that child like she was the heiress to an empire."

"So you're saying..." Jessica's head swam. "You're saying I had another sister, and the only reason I don't anymore is because of you."

"Yes."

"And my mother killed you in revenge."

"Yes. And now I'm going to kill her, and you're going to help me. I just thought you should understand everything before we get to work."

Jessica's thoughts wavered, the fog rolling back into her mind. It all made so much sense. They'd discussed a lot of this already. For some reason, she just kept forgetting. Of course, Jerry would need her to help him. A spirit like him would not be able to hold Maria down or use a weapon against her.

"We have so many things to get done," Jerry said.

"You're right." Jessica looked at the burrs sticking to her clothes and remembered they'd accomplished much already this evening.

The university campus melted away, and it was just the three of them, alone together: Jessica, Jerry, and a murky presence she couldn't quite identify. The presence was amused, and she could hear its laughter inside her.

As if watching from afar, Jessica saw herself starting the car and leaving the nearly empty parking lot behind.

She didn't know where they were going. Somehow, it didn't matter very much. She would just sit back and enjoy the ride.

32

Sidney spent the next hour patrolling streets in northern Kentucky with no success. She'd gone back to the park to see if Jessica would try to waylay her mother there, but the family reunion had concluded, and the park was vacant.

Was Sidney stupid for having left the house when Wayne had expressly told her not to? Maybe. Did she regret ignoring him? Not yet.

Sidney pulled into a gas station and hit Rachel's number on the speed dial. "Hey," she said in a low voice when Rachel picked up. "Are you at your uncle's place?"

"Yeah," Rachel said just as quietly. "No sign of Jessica yet, but my parents are here. We just had an incredibly awkward dinner, and I can tell Mom is about to give us a 'talk.'"

"I'm sure that's going to be loads of fun for you. What's the address there?"

"223 Martin Court. Why?"

"I thought it might be important information to have. Talk to you later."

She ended the call, wishing she didn't have a "dumb" phone. How was she even supposed to find Martin Court? It could be anywhere.

Then she turned toward the gas station's convenience store, where neon signs blinked on and off and a man swaggered out the door, holding a carton of Winstons.

"Of course," she said out loud. "I'll have to go in and ask for directions."

"We are going to have a talk," Maria said, giving her daughter and son-in-law the most businesslike stare she could conjure. The couple had taken a seat on Esteban's couch and were squeezing each other's hands like they thought this evening would be their last.

Esteban and Sharon had brought in chairs from the kitchen. Stephen sat in a swivel office chair to Maria's left, staring down at his loafers.

"Don't act like we're the ones in trouble here," Rachel said in a defiant tone. "I'll get straight to the point: you tortured a man to death just a couple months before I was born. Give me one good reason why I shouldn't call the cops on you both right now. Or it is all four of you?"

"That isn't what happened, Rachel," Stephen said softly. "You weren't there."

Rachel pursed her lips. "But I was, wasn't I? Seems kind of dangerous, bringing a pregnant lady to an execution."

"Enough!" Maria's eyes watered. "Yes, I was pregnant with you when…when Sarah died. Your father and I were both at work when we got the news. You have to understand—her death destroyed us. Everything we'd lived for was gone. And it was so *unnecessary*. We knew that Jerry struggled with his mental health, but we never imagined he would take things so far."

"You knew Jerry before?" Rachel asked, her eyes widening.

"Clarkville was such a small town in those days." Maria remembered the charming brick houses and the broad maples that had dominated Main Street. "Jerry lived on the same road as us, just a couple of houses down. We knew he'd been through a bitter divorce right before we met him, and I know it still ate at him, even years later. He could get so moody, but on his good days, he was a pleasure to be around."

"We played a *lot* of five-card stud with him," Stephen added with a humorless smile. "He won more of my money than I'd like to admit."

"But he'd use his winnings to pay for your beer," Maria reminded him.

Stephen's expression grew stony. "For some reason, I'd forgotten."

"So, you were friends with him," Rachel said. "Wonderful. You still killed him."

Maria silently counted to ten before speaking. "Yes. I did. But please, hear me out." She thought back to all the things she'd long ago relegated to a closet in the back of her mind, sorting through them, putting them in order. "We loved Sarah—she was our everything. And to learn that she'd died in such a horrible way, doing nothing more than playing outside with her friends…it destroyed us. You can't understand it until you've been there. The only thing that kept us going was knowing that you would be arriving soon, Rachel.

"A police officer showed up at the house the day after Sarah died. He told us he'd seen what happened and that he had a way to take care of it, if we were interested in participating. We were horrified when he told us who'd killed our daughter and her friends—horrified and betrayed. We agreed to go with the police the following night.

"We were distraught. We didn't know what to expect. We waited in the woods until they brought Jerry there. They tied him to a chair that was chained to a tree, and people started hurting him. It was the most awful thing I've ever had to watch. He *begged* for mercy, and no one gave it. What he'd done to our daughters was unspeakable, but nobody deserved *that.*

"I'd brought a dagger with me, just in case. I know it was stupid of me. But they tortured him for so long, and he was still alive, despite the injuries. I could tell he wasn't going to survive, and I thought, he's suffered enough now. So I stabbed him in the heart." Maria sucked in a ragged breath. "But Sarah was still dead."

Tears streaked down Rachel's face. It broke Maria's heart to see her so upset—but what else had she really expected? The truth hurt.

"Who else was there that night?" Rachel asked quietly.

"I was," Esteban replied, his shoulders slumping. "I didn't touch the guy, though. I just wanted to be there for Maria and Stephen."

"My father was there too," Maria added. "As well as the other victims' families."

"I didn't tell my family about it." Stephen rubbed his eyes. "They wouldn't have understood. My parents died thinking that Sarah and the others were killed by an unknown gunman. The Clarkville police made sure to keep it all under wraps, for everyone's sake."

"How could you both have kept this from us for so long?"

Stephen gave their daughter a thin smile. "Do we really need to answer that?"

Rachel had no reply. Maria could feel her growing more distant than she'd ever been before, and it was all her fault.

"So, what happens now?" Esteban asked, looking up at the clock.

"That depends," Rachel said, recovering. "I'm sure you all know by now that Jerry isn't as 'gone' as you'd like to think. He's gotten into Jessica's head, and he's coming for Mom. So, we're going to wait here for Jessica, and we'll restrain her before she hurts anyone."

"And then what?" Sharon asked, speaking for the first time. Her face looked vaguely green.

Rachel frowned. "I wish I knew."

Wayne's hardware store hunch was turning into a fruitless endeavor. He'd gone up and down the parking lot rows outside of every Lowe's and Home Depot he could find between Eleanor and Clarkville and hadn't seen Jessica's rattletrap Taurus at any of them.

Maybe she didn't need duct tape and nail guns to do what Jerry needed her to.

Or maybe she'd been prepared already, unbeknownst to everyone except Jerry.

Wayne picked up his phone and called Rachel. "Hi. What's your uncle's address?"

A gas station clerk smelling faintly of sweat and cannabis gave Sidney the directions to Esteban Reyes's street. She scrawled them onto a paper bag the clerk had given her and dashed back out to her car.

"Left onto Briarpatch Drive, left onto Sunshine Drive, right onto Martin Court," she muttered, gunning it out of the parking lot. "Briarpatch, Sunshine, Martin. Briarpatch, Sunshine, Martin."

Briarpatch and Sunshine were easy enough to find, but the cross street was Martinez Street, not Martin Court.

She beat the steering wheel with one hand. "Dammit!"

There was no point in going back to the gas station to tell the clerk he'd made a mistake. She would just have to start turning down streets at random until she found the right one.

The sky turned black with nightfall as she cruised down a street where the houses were sandwiched together almost too close for comfort. Porch lights had flickered on at some of the residences, illuminating their house numbers.

She passed a 223, but she still hadn't found Martin Court.

Sidney sighed. This was going to take a while. Would she get there in time?

The night was serene.

Jessica strolled along the sidewalk in a flashy, newer subdivision not far from the campus, where the houses were all practically built on top of one another, like books competing for space on a crowded shelf. She'd parked her car on another street and had been walking for about five minutes.

There was no need to hurry. She'd arrive at her destination soon enough.

Feeling somewhat elated at the thought of what was to come, she entered the shadows where the light from the two nearest street lamps did not quite reach. A dark figure materialized beside her, and she stopped.

"Hi, Jerry," she said.

"Hello, yourself."

Jerry's gaze appeared distant, and Jessica had the odd sensation they'd recently had a disagreement. What had they been arguing about earlier? It must not have been anything important, or she would have remembered.

"Is there something you wanted to say to me?" Jessica asked.

Jerry's forehead creased. "I'm not sure." He shook his head. "It's okay. Sometimes, I'm a little forgetful."

"I understand. It happens to me too."

"It must be contagious."

"I'm glad you're here with me," Jessica said after a brief pause. "Can I hold your hand?"

Jerry shrugged. "If it makes you feel safer walking in the dark."

Jessica took Jerry's left hand in her right, and they continued down the sidewalk side by side, like any ordinary couple, though Jessica felt no romance between them. Their relationship was something different: two people focused on a single goal, neither of them able to accomplish it without the other.

That third, unseen person with them—the voice whispering in the darkness of dreams—was the glue tying them both together. Jessica understood now why Vindictam had wanted her to let it in. It could truly end her pain, both physical and mental, if only she'd allow it to do so.

Her physical pain had been cured the moment she welcomed Vindictam inside of her.

The source of her mental pain—Maria Roman-Dell—grew closer with every footstep, and she would end soon as well.

The street she was on now seemed familiar. The houses were spaced a little farther apart from one another, similar to how they were in Eleanor. The house numbers increased the farther she went.

151.

175.

203.

223.

Light glowed through thin drapes in the front window of 223. Misshapen shadows glided across the fabric like wraiths.

Anger flared deep within her. *She* was in that house. The woman who'd murdered not only a man, but her entire childhood and interred both in unholy ground.

Vindictam's murky presence prodded at her mind like a fist rapping lightly on a door. *Don't allow yourself to be seen.*

Okay, she thought. *I can manage that.*

Jessica turned to face Jerry. "We're here," she whispered.

"Good."

He vanished, his thoughts swirled through her mind once more. Jessica slipped into the shadows between 223 and the next house. Her foot caught on a coil of garden hose, and she stumbled, careful not to swear and alert the house's occupants to her presence.

The backyard was much darker than the front. Jessica felt her way along the rear wall of the house until she located the back door, where faint light spilled from a grid of square panes. She held her face to the glass and watched as a dark-haired woman passed by inside without noticing her.

Maybe she, like Jerry, had become insubstantial and unseen. Perhaps she was even a ghost herself now, dead to the world but so very, *very* alive.

Jessica tried the knob. It turned.

Ever so quietly, she stepped inside.

Wayne's headlights caught a flash of white just a few minutes after turning into Esteban Reyes's subdivision. To his right, parked along the curb, was Jessica's Taurus.

"What the hell?"

He threw the truck into reverse and backed it into an empty place behind the Taurus, heart hammering at light speed. Wayne climbed out as fast as his legs would allow and peered into the driver's side window of the car.

No Jessica.

The house Wayne had parked in front of had darkened windows and a For Sale sign staked in the grass. Why had Jessica left her car here?

A horn honked behind him.

Sidney's Camry had stopped in the center of the road. The window rolled down, and Sidney poked her head out and called, "This isn't the right address!"

Wayne didn't even bother asking why Sidney wasn't at home, keeping an eye out for an erratic Jessica. "This is her car."

"True…"

"Jerry must have thought that pulling into Esteban's driveway might be a little too obvious. Rachel hasn't called me yet, so we might pass Jessica on the way there."

Sidney's face lit up. "Ooh, good point. I'll follow you, if you know where you're going."

Wayne clambered back into his truck and proceeded through the subdivision with one eye on the road and one on the sidewalk. His headlight beams soon illuminated the sign for Martin Court.

He took a deep breath. This was it.

33

The presence told Jessica the woman who'd walked past the door was named Maria. A few memories of the woman resurfaced, like rotting logs in a rancid lake. Maria was the one who'd never loved her. The hateful one who'd taken Jerry's life. The one who deserved to die perhaps even more than Abigail.

Jessica paused in the back hallway. More memories trickled into her consciousness. This was her uncle's house, and if Jessica remembered correctly, there was a closet right about…there. She found a knob and slowly pulled the closet door open without a sound.

A babble of voices conversed in the next room. That was good; they'd be too distracted to hear her if she made any inadvertent noises while settling in. She stepped over some boots piled in the bottom of the closet and latched the door.

The space was cramped, and the only light she could see came from the crack under the door. The coats hanging above her smelled like mothballs. Her sinuses itched—but if she were truly a ghost, how could that be possible?

But she had to be a ghost because she was slowly remembering what it had been like to be alive. Old friends. Family gatherings. A blond woman in a wedding dress walking up a church aisle. Jessica could even remember dying in front of all those people in the forest. She remembered their hatred, then the sudden cessation of feeling when soul separated from flesh.

A knocking sound echoed through the house, and the voices fell silent.

"I'll get it," a man said.

Seconds later, the dull thud of footsteps entered the living room. More voices babbled. They seemed to mostly be talking about *her*.

Jessica ignored them, drawing her knees up to her chest and closing her eyes. She was bound to have a long night ahead of her.

Even ghosts needed as much rest as they could get.

Jessica still hadn't arrived at her uncle's house, and a thorough search of Esteban's quarter-acre lot around 8:30 p.m. revealed she wasn't hiding there either.

Wayne wished he could call the police. There was no reason for Jessica to have been gone for this long.

Someone could have nabbed her off the sidewalk. Sure, it was a nice neighborhood, but that wouldn't stop a dedicated pervert from committing such a crime.

Maybe she'd cut through backyards and gotten lost in the dark. Or maybe she'd gone back to her car for something, or even driven it back home.

Jessica's family went to bed around 10:30 p.m. Sidney slouched over in a recliner in Esteban's living room, snoring lightly. Every once in a while, she twitched as if pursued by a phantom in a dream.

Wayne stayed by the front window while everyone slept, watching the deserted street. Part of him wanted to believe Jessica really had returned to her car and gone home. She could be sitting on the couch with a bowl of popcorn, watching one of her favorite Tim Burton films, wondering where everyone had gone.

But if that were the case, Jessica would have called him.

It still wouldn't hurt to check for Jessica's car. It would take him five minutes to drive to where she'd parked and see if it was still there, and another five minutes to get back.

He removed his keyring from his pocket and went outside.

Jessica opened her eyes.

She'd fallen asleep, and since her cell phone still had a dead battery, she had no way to determine how long her siesta had lasted unless she snuck out of the closet to find a clock.

The sliver of light at the bottom of the door was gone. She listened, hearing nothing but the sounds of her own breathing and the muted hum of vehicles speeding along on a more distant road.

The house itself was quiet. Not even the walls or floor creaked.

Jessica rose, feeling for the knob. She turned it and stuck her head out into the hall. The silence continued without interruption.

Esteban and Sharon's twins, Tina and Henry, were freshmen at The Ohio State University way up in Columbus. Neither of them had come to the family reunion, so their bedrooms had likely been allotted to the Roman-Dells and Rachel and Eric for the weekend.

Jessica crept toward the kitchen, where a nightlight glowed beside the sink. She set her purse on the center island and withdrew a roll of duct tape from the larger compartment where she kept her wallet. Jessica put the roll around her wrist like a clunky bracelet and left her purse behind, having no further use for it.

What she did need were the keys to the Lexus. She wasn't sure if Stephen or Maria would have them. If Maria had left her purse downstairs somewhere, Jessica could check it and find out.

A fraction of the soft light splayed across the living room walls. An inert form lay in one of the chairs. Sidney? Of course, she would be here. Sidney cared about her. It was all very touching.

Sidney's own purse lay in a lumpy heap next to the recliner. A simple solution presented itself, and Jessica deftly swiped the key to Sidney's Camry from within it and transferred it to the pocket of her jeans.

Sidney murmured something and changed positions but did not wake.

Jessica crossed back through the kitchen to the staircase leading to the second floor. Some of the steps creaked when she climbed, so she slowed her pace to avoid unwanted attention.

The first bedroom doorknob in the upstairs hallway did not turn, having been locked from the inside. The occupants must have been paranoid. The poor things.

Help me, she prayed.

The knob emitted a soft click. She turned it again and pushed the door open with ease.

Like fish in a barrel.

Darkness cloaked the room so well, she couldn't see who slept there. However, the exhalations of the pair huddled in the bed did not sound like Maria or Stephen.

Jessica backed out of the room and continued to the next, where the door had been left ajar. The atmosphere in this room was markedly different than that of the room preceding it. The faint smells of sweat and tears passed through Jessica's sinuses and were gone almost as soon as she detected them.

She pulled the roll of duct tape off her wrist and crept closer to the bed with the silence of a feline stalking a rodent. One of the figures on the bed let out a garbled syllable that made her tense, but she relaxed when she realized it was only sleep-talk.

Stephen Roman-Dell slept on the side of the bed closest to the door. Jessica's eyes had adjusted well enough by now, she could see him with perfect clarity. One of his hands reached up and scratched at his right sideburn before lowering itself back to the blanket.

Oh, Stephen. The fun they'd had all those years ago, drinking and playing cards…

Stephen had not lifted a finger to harm Jerry, which is why he would survive this night. The man's presence did pose a problem, though. If he woke up while Jessica was dealing with Maria, he might stop her.

Jessica's heart began to flutter.

She would just have to stop him first.

Jessica's car *was* still parked down the street.

Not good.

Wayne executed a perfect three-point turn in the middle of the road and gunned it toward 223 Martin Court once more, begging all the powers that be in the universe to keep Jessica safe and praying they would listen.

Jessica had to immobilize Stephen so he wouldn't stop her from extracting Maria from the room. The trick was to do it without waking anyone else.

She tore a strip of tape off the roll. The sound of it could have roused the dead, but neither Roman-Dell stirred.

The floor creaked when she leaned over Stephen. She secured the tape over his mouth, tore another piece from the roll, and did the same to her mother.

To execute the next step of the plan, she needed something heavy and solid. The lamp on the bedside table would make too much noise if the bulb or base shattered on impact. A suitcase, perhaps? Perfect.

She lifted a boxy piece of luggage from the floor, held it high, and smashed it down onto her sleeping father's head.

Something slammed into the bed beside Maria, jolting her awake. She leapt up and stumbled, her legs catching in the blanket as if it were a snare.

The entire bed shook again. In the dimness, a figure hefted a large object over her husband's head for a third go.

Maria tried to scream, but her mouth wouldn't open. She slapped her hand to her face and felt something smooth and rectangular where her lips should have been.

Moaning as loudly as she could, Maria lunged toward the attacker and got knocked backward by a blow to the head. Stars danced before her eyes, and for a fraction of a second, she wondered if this was only a bad dream.

Cold fingers clamped around her arm. She was yanked to her feet, and she almost fell again as she was pulled to the door.

"We're going on a little trip," the attacker snarled.

Maria's blood turned to ice. The voice belonged to Jessica, but its inflections were that of her old friend who'd lost his mind and murdered her daughter.

Maria tried to pry Jessica's fingers from her arm with her free hand. They wouldn't budge.

The other bedroom doors banged open as Jessica dragged Maria toward the stairs.

"What's going on?" asked Esteban.

Rachel's voice joined in. "Who's that?"

"Jessica? Maria?"

"Someone, stop them!"

Now Jessica was pulling Maria through the kitchen. Maria hooked her foot around a chair and managed to drag it for a few feet until it caught the side of the refrigerator, jolting the unit so hard that cereal boxes lined up on top of it went toppling over.

It barely even slowed Jessica down. Her daughter hauled her through the living room, heading for the front door. Sidney leapt out of the recliner where she'd been sleeping.

"Holy crap! Hey, stop!"

Someone upstairs let out a scream.

Jessica acted deaf to the commotion. She threw open the door, pulled Maria toward a Toyota Camry parked behind Maria's own Lexus, and grabbed out a set of keys.

"Jessica!" Esteban was right on their heels. "Let go of her!"

Jessica whirled, putting herself between him and Maria without letting go of Maria's increasingly sore arm.

Esteban stepped toward them with his arms at his sides. "Jessica, snap out of this. Please?"

Jessica brought her free fist back and punched him squarely in the nose. He staggered backward, swearing and covering his face with his hands.

Jessica shoved Maria into the car with the strength of a bodybuilder and dashed around to the driver's side, just as some of the others began spilling from the house. Maria scrambled for the door handle, but it stuck tight. Esteban rushed forward and tugged at the outer handle, but the car was already moving in reverse.

Jessica backed onto the street, threw the Camry into gear, and stomped her foot onto the accelerator so hard, Maria was flung backward into the seat.

Tears blurred Maria's vision as houses swept by them. It looked like what had begun twenty-four years ago was finally coming to an end.

34

Sidney's car squealed past Wayne the moment he turned onto Martin Court, but Sidney wasn't the one driving it.

His heart plummeted. He'd been a fool to leave, and now it was too late.

Up ahead, people poured out of the Reyes driveway into the street. Wayne screeched to a halt and lowered his window as Sidney and Rachel raced toward him.

"Where the hell have you been?" Sidney panted. "Jessica just dragged Maria out of here like she was a ragdoll and took off in my car!"

Esteban jogged up to the truck. Blood trickled from his swelling nose. "Stephen's in bad shape."

Wayne's stomach twisted into knots. "Has anyone called an ambulance?"

"I don't know. Sharon's with him right now. It all happened pretty fast."

Sidney and Rachel squashed themselves into the truck cab beside Wayne. "Follow her," Rachel ordered in a dark tone.

"You don't need to tell me." To Esteban, Wayne said, "I'll get them back. I promise."

And then he went off after Jessica and Maria, who were already out of sight.

Maria considered her options.

Since the door handle was apparently broken, she couldn't jump out of the moving car to save herself. Jessica did have a souvenir baseball bat she'd removed from the passenger floor mat and tucked beside her, out of Maria's reach. Could she find a way to take it from Jessica and smash a window?

In the meantime, Maria worked at the edges of the tape on her mouth and managed to peel it off without removing her skin. "Jessica, please—"

"I know what you're thinking," Jessica said, cutting her off. "You want to run away. Go ahead and try it. You won't get far."

Her daughter's words were frigid and callous, and Maria knew they weren't Jessica's words at all, but Jerry's. "Where is my daughter?" Maria asked.

Jessica shrugged, keeping her eyes on the road. They were traveling down a highway now—the one leading through Clarkville down to Iron Springs. "She's here just as much as I am."

"Why isn't she stopping you?"

One corner of Jessica's mouth turned up in a sardonic smile. "Why should she? She doesn't care anything about you. She begged for your attention. Your approval. Your *love*. And you ignored her. I wish you'd done the same to me."

Jerry's words stung. She *did* love Jessica. Was Maria so damaged that Jessica hadn't seen it? "I'm sorry," Maria said. "What happened in the woods that night—it wasn't my idea."

"Yet you were there. I asked you for mercy, and you refused. How do you think that makes me feel?"

Maria's anger briefly drowned out her fear of the dead man speaking through her daughter's mouth. "Have you forgotten why you were there in the first place?"

"No."

That single word, layered with meaning, sent chills through Maria's body. "Why did you kill Sarah and her friends?" she asked.

Jessica—or Jerry, rather—seemed to think about it. "Because Vindictam told me it would make everything better."

Maria frowned. "I don't understand."

"Vindictam said that if I killed those girls, all my pain would stop."

"Who's Vindictam?"

"I don't really know. But it's here now. Can't you feel it?"

Maria began to feel dizzy, and she forced herself to breathe. "No."

"That's too bad. Maybe if you could, you would understand."

"Try me."

Jessica's shoulders drooped. "Do you remember me talking about my wife? Abigail?"

"You said she had terrible mood swings and would throw dishes at you when she got angry."

"Yes. She took the one thing away from me that I'd ever wanted."

"I remember you saying she had an abortion. We told you to talk to a therapist to work through it."

Jessica was quiet a moment, then said, "Jessica would like to know if you and your husband ever went to therapy following Sarah's death."

Maria pressed her lips together in a thin line. "We aren't talking about me. We're talking about you."

"Very well. June 27, 1986—the day I did it—was the sixth anniversary of Abigail's due date. Vindictam said…It said that I shouldn't have to be sad about that day anymore."

They were now driving down a tree-lined road in the middle of nowhere, the lights of the northern Kentucky suburbs dwindling behind them. A sign read: "Iron Springs: 2 mi."

The car turned right onto a road heading south.

Oh, no. Oh, no, no, no. Not here. Not this place. She'd vowed never again to come here because the torment of doing so would kill her.

Maria had to get out of this car.

Her heart thudded against her ribcage, and her skin was slick with sweat.

"Don't be scared, Maria," Jerry said with Jessica's voice. "Dying hurts, but that pain doesn't last."

A church sign in the distance grew nearer. The Camry slowed.

This was it.

They were driving down a lane. It had been gravel back then, but now it was paved, like the road. Shadows danced out of their way when the headlights cut through the darkness.

The parking lot and church came into view.

Memories Maria had suppressed for so long flooded back to her. The heaviness she and Stephen had felt as they'd come here with Esteban and their father, not knowing precisely what they were about to witness. Following a uniformed police officer through a cemetery and into the woods to a clearing where other Clarkville residents had already gathered near a glowing bonfire.

The interminable waiting for the murderer to arrive.

Jessica put the car into park and killed the engine. She pulled a roll of duct tape from her left wrist. "Give me your hands."

Maria lunged for the baseball bat, grabbed it, and swung it into the windshield in a single movement. Crumbling glass cascaded over the hood, and Maria shimmied through the opening while Jessica tried but failed to grasp her by the ankles.

Maria bolted toward the lane—toward *freedom*—but since she'd literally been dragged from bed, she wore no shoes. Pebbles and bits of other sharp detritus bit into her feet with every footfall, and the pain slowed her.

Jessica let out a startled cry behind her. Maria knew she should see if her daughter was okay, but it could have been a ruse to make her falter.

The temperature suddenly dropped to almost freezing, and a man materialized in the center of the lane before her. The light from a nearby mercury vapor lamp illuminated his yellow boxer shorts and shreds of a white T-shirt. Blood oozed from the wounds carved into his body, and his eyes! Dear God, she'd forgotten the eyes—the sclera had turned a deep red in both of them, so his irises stood out like icy blue rings.

Despite his injuries, he was grinning.

Maria's vision wavered, and the world went dark.

"It's not much farther," Wayne said to his passengers.

"Good." No matter how hard Sidney tried to hold still, her whole body continued to tremble. To say she was scared would have been an understatement. She was flat-out terrified.

They were driving down a tunnel of trees into hell itself. Okay, maybe that was a little melodramatic. But either way, she wanted her mom.

Marjorie had always made her feel secure in the face of trouble. Now, though, Sidney would have to cope with the terrors life threw at her with no one's help but her own.

The truck was slowing down. A sign beside the road read: "Iron Springs United Methodist Church."

They turned.

Jessica felt so confused.

Her thoughts tumbled and turned like images inside a kaleidoscope, always changing before she could fully grasp what she'd just seen and heard. She was peeling potatoes in Wayne's kitchen. Arguing with her mother in front of relatives. Picking over lunch. Peeling potatoes again. Arguing with her mother. Arguing with Rachel. Talking to Jerry. Arguing with Jerry? Hiding in a closet. Driving. With her mother. In a car that wasn't hers.

Something was in her head, like a splinter that had gotten wedged so far up under a fingernail she couldn't get it out. It wouldn't leave. Sometimes, it let her take partial control of herself to do some basic things, but in the end, it had her.

Memories! It needed her memories to know just what to do. It fed off them like they were delicacies, and it wanted *more.*

Jerry was trapped inside her head too. It was all so puzzling. The thing, Vindictam, was using them. It didn't want them to know which thoughts were their own. It wanted them to think the three of them were one, like some unholy trinity.

Jessica's mouth was moving. She didn't know what she was saying anymore—not that it was her speaking in the first place. Words were meaningless noises echoing in her eardrums.

She tried to pray for help, but her mind drew a blank.

They were in a familiar place. They'd all been here before. Old church. Chain link fence. Headstones.

Her mouth moved again. The woman with her smashed a window and fled.

Suddenly, Jessica was outside. Her thoughts cleared long enough for her to see her mother making a run toward the road.

"Mom!" she tried to scream, but something constricted her throat before she could get the whole word out.

A humanlike thing appeared in the lane on the other side of Maria. Yellow shorts, lots of blood. It looked like Jerry, but it couldn't have been because he was still inside her head.

Ahead of her, Maria crumpled in a dead faint.

Jessica's legs propelled her forward. The apparition vanished as soon as she reached her mother's side.

Anger flooded every cell in her body. *Murderer.*

A roll of duct tape was in her hands. Maria didn't stir. That simplified things. Jessica bound the woman's wrists and ankles without any trouble.

Jessica paused to scratch an ear. What had she just been thinking about? She'd forgotten again. What a bad habit. If it were important, she'd remember it later.

For now, she had work to do.

35

Jessica had parked the Camry without giving regard to the lines demarcating the parking spaces. Wayne drew the truck up beside the vacant car, noting the Camry's windshield had been busted out and lay in a thousand pieces across the hood and onto the blacktop. He pocketed the bottle of holy water, climbed out of the truck, and cupped his hand over his ear to try to determine how far ahead of them Jessica and Maria were but could hear nothing.

Sidney clicked on a flashlight she'd dug out of the truck's glovebox, took one look at her car's crumbled windshield, and sighed. "Dammit."

"What do we do now?" Rachel stood beside them, shivering. She wore a light sweater over her pajamas and a pair of soft slippers.

Wayne nodded toward the graveyard. "We go that way."

Rachel accepted his words with a nod and turned to go, but Wayne added, "Look, I know you're pregnant. If you want to stay out of this, I understand."

"They're my mom and sister. I have to be there."

"Okay, then. Let's go."

Rachel shot off down the graveyard path faster than Wayne could keep up with, seeming not to notice she didn't have a flashlight of her own.

"Rachel, wait," Sidney called. "We should all go in together."

Rachel halted. "Sorry. You're right. Do you know exactly where we're going?"

"I'm pretty sure they'll be in the place where Jerry was murdered," Wayne said, catching up to the woman. "Jessica and I dug up his remains Friday afternoon. It's a *long* story."

They followed the gravel path until it veered to the left, then kept walking straight through the grass among the headstones. Wayne's chest tightened at the memory of the skull staring up at him in a silent plea. What he hadn't known then but knew now…

"What did you do with him?" Rachel asked.

Wayne snapped back to attention. "Hmm?"

"What did you do with Jerry's body?"

He clenched his jaw. "Jessica had us put him in an old cabin back there. She wanted to wait until after the family reunion was over to notify the police about it. Only now I think I know a little better."

A hush fell over their group with a swiftness that made Wayne uneasy. The darkness transformed the forest into a far more sinister place than it had been by day. It didn't help that the branches closing in around them reminded him of grasping arms. He recoiled when he walked face-first into a spiderweb stretched between the trunks.

"You all right?" Sidney whispered.

Wayne clawed the offending web from his skin. "Yeah. I'm fine." But now his hands were shaking and wouldn't stop.

Flames crackled among the trees ahead of them and to the left. They flared brighter as Wayne angled toward them.

"How could she have built a fire already?" Rachel asked, hugging her sweater tighter against herself. "We weren't that far behind them."

"She might have come here earlier and started one, then rekindled it just now," Wayne said. "She probably came straight here to prepare before heading to your uncle's house."

"Prepare? Oh, God."

"Yeah. So let's try to make this fast."

Maria came to but did not open her eyes for fear of what she might see. An orange glow flickered through her eyelids, and the sudden pop of a burning stick made her twitch.

She tried to move, but her arms were pinned behind her, growing increasingly numb from the awkward position. Maria opened her eyes and gasped.

She'd been bound to an aluminum lawn chair with copious amounts of duct tape. Her ankles were taped so securely, she couldn't even wiggle them. More tape crossed her upper torso, preventing her from leaning forward.

Though unable to twist far enough around to see it, she *knew* the lawn chair was chained to a tree trunk.

Jessica sat cross-legged on the ground a few feet in front of her with her hands folded in her lap. The baseball bat lay at her right hip, next to a tarnished dagger Maria recognized immediately.

"How are you feeling?"

Maria licked her lips. They were chapped, and she was badly in need of a drink. "Let me go."

"You know I'm not going to do that."

Maria saw past Jessica then, and her eyes widened. Another lawn chair leaned against a tree about twenty feet away from her. A mound of bones had been piled in it, topped by a human skull that was looking right at her.

Jessica followed Maria's gaze and smiled. "Ah. You've found me."

"But we *buried* you."

"And Jessica and her friend Wayne exhumed me. They left us a very convenient hole to use when we're finished here tonight."

Nausea swept through Maria. "I don't want to die."

"Neither did I."

"Neither did Sarah."

That made Jessica—*Jerry*—pause. "You had the opportunity to change my fate. I asked you to let me live, and you didn't."

"You weren't going to live, Jerry. They'd tortured you too badly. God knows I'll never forgive you for what you did, but I couldn't let them keep hurting you."

Jerry cocked Jessica's eyebrow at her. "What you're saying is, you put me out of my misery, like a dying dog?"

"That's exactly what I'm saying!"

"Pfft. You're no physician. You don't know that I couldn't have been patched back together."

Maria disagreed—she'd *seen* those injuries—but chose to drop that argument. It was more than clear to her that Jerry meant to end her in much the same way she'd ended him, but if she kept him talking long enough, she might be able to find a way out of this.

"Are you going to torture me?" she asked, looking back to the baseball bat and the dagger. She couldn't remember all the implements that had been used against Jerry that terrible night, but she knew it had been more than that.

Jerry tilted Jessica's head. "Should I?"

"I didn't do those horrible things to you."

"You didn't stop them until it was too late."

Maria swallowed. "Do you remember how awful it felt when Abigail told you she'd gone and had an abortion?"

Jessica's face clouded over with dark emotion. "I've never forgotten. Why?"

"I imagine it's similar to how I felt when a police officer came to my door and told me my daughter was dead. The whole world just stopped. But what you felt was the loss of a potential life. You'd looked forward to raising a child and watching them grow. I already had a child, and you stole her from me.

"You *knew* Sarah, Jerry. She was the sweetest child…She loved dolls and chocolate cake. She loved singing and dancing. She always begged us to get a dog because the family next door had one, but we always said no. In the evenings, she would always bring me and Stephen a stack of books for us to read to her before bed. She was looking forward to starting the first grade in the fall because, according to her, she would finally be a 'big girl.'"

"What are you getting at?"

"You...You can't take your own pain and force it onto other people. That's not how life works."

"Jessica thinks you've been forcing *your* pain onto *her*."

Maria bowed her head, and shame flowed through her. "Maybe I have. I—I wanted to be the same mother to Jessica and Rachel as I was to Sarah, but the flashbacks...I know I needed to get help. But how could I have gone to a shrink when part of my trauma was killing you?"

The spirit residing within her daughter was silent for a time. Jessica's face appeared almost contemplative. Were Maria's words getting through to them both?

"I told you I didn't want to kill the girls," Jerry finally said. "Vindictam told me I had to, to make my pain stop."

"And did it?"

Jessica's jaw clenched. Before Maria realized what was happening, Jessica had risen, plucked up the baseball bat, and swung it into Maria's ribcage. Agony radiated through Maria's side, and she screamed.

36

As Wayne and the others approached the firelight, he could see one person sitting in a lawn chair chained to a tree and one rising from a seated position on the ground.

He let out a small breath of relief when he realized the second person was Jessica. The danger seemed far from over, but at least she was in his sight.

Jessica was still moving. Wayne watched in horror as she began pummeling Maria with a baseball bat, with a strength Wayne knew she didn't possess on her own. Maria sobbed with every sickening impact, yet Jessica—or the thing that *looked* like Jessica—showed no signs of relenting.

Sidney and Rachel ran straight toward the two women. Wayne trailed after them, cursing his disability for making him so slow in such a vital moment.

He emerged into the clearing fifteen seconds behind them. Sidney, who weighed about 110 pounds on a bad day, threw herself at Jessica without a second of hesitation and shoved her to the ground. Jessica landed hard on her back and seemed briefly dazed, and Rachel struggled to wrestle the bat from Jessica's clenched fist.

While they were thus distracted, Wayne knelt beside Maria, whose face was already bruised and swelling. Blood ran from a split lip that looked in need of stitches.

"We need to get you out of here," he said in a low voice, casting a wary glance over his shoulder at the others, who were still fighting to subdue a flailing Jessica.

"Dagger," Maria gasped. "On the ground. For the tape. My ribs—I think they're broken."

Wayne let out a curse and began to search for the dagger on his hands and knees.

"Watch out!"

The baseball bat swung out of nowhere and cracked Wayne across the side of his head, sending his glasses flying. Sidney lay sprawled on the ground a few feet away, clutching her arm against her chest, and Rachel stood a short distance beyond that with one arm out in a warding gesture. Jessica had regained her feet, panting, and seemed to be reassessing the situation.

"Please don't hurt me," Rachel said, almost in a whimper. "I'm pregnant. I didn't have anything to do with any of this…"

Jessica's gaze slid back to Maria. Even with Wayne's blurred vision, he could see her bend, pluck up the dagger, and move in for the kill.

"Jerry, stop it!" Wayne shouted. His voice reverberated through the forest, and Jessica actually stopped and stared at him, the dagger gleaming in one pale fist.

"Why?" Jerry asked, using Jessica's voice.

"It doesn't solve anything. You're dead. Killing Maria isn't going to fix that."

"You need to stay out of this."

"*You* need to get out of Jessica."

"Only when I'm finished."

Wayne blinked. His nearsighted eyes had caught onto some movement in their periphery—Sidney, crawling haltingly across the ground toward the abandoned bat. She closed her fingers around the handle and dragged herself to her feet behind Jessica, then poised herself, waiting.

"And you'll be finished once you've killed Maria?"

"Of course not. Many people hurt me that night. Jessica can help me find them—and Abigail."

"I don't think that's a good idea."

"Vindictam says it is."

"Who?"

"Vindictam."

The name slid from Jessica's mouth like a silken ribbon, and it made Wayne feel cold inside. He finally understood the full reality of the situation.

"It says hello."

The unwanted pair inside Jessica's skull let her take a backseat for a while, giving her time to think about how stupid she'd been.

She could finally see the deceptions and distortions that had caused her so much recent confusion, and it made her *angry.*

All she'd wanted was to find a ghost so her YouTube channel could take off. Money would start rolling in from the ad revenue, and she might actually have enough income to feed herself and fill up her gas tank. It had all seemed so straightforward.

But ghosts were people, and people had baggage. In Jerry's case, that baggage seemed to be named Vindictam—a being whose nature was becoming increasingly clear to her the harder Jessica tried and failed to reclaim her body for herself.

Since Vindictam seemed to be fully preoccupied with Jerry, the clouds had parted in Jessica's mind, and she'd regained complete awareness of who she was. At least, it felt like complete awareness. Would she know otherwise? But now, all she needed to do was expel it. Subterfuge wouldn't be a likely course of action against a being such as Vindictam. She'd opt for directness.

Jessica thought hard about a forest and a comfortable wooden bench, and the images of both came to life around her, like a mind's eye on steroids. She sat on the bench and said, "Vindictam? Can you hear me?"

The young man she'd seen in a vision before appeared in front of her, leaning jauntily against a tree trunk with his arms crossed. "Is there a problem?"

"Yeah. You tricked me."

"Did I?" His platinum eyebrows rose. The edges of him flickered, as if he too were simply an image.

"You told me my pain would stop if I let you in," Jessica said. "But you were causing the pain to begin with, weren't you? You took my pain from moving furniture and amplified the hell out of it so you had me all worried that there was something wrong with me, but the only thing wrong was *you*."

Vindictam's dark eyes bored into hers. "I am not *wrong*."

Jessica rose from the bench. The hatred oozed from Vindictam like a viscous tar.

"I've wanted to find a ghost for as long as I can remember. I had no idea I'd find a demon too. That's what you are, right? A pathetic little demon who feeds on weak people until they snap. You're probably so junior that the devil doesn't even know your name."

Vindictam said nothing, though its wrath intensified. Jessica knew she should be scared—this was an honest-to-God *evil spirit* that could probably turn her into a bloody stain with the snap of its fingers—but this was *her* body, dammit, and she'd stand her ground if it was the last thing she did.

"What do you even get out of all of this?" Jessica went on, feeling emboldened. "Jerry was just a sad divorcee who wanted to be a dad. If you'd left him alone, he would have eventually moved on with his life, but no, you had to poke him and prod him until he turned into a mass murderer." Her eyes stung as she replayed the conversation she'd had with Jerry in the university parking lot. Jerry had killed four children, including Jessica's own sister. An unforgiveable act.

Vindictam licked his lips. "I would see all of creation burn, if only because I want it to."

"Well, you're just a swell guy, aren't you?"

The demon lunged at her. In the real world, Jessica wouldn't have stood a chance in hand-to-hand combat, but this was inside her head, so the rules of physics didn't exactly apply. She grabbed the demon's arms and shoved him hard, causing him to stagger backward.

"Get out of my mind!"

The demon lashed out with one hand, raking its nails across her face. Jessica kicked it between the legs and received a punch to the jaw for her efforts.

"Jerry?" she panted. "A little help here?"

Despite the fact Vindictam was fighting with her *mano a mano*, she could also feel him elsewhere in her mind, controlling her actual body. Maybe if she tweaked her surroundings just a little bit…

She tried to home in on Jerry, and the mind-forest melted away, revealing a cemetery full of headstones towering like skyscrapers, as if Jessica were the size of an ant. A black, pulsating form huddled at the base of the nearest headstone, screaming like one of the damned. Jessica took a few tentative steps closer and saw that the amorphous shape before her was a human wrapped in tangles of black tentacles—one pale, clawing hand protruded from the mass as if pleading for help.

God, she thought, *if you can hear me, help me end this thing.*

She strode forward before her nerve broke. The screams were echoing through her mind so loudly she could hardly think. Drawing on every ounce of resolve, Jessica grabbed the human hand and pulled, hard, like she was tugging a car out of quicksand.

Pain lanced through her—the same mysterious pain that had troubled her for days before Vindictam had fully settled in. She only gripped the hand tighter, resisting the urge to let go and run. The black tentacles tried to twine themselves around her arms, but she willed them away with everything she had in her.

A man's arm slowly emerged from the mass. *Come on*, Jessica thought, refusing to let go, even though every nerve inside of her had ignited with agony. *Come on…*

Jerry's full form surfaced from the black tentacles with a sickening sucking noise, and he and Jessica fell into a heap together. The tentacles retreated into a tight, pulsating ball. The pain lessened to some extent but did not fully dissipate.

"Are you okay?" Jessica panted, trying to get her feet back under her.

Jerry tried to sit up. His hair was wild and slick with slime. "What's happening? Where…?"

"We're inside my head, and we're possessed by a demon named Vindictam. We need to get out of here."

He's a murderer, hissed a voice. *Why would you ever help him?*

Because if I don't, Jessica thought back, *this will never end.*

Jerry opened his mouth in surprise. Jessica whirled just in time to see the platinum blond human-shaped apparition of Vindictam swinging a baseball bat at her head, his face twisted in a snarl. She tried to duck, but she was too slow…

…and suddenly, she was standing in a forest clearing in the real world.

Jessica beheld a chilling tableau. Ahead of her and to Jessica's right sat a lawn chair heaped with bones and a skull. To her left, another lawn chair had been chained to a tree. Her own mother had been lashed to it with duct tape. A crackling bonfire illuminated the scene, making the shadows writhe and dance.

Jessica stepped forward. "Mom?" she started to say, then noticed the dark-haired young woman in jeans and a ratty old hoodie standing a few feet away from her, holding a dagger.

She was looking at the back of her own head. Vindictam had

thrown her out of her body, completely hijacking it for himself.

A greater fear than Jessica had ever known surged through her. It wasn't supposed to happen like this! She was supposed to grow old and gray, not stop at the tender age of twenty-one while an actual monster continued to dwell inside her living corpse.

Jessica held her hands out in front of her. They looked solid. She flexed her fingers and toes. All seemed to be in working order, except the fact she was now a soul without a body.

Movement in front of her caught her attention. Sidney crawled across the ground toward an abandoned baseball bat. Wayne was doing his best to keep Vindictam talking so the demon wouldn't notice Sidney, who then rose and struck Jessica's body on the back of its head.

Though she couldn't feel it, Jessica winced. Her body crumpled to the ground, dropping the dagger, and Sidney, Wayne, and Rachel rushed in to pin her—it—down.

Wayne fumbled with his pocket and removed the small bottle of holy water. "I don't have any idea how this is going to work," he said to nobody in particular, "but it's the only thing I've got. I suppose you could say I have faith in it."

He splashed some of the holy water onto Jessica's twisting body. It chilled her, hearing a scream emerge from its mouth, because while it sounded just like her, it *wasn't* her.

"I command you to leave Jessica's body!" Wayne's voice boomed. Tears streaked his face. "You have no place here."

"It's all Abigail's fault!" Jerry shrieked via Jessica. "She did this to me!"

Wayne closed his eyes and drew in a deep breath. "Jerry, as much as I hate to say it, you're a victim here too. I think there's a demon inside you. That's what Vindictam is, right? You've got to let go of what happened. Otherwise, I don't think the demon will ever let go of you."

"How can I ever let go?" Jerry sobbed. "Abigail killed our child. I need to find her. She needs to be *punished*."

"Abigail is dead," Wayne said quietly. "So there's really no need to obsess about her anymore."

Jessica frowned. What kind of tactic was Wayne using here?

Jessica's body had stopped struggling. Sidney and Rachel each sat on one of its arms, and Wayne kneeled on its legs.

"How would you know anything about Abigail?" Jerry asked, sounding more perplexed than angry.

"Be careful," Sidney said in a warning tone.

"Just let it go," Wayne said to Jerry, ignoring his cousin. "What happened in the past is done."

Jerry made Jessica's lip curl. "Don't spout psychobabble at me. How do you know Abigail is dead?"

Wayne closed his eyes again and seemed to be counting off several silent beats. "Because I killed her."

Jessica put a hand over her mouth. "No," she breathed.

Jerry narrowed Jessica's eyes. "I don't understand."

Wayne swallowed. "You've been hanging around for a few days. Have you ever heard anyone say my last name?"

Jerry paused. "No. Why?"

"It's Thompson." Wayne let his words hang in the air like smog.

"But…that was Abigail's maiden name. I don't…"

The firelight danced in Wayne's eyes. "Abigail Thompson was my mother. She suffered from addiction and untreated mental illness. She tried to kill me with a fireplace poker when I was thirteen years old. I got it away from her…and you can imagine the rest."

Jessica's eyelids blinked. "You mean that Abigail had the audacity to go and have a child with *someone else* after what she did to me?"

"You're not quite understanding." Wayne was shaking his head. "I was born on May 2, 1980. Does that date mean anything to you?"

Even in the firelight, Jessica could see the color empty out of her own face. "But that's impossible."

"It's not." Wayne's voice became almost strangled as he spoke. "My mother had a saline abortion when she was seven months pregnant with me, but they didn't inject enough of the stuff into her. She was supposed to go back the next day and deliver my body, but she went into labor in the middle of the night at her parents' house. They rushed her to the hospital. I was born an hour later."

Wayne paused to wipe at his eyes.

"She told me the story so many times. I never knew if she was sorry about it or disappointed that I was too stubborn to die, even though the abortion had permanently damaged my brain. I spent the first couple months of my life in an intensive care unit. My grandparents said they would come and sit with me sometimes. They were in so much denial…When I was finally discharged, they took me home. They were my legal guardians, but my mother still lived with them."

Jessica could feel her mind spinning in circles, unwilling to accept Wayne's words but knowing they had to be true. But that meant…

Frost began to spread across the ground at Jessica's insubstantial feet, and her actual body went slack. Jerry's apparition materialized beside Wayne. Jerry stared down at Wayne with wide eyes.

"You're telling the truth," Jerry said, his voice full of wonder.

Wayne got to his feet, brushed off his slacks, and plucked his glasses off the ground. He put them on, adjusted them, and stared at Jerry, who'd apparently drawn enough energy from his surroundings to manifest himself to everyone present, if Jessica were to guess from the astonished gasps coming from Rachel and Sidney.

Jerry was taller than Wayne by a good three inches. His face was narrower, and his eyes were blue, not brown like Wayne's.

Except for the hair, Wayne must have resembled his long-dead mother.

Jerry reached out a hand as if wanting to touch Wayne but quickly withdrew it. "Why didn't she tell me? I would have taken you away from there."

"I never knew your name, or saw pictures of you." Wayne paused. "I think she was afraid of you." Tears were running freely down Wayne's cheeks now. "I didn't even make the connection until this morning, when Jessica was telling me about your ex-wife and described my mother down to the last detail. She *was* blond, she *would* be fifty-seven years old, and she did work at Lyle Mercer High School. It was wrong how Abigail treated us. But it's all over. She's been gone for seventeen years. I've moved on from it, and you should too."

Jerry hung his head in shame, but Wayne wasn't finished.

"That *thing* possessing you has spoon-fed you nothing but lies. Hell, maybe it even got to Abigail too. But the fact is, I'm your son, I'm alive and well, and you've *got* to put this all behind you before anyone else gets hurt."

"Oh, God." Jerry looked nearly ill. "Oh, *God*. What have I done?"

A log popped in the fire. Wayne looked around wildly. "Where did he go? Jerry? Are you still there?"

Jerry was still visible to Jessica, speechless and bewildered. "Jerry?" Jessica said softly. "We need to get that demon out of my body. Can you help?"

Jerry turned toward her, surprised, but then his face fell at the sight of her. "You're dead."

His words sent a mild panic through her, but she said, "I don't think so. Look, I'm breathing. See?"

Her body's chest rose and fell with rapid breaths. It was uncanny to watch, like something out of one of the horror flicks she and Sidney had devoured so much of.

Then its eyes snapped open, and it tried to rise, taking both Sidney and Rachel with it. Jessica watched helplessly as Wayne joined them in trying to hold her body back down.

"I think Wayne is right," Jessica said, knowing she needed to act fast before Vindictam caused more harm to her and her loved ones.

"That demon still has a hold on you."

"It still has a hold on you too." Jerry's tone was dark. "Otherwise, you wouldn't be standing out here with me."

Jessica gritted her teeth. "What do I need to let go of?"

Jerry nodded toward Maria, who was sobbing quietly in the lawn chair with her head bowed. "It's my fault that she treated you the way she did. I hurt so many people. I wish I'd been strong enough to resist it." He shook his head. "You need to forgive her."

Jessica stared at her mother long and hard. Could she forgive the woman who'd caused so much hurt? It seemed as impossible as reaching up one skinny arm and touching the stars.

"It's hard," Jessica admitted.

"Yes."

"Can we do it?"

Jerry gave her a thin smile. "For your sake, we have to."

Jessica thought about the lonely years when she'd longed for nothing more than a mother's attention, a word of encouragement, a warm embrace. Maria had been distant and refused it all. And yes, it hurt, but it was also in the past now.

Where it belonged.

Jessica said, "Growing up with that woman wasn't easy. But she was hurting too. I acknowledge that. I let it go."

Vindictam let out a snarl through Jessica's own mouth. Wayne was sprinkling holy water again, muttering prayers.

Jerry bowed his head and said, "I've done horrifically cruel things. I know I have to face judgment for that. I'm terrified about what that will feel like, but it's what I deserve." He twitched as Jessica's body let out another cry—the holy water must have stung. "I don't understand why Abigail did the things she did. Maybe we should have worked on communicating better. Maybe we both should have gotten help for our problems. None of that matters anymore, though. She's gone too. And...I let it go."

Jessica's body flopped onto its back once more. From her disembodied vantage point, Jessica could see a writhing black mass rise and dissipate into the air. A distant, inhuman scream faded and then cut short. Vindictam?

"She's not breathing!" Sidney cried, shaking Jessica's shoulders as if that would help.

The lips on Jessica's body were turning blue. Wayne immediately set to work administering CPR.

Jessica turned away, unable to stomach watching something so terrible.

"It hurts, doesn't it?" Jerry said, sensing her thoughts.

"Yeah." She swallowed. "I don't want to die."

Jerry's mouth quirked up in a smile that reminded her now of Wayne's. "You'd better get back in there, then. There seems to be a vacancy."

God, she hoped so. Jessica faced her body again, stepped up to it, and—

A rush of wind entered her lungs, and the next thing she knew, she was staring up into Wayne's tear-streaked face. "I'm alive," she breathed. And it felt *good*.

Though Wayne was smiling, he also had a look of uncertainty about him.

"It's just me in here now," Jessica said. "Vindictam is gone. Jerry and I…we let it go."

Wayne sat back and folded his arms. "Tell me something that only you would know."

Jessica thought about it. "You're practically an honorary Boy Scout."

"That works for me." Wayne let out a long breath. "Rachel, call an ambulance for your mom. Sidney, try to get that tape off of Maria." He looked back to Jessica and lowered his voice. "You're sure that thing is gone? For good?"

Jessica searched through her thoughts and came up dry. "I can't feel it anymore. It's like it was clouding my mind for days and I didn't even realize it." Vindictam was obviously what Sidney had seen in the kitchen—her friend had not been completely blind to it, as she was.

Jessica tried not to let the guilt overcome her. What was done was done.

She joined Sidney at her mother's side and used the old dagger to rip through the layers of duct tape binding Maria to the chair.

"I'm so sorry," Maria kept saying as they freed her. "I'm so, so sorry."

"It's okay." The words felt strange in Jessica's mouth. "It's over now."

Maria leveled a pained look at her. "No, it isn't. Is Jerry still here?"

Jessica looked over her shoulder. Jerry was gazing sadly at the bones Vindictam had forced her to pile into the old lawn chair, like some morbid spectator.

"Yeah."

Maria cleared her throat. "Jerry? May I say something?"

Jerry swiveled toward her, his expression darkening, not with anger, but regret. "Should I manifest myself again?" he asked Jessica.

"I'll leave that up to you," Jessica said. "Mom, wait a minute." She suddenly felt more tired than she'd been in her entire life, and she sank to the ground beside Maria, who seemed to be in too much pain to get up from the chair.

Jerry approached them with uncertainty in his step. He stopped in front of them, then sat cross-legged in the bed of fallen leaves coating the ground.

The air grew frigid once again, and Sidney let out a small whimper as Jerry became visible to her for a second time.

Maria lifted her head and stared stoically at her old friend. "It's just you now, yes?" she asked in a low tone. "No demons?"

"It's just me," Jerry said. "Maria, I know that nothing I say will ever make anything right, but…I'm sorry."

Maria accepted that with a small nod. "I'm going to turn myself in," she said. "None of us had the right to do what we did. Your family deserves to know the truth."

Jessica's heart skipped a beat at the same moment Rachel said, "Mom, no!"

"I have to," Maria insisted. "I took this man's life. Turning myself in is the right thing to do."

Jerry tilted his head, studying her. "You don't have to do that. You were right—I wouldn't have survived that night anyway. I might have suffered even longer, if not for you."

"Police and paramedics are going to be here soon," Wayne reminded them. "There are obvious human remains in that chair over there. It's going to be awfully hard to explain all of this without pointing any fingers."

"Then lie," Jerry said. "I think that Maria has suffered enough."

Maria's eyes widened. "You're sure?"

"If you can forgive me for what I did to Sarah, then I can forgive you for what you did to me." Jerry smiled. "Let's call it even."

Jerry watched them leave.

The young women named Sidney and Rachel helped Maria along in the direction of the parking lot, presumably so the paramedics would have easier access to her. Jessica threw one final look over her shoulder at Jerry and gave him a sad smile before departing. Then she turned back to Wayne, and they were gone.

As the bonfire cooled to embers, Jerry sat on the ground beside the lawn chair he'd been murdered in, once again eyeing the heap of bones that had once been him. It hurt to see what time and death had done to him, but the truth was never an easy thing to accept.

The truth was, he'd murdered four children. There was no excusing that—and he'd gotten exactly what he deserved for it. Pain begat more pain. The families had gotten even.

The fire's embers cooled to ash. For the first time in thirty years, no voices preyed on Jerry's conscience. His mind was completely clear at last, and he felt like his old self again, except for the fact he was very, *very* dead.

He thought about Abigail and what she'd hidden from him. For once, he felt no bitterness toward her, only emptiness.

Jerry wished he could talk to her.

"God, please take me," he rasped, emotion overcoming him. "Do whatever you need to do with me. Just don't leave me here all alone anymore."

A sudden calm came over him. Nothing moved him onward to bliss or the inferno; he simply remained sitting on the ground, unseen, in a Kentucky forest.

But now he had an understanding that maybe—just *maybe*—he might have a second chance.

37

"How are your parents doing?"

Jessica twitched and paused the television, where the ghosts of Alec Baldwin and Geena Davis were busy trying to haunt Catherine O'Hara and Jeffrey Jones's new house. Wayne stood in the doorway in his work clothes. She'd been so absorbed in the movie, she hadn't heard him come in.

It was Wednesday evening, four days after what she was coming to think of as The Fiasco. She'd spent most of the time curled up in a ball on the couch, drowning her thoughts in fictional people's problems and cheap Mexican food.

"Better," she said. "Apparently, I gave Dad a pretty bad concussion with that suitcase, but he'll be all right. And they say Mom's ribs should heal okay."

To save Jessica from assault charges, Uncle Esteban had told the cops that a drug addict had snuck into his house, attacked his brother-in-law, and kidnapped his sister. The "drug addict" had mysteriously vanished once "Jessica and the others" found Maria in the woods. The cops seemed dubious but didn't press the issue since nobody had been killed. As for the old bones in the lawn chair? That was anybody's guess.

"For the hundredth time, it wasn't *you*, Jessica." Wayne came into the room and sat in his recliner. "You really shouldn't beat yourself up about this."

She crossed her arms. "I know it wasn't *me*, but part of me was still there. I can remember it."

"Okay…"

"And if I hadn't been so naïve, it wouldn't have happened in the first place. So there."

Wayne gave her a kindly expression she didn't feel she deserved. "Everyone is okay. Nobody died this time around."

"Yeah."

"Which reminds me, there's something important I want to talk to you about."

Jessica raised her eyebrows—that could definitely either be a good thing or a bad thing. "You want me to move out of here, don't you? I know I've caused nothing but problems for you. I can pack my things and go somewhere else."

Wayne studied her long and hard. "Is that what you want?"

"No. But it might be better for you that way."

His expression grew more serious. "This thing between you and me—I want to know where we stand."

Jessica sat up straighter. "What do you mean?"

Wayne sat in his recliner and took off his shoes and ankle-foot orthotics. "Have you thought about how fucked-up this whole thing is? My mother aborted me. My father flipped his shit and murdered your sister. Your mother murdered him. And then I killed my mother. I don't know if we need to be on the *Jerry Springer Show* or the *True Crime Network*."

"Or *Ghost Hunters*." Jerry had been distant ever since The Fiasco, but Jessica had spotted him a few times lurking on the back deck, where he apparently thought she wouldn't see him.

Wayne didn't smile. "The fact is, we both have a lot to cope with. It took me years to get over what happened with my mom, and now I have to accept the fact that my father was a mass murderer."

"But it wasn't *him*, remember?" Jessica said wryly.

Wayne's shoulders drooped a bit. "Yeah. I know. Honestly, it does make it a little easier to wrap my mind around it. But regardless, my parents were two incredibly shitty people. They must have clashed like ammonia and bleach, and I'm the result."

"Are you trying to tell me you're toxic fumes?"

"I'm *saying* that that's where I come from. Abigail plus Jerry equals me. Do you still want me around, now that the truth is out?"

It made Jessica's heart ache, knowing Wayne was struggling so badly with his genetic identity. She rose from the couch and sat on the arm of his recliner, taking his hand in hers.

"Wayne," she said, "you are one of the kindest people I've ever known. You make me feel like my weird little hobbies and I are worth it. If you can accept the fact that I rather foolishly let a ghost and a demon into the house and into my head, and if you're fine with the fact that my mom stabbed your dad to death, then yes, I still want you around. We are *not* our parents."

"Thank God for that."

"So, do we start over, you and I?"

Wayne tilted his head and held out a hand to her. "Hi, I'm Wayne. I'm a disabled accountant who loves to moisturize and wear pastel colors."

Jessica shook his hand. "Hi, Wayne. I'm Jessica. I see dead people. It's nice to meet you."

"Has anyone ever told you you're gorgeous, Jessica?"

"Once or twice." She smiled at him. "And I think you're fucking hot."

Jessica leaned in and kissed him, and he pulled her close to his chest. His heart beat against her. It made her feel content and warm, and if they could have stayed like that forever, she wouldn't have batted an eye.

After a time, the air grew cooler in the living room, and a soft voice said, "Excuse me."

Jessica lifted her head from Wayne's shoulder. Jerry lurked in the doorway to the kitchen. His face still held a deathly pallor, but there was something lighter about him, like a great burden had been lifted.

Wayne scrambled upright. "Holy shit. You're still here."

The lights in the kitchen winked out, and Jerry looked a tad regretful. "Sorry about that. I think I just tripped a breaker trying to get you to see me. I'm not sure how long this is going to last..."

"You wanted *me* to see you?" Wayne asked.

"Yes, for obvious reasons. Um...do you care if I sit down?"

"Go ahead." Wayne sighed. "Because there's absolutely nothing weird about me sitting down and having a chat with my dead dad."

"You've inherited my sarcasm, I see." Jerry took a seat on the couch cushion Jessica had vacated earlier. "I pity your friends."

"They're used to it by now." Wayne adjusted his glasses and leveled his gaze at Jerry. "So. What's up?"

"I wanted to discuss my remains."

"The cops have them right now. Maria still wants to turn herself in, to save them the trouble of hunting down a killer, but hasn't committed yet. So, I don't have any idea when the remains are going to be released to your family."

Jerry accepted this with a nod. "Well, *when* they're finally released... I've decided what should be done with them. I've spent long enough in a graveyard to know it's not for me. I would like to be cremated."

"I'm sure that can be arranged," Wayne said, his voice starting to crack.

Jessica squeezed his hand tighter, and he squeezed back.

"What are you going to do now?" Jessica asked Jerry. "If you want to stay here with us, we've got room."

"You both know I have no place here." Jerry closed his eyes. "I've been clinging to this world far past my expiration date. I need to go and face my judgment."

"Are you scared?"

"I'm terrified. But I believe that I'll be judged rightly."

"You're starting to flicker out," Wayne said, though Jessica could still see Jerry just fine.

Jerry shifted uncomfortably. "Sorry, hang on… "

Downstairs, the furnace shut off with a soft thud.

"Remind me to reset the breakers before bed," Wayne said to Jessica in a long-suffering tone.

"When are you going?" Jessica asked Jerry, feeling a lump form in her throat.

"Soon. There's just a few more things I want to say. One: if you would reach out to my niece Casey, please tell her that I love her and all the rest of my family. Tell them the truth about what happened. It will be hard for them, but they need to hear it so they stop wondering."

"We can do that," Wayne said.

"I appreciate it. And Jessica: are you still going to work on your YouTube? I haven't seen you make any new videos in days."

Jessica couldn't help but grimace. "My heart hasn't been in it. I feel like I was exploiting you. You were like the pot of gold at the end of the rainbow, and I apologize for that."

"Apology accepted. But I was going to say, whether you like it or not, you have a gift. You can see me with little effort on my part. Why don't you go out and help other people like me?"

"Help them *how*?"

Jerry shrugged. "They're lost, like I was. Help them find the right way to where they need to go."

Jessica thought about it. Could she keep doing that kind of thing and stay safe from the dark, evil things lurking in the cracks? What if there were other "Vindictams" out there, waiting for her when she least expected it?

She would be on her guard, though. Boy, would she be on her guard.

"When do you plan on going?" Wayne asked Jerry.

Jerry's forehead creased. "Soon. I'd like for both of you to be there."

"Where is 'there,' exactly?" Jessica asked.

Jerry told her, and she smiled.

"We can do that too."

Saturday morning, Jessica rode with Wayne to the Cincinnati Nature Center. It was the day before Halloween, the sun gleamed brightly, and the air was crisp with an autumn chill.

Jessica slowed her pace so Wayne could walk beside her. They trudged into the woods and followed a trail around the curve of a hill. After a few minutes, they came upon a bench, and Jessica said, "Is this a good spot?"

"It's as good as any," Jerry replied with a nervous smile. Then he appeared to concentrate hard for a moment, and Wayne said, "I see you now."

The two men regarded each other for several long moments without speaking.

"I keep trying not to think about what might have been," Jerry finally said. "I'm just glad you're okay, in spite of everything that happened."

"Me too." Wayne fidgeted, shifting his weight from one leg to the other. "So, what happens next?"

Jerry tilted his head toward the cloudless blue sky. "I have to let go of this world."

"Easier said than done?" Jessica asked.

"*Much* easier." Jerry scanned the sunny, wooded, hillside. "It's a beautiful world. I'm going to miss it terribly."

"What do you think will happen to you?"

"I suspect," Jerry said, "that I'll have to face the children I killed.

I'll have to look them in the eye and submit myself to their mercy. Maybe they'll even be kind."

Jerry stepped away from them. Squirrels raced up a tree nearby, and birds swooped through the air. A few stray leaves wafted down from the canopy and fluttered to the ground.

"I hope we see each other again someday," Jessica said, a lump of emotion rising in her throat. "But not for a long time."

"Ditto," Wayne said. "Goodbye, Jerry. Um, Dad."

That single word lit up Jerry's face brighter than Jessica had ever seen it.

"Goodbye to you both. And don't forget what I said."

Jerry strode off down the hillside, fading away, even to Jessica's watering eyes. Then he was gone.

Jessica cleared her throat. "So. Um. Now what?"

"Let's stay a while. It's a nice day."

"Fine with me. I've got no plans."

They sat on the bench. Jessica leaned her head against Wayne's shoulder, and they watched the autumn morning go by, nodding to the occasional hiker who passed them.

"Do you think he'll be all right?" Jessica asked at length.

Wayne sighed. "I'm afraid the answer to that is well above my paygrade."

"It sucks, not knowing."

"Maybe it's better that way." Wayne drummed his fingers on his leg. "Are you going to take his advice and help more ghosts?"

"I'll have to think about it. I don't know if I'm cut out for the drama."

"Did you say drama, or trauma?"

Jessica forced a laugh. "I think they amount to the same thing."

She thought about her channel and its growing list of followers who thirsted for anything paranormal. Could she really keep going, after everything that had happened? Things had gotten far too close to home. What if something like this happened again, with a less favorable outcome? Did she really want to involve herself in this kind of thing on a regular basis?

"You know," Wayne said, "I'm here to help whenever you need it. If some other lost soul comes traipsing over our doorstep, you won't be alone."

"I appreciate that."

"And you're more than welcome to ignore any advice I toss your way, but I really think your channel could become big if you take the right steps."

She smirked at him. "Like *not* exploiting insane ghosts?"

"For one." Wayne smiled. "And you don't even have to think about it today, or even tomorrow. Try to heal from this first. Then you can move on to the next thing."

"Like Jerry did?"

"Like Jerry did."

A darkness deeper than night surrounded Jerry.

Time had lost all semblance of meaning. He had been here for either a moment, or for an entire age of the world. It didn't really seem to matter either way. If he still had a heart, it would be racing, and he would be trying not to hyperventilate from the fear crushing him from all sides.

At least there was no pain. There was no sound, no sight, no sensation whatsoever. Only his emotions…and his memories.

"Is anyone out there?" he asked, but the void devoured the words before he had a chance to hear them.

So, this was hell. Unlike the lake of fire preached from judgy pulpits, Jerry's eternity would be one of nothingness. He supposed he could accept that, difficult as it was.

"I'm sorry," he said to the void. "I know I can't ever take back what I did—what Vindictam made me do. But I can speak their names: Megan Smith. Josie Smith. Lauren Scott. And Sarah Roman-Dell. I don't think they should ever be forgotten."

More time passed. It could have been five hundred million years or five minutes.

Oddly enough, the darkness seemed to be lightening. A scene began to take shape: rows of houses on half-acre lots, in the heart of summer, when everything was green and in bloom.

With a start, he realized it was Clarkville, as it had appeared on the day of the murders Jerry had committed.

A picnic table stood in the grass behind one house. Four girls sat around it, playing a board game. Three looked to be kindergarten age, and the older one appeared to be supervising the others with an expression of detached boredom.

Sensing it was the right thing to do, Jerry approached the girls with caution. The oldest one turned her head his way and said brightly, "Oh, hi, Mr. Madison!"

Jerry swallowed. "Hi. It's Megan, right?"

"Yeah." Then, to one of the other girls, Megan said, "Hey, it's Sarah's turn! You've got to be patient!"

Josie—one of the six-year-olds—guiltily drew her hands back from the board game and gave her friends a sheepish smile.

"You don't have to keep standing there, you know," Megan said.

Jerry hesitated. "I'm not sure what else I'm supposed to do."

She looked him right in the eye. "I know you feel guilty about what happened."

"As you should," said little Sarah, in a tone no real six-year-old ever would have uttered.

Josie and Lauren, the fourth girl, looked up from their game as well. It felt unnerving to have those four sets of eyes staring at him, especially considering what Jerry had done to them.

"Is this real?" Jerry asked when a monarch butterfly flapped past his head.

"Do you have any reason to believe otherwise?" Megan asked.

Jerry opened his mouth and closed it. He was starting to notice odd little things here and there, like twinges going up and down his arms and legs.

Something banged against the inside of his ribs—he had *ribs* now?—and he gasped in an actual breath.

The girls smiled at him as if they understood what was happening. "It'll take some getting used to," said the girl named Lauren. "You haven't breathed in a long time."

"But…how…?"

Megan shrugged. "That's just the way of things. Or so we've been told."

"But I'm *dead*. And so are all of you."

"Well, yeah. But that's just the first life. Welcome to the second one."

Jerry gaped at them. "I *killed* you. You…you should be punishing me right now. You should be punishing me for *eternity*."

"That sounds like an awful lot of work," said Sarah dubiously.

"Yeah," agreed Lauren. "I'd rather just sit here and keep playing games. I can go get *Mouse Trap* when we're done with this one."

Jerry practiced breathing in and out for a few moments while he took this all in. He could actually feel blood rushing through his veins. His stomach even growled. Was there actual food here?

"Come sit with us," little Josie piped up. "We don't bite."

Jerry couldn't help but grimace. "You're sure you want me to, after what I did?"

"Why not?" Megan gave him a mischievous grin. "I know *Candy Land* and *Mouse Trap* probably aren't your thing. How about I go grab a pack of cards? The girls and I have had a long time to learn some new stuff. We can all play five-card stud."

Shaking his head in disbelief, Jerry sat down at one end of the picnic table, beside Megan and across from Sarah, who looked like a miniature version of her sister Jessica. Megan rose, disappeared into her house, and came back with a red pack of Bicycle playing cards, then shuffled and dealt them.

And thus began the first day of forever.

EPILOGUE

2011

"Hey, everyone! It's your Friendly Neighborhood Ghost Hunter again. If you're following my channel, you may have noticed I've been gone awhile. A lot of big things came up, and I've had to sort through them one by one. I'm sure some of you can relate."

Jessica stopped recording to think about what to say next. The past six months had mostly been her trying to figure out a new normal. She was still living with Wayne—which was absolutely *not* a problem—and she'd actually picked up a small, part-time job answering the phone and penciling in appointments at a hair and nail salon down the street. The pay was minimal, but she'd take it over *no* pay any day.

Plus, to Jessica's absolute delight, a popular paranormal blogger had written a small piece about Jessica's channel early in the year, which had driven enough traffic there to throw her over the minimum threshold for monetization. And as long as she kept posting, it would only grow from there.

Things were looking up for her friends as well. Wayne had finally gotten the raise his employers had promised him, and Sidney found an office job at a nearby HVAC company.

Since there no longer seemed to be any demons or angry spirits lurking around, Sidney had moved back into her bedroom, and she and Jessica had resumed their tradition of sitting on the couch late into the night, watching terrible movies while Wayne made snide remarks that had them in stitches.

Those things were just the easy things—after all, there wasn't anything overly taxing at her new job, and watching movies required minimal effort. What Jessica had been focusing on the most these past six months was trying to establish a relationship with her parents. She drove to Indianapolis every other weekend and forced herself to sit and talk with them about the goings-on in her life and about the painful past. To her surprise, Maria began opening up to her, describing her grief over her lost daughter and how hard it was to become a parent all over again after that devastating loss. Stephen recounted stories of their time with Sarah, telling Jessica about the things Sarah had loved and done.

A few weeks ago, Jessica had even gone with her parents to visit Sarah's grave, something they had apparently not done in more than twenty years. It had been a somber affair, and Jessica laid a bouquet of flowers atop the small headstone marking her sister's resting place.

In the present, Jessica leaned forward and hit the Record button on her camcorder again. "Do you remember me talking about a ghost named Jerry who followed me home from a graveyard back in October? It was scary, but I was also thrilled because it was like hitting the jackpot for me. I'm a ghost hunter, right? And I'd found my very own ghost.

"But it turns out, Jerry wasn't the only thing that came home with me that night. There was a demon attached to him, and it got to me too. It started to warp my thinking in ways I didn't even realize. I may not be the most level-headed person around here, but when I started thinking that murder was a perfectly logical solution to my problems, well, that should have been a major red flag. But it wasn't because I was no longer myself. I completely lost the ability to determine right from wrong."

She paused the camcorder again, remembering the bloodlust that had overpowered her just *thinking* about her mother. If her friends hadn't been able to intervene…

Jessica hit Record again. "The only reason I'm alive and well today is because I was able to let go of the things that the demon was feeding off of. And trust me, it was *hard*. But it was do that or die—because I know I wouldn't have survived the possession otherwise.

"Jerry ditched the demon too, in the end. He was finally able to move on. I know it all sounds so crazy, and you can believe as much or as little as you want. But I'll tell you this: there are terrible things lurking out there. Things that won't think twice about hijacking your own minds and bodies for their own gain. So beware, if you're ever considering digging around in the paranormal. Not every spirit you meet is going to be friendly.

"You might be wondering, am I going to give up ghost hunting? Not a chance." She grinned at the camera. "I don't actually know if I'm able to see all ghosts, or if Jerry was just a special case. Either way, ghosts are people too. If I run into more ghosts someday, instead of exploiting them for likes and views, I'm going to focus on helping them get to where they need to go. Any questions?"

She ended the recording and looked over at her audience, which consisted of Wayne, Sidney, and Rachel.

"So, what do you guys think?" Jessica asked them.

"Not bad," Rachel said. "And thank you for not going any deeper into our family's issues." Rachel and Eric had moved into a house two streets away from Wayne's the previous month. Rachel was starting to look like she'd swallowed an entire honeydew melon, and she'd propped her swollen ankles on an ottoman while sipping at a bottle of ginger ale.

"I didn't think the internet needed to know about all of that," Jessica admitted.

"You're sounding more confident than you used to," added Wayne. He sat in his usual recliner with his orthotics off. "I like it."

"Thanks." Jessica blushed. "I just want to be authentic. I think people might connect with that."

"I have one question," Sidney said, frowning in thought. "If you're not going to be 'exploiting ghosts' anymore, what exactly are you going to be showing people in your videos?"

"The journey." Jessica shrugged.

"What do you mean by that?" Rachel asked, then held a hand against her increasingly large baby bump. "Ow, that was a hard kick."

Jessica couldn't help but smile, knowing that her tiny, unborn niece was growing stronger by the day. "I'll be teaching my viewers how to use their own equipment if they've got it. I'll show them how to debunk things that aren't really ghosts. And I'll teach them the right way to interact with spirits if they do get the chance to meet one."

"And if you run into another one like Jerry?" Sidney asked.

"Then I'll do my best to help them. It's what he wanted."

While Maria was slowly warming up to the fact she had two living, breathing daughters who would probably be scarred for life due to her lousy parenting, the guilt was by no means diminishing.

Her nightmares had been getting worse. Every time she closed her eyes, she saw the bones in the lawn chair and Jerry's apparition coming toward her, like something straight from hell. She'd woken up Stephen by screaming a few times, yet nothing he said would calm her.

He hadn't been there the second time around. Stephen knew, but he didn't *know*.

One morning at the beginning of May, Maria rose early, left Stephen the long note she'd handwritten the night before, and got in the car. She drove for more than two hours and pulled into a parking lot in Clarkville, Kentucky. Her eyes wet with tears, she got out of the car, took a deep breath, and strode into the police station.

"How can I help you?" asked an overly cheery receptionist.

In a small town like this, the cops mostly dealt with speeders and drunks. *Except for the summer of '86...*

Maria cleared her throat. "I have information about a case that I believe your department is working on."

"Would you like to speak with one of our officers?"

"Yes, please."

Maria was shown to a room. Not the kind with two-way glass, thank God, but just a regular room with a desk, some filing cabinets, and a few chairs. She didn't have to wait long before a man rapped on the doorframe and said, "You wanted to speak with an officer about a case?"

Maria turned to face him and felt her insides go cold. She hadn't seen him in decades, but there was no doubt it was the same man, just with much grayer hair. His nametag confirmed it. This was Officer Ridgeway, the man who had organized Jerry Madison's death in the woods behind the graveyard.

The man's eyes widened when he recognized her too. "Maria Roman-Dell? It's certainly been a while, hasn't it?"

"Yes," she said and swallowed.

"The family been good?"

"Yes."

They continued staring at each other. Maria could see a shift taking place behind Officer Ridgeway's eyes. He might have been surprised at first, but he definitely knew now why she was here.

"So, Maria," Officer Ridgeway said, a sardonic smile spreading across his face. "What is it you came here to talk about?"

ABOUT THE AUTHOR

J.S. BAILEY is an author and bookseller hailing from Southwest Ohio. She enjoys crafting, walking in the woods, and spending time with her family. Learn more about Bailey and her work at www.jsbaileywrites.com.

AUTHOR'S NOTE

Memory and Bone is the reincarnation of a very early novel I published at the tender age of twenty-four. Movies are constantly being remade, after all, so why not novels?

When the rights to that early novel reverted back to me, I chose to rewrite it in its entirety rather than republish it as it was. The characters became more relatable, and perhaps more sympathetic. Instead of presenting a world starkly in black and white—the way I myself viewed the world when younger—I shaded it with layers of gray.

Some of my favorite novels have a strong sense of time and place, and I hoped to convey that here by setting *Memory and Bone* in the Greater Cincinnati region during the aftermath of the Great Recession, when so many of us were still struggling. Many of the towns in the novel—Eleanor, Clarkville, and Iron Springs—are fictitious. Other locations, such as the Cincinnati Nature Center and Northern Kentucky University, are very real and are both places where I have spent a great deal of time.

If you enjoyed this book, please consider telling others about it. This can be via an online review, sharing it with your book club, requesting it at your library, or gifting it to a friend.

Thank you for reading, and happy hauntings.

LIST OF TRIGGER WARNINGS

- Abduction
- Abortion
- Alcohol abuse
- Attempted suicide
- Child abuse
- Child neglect
- Death of children
- Death of parents
- Domestic violence
- Gun violence
- Hauntings
- Homophobia
- Mental illness
- Murder
- Physical assault
- Poltergeist activity
- Spiritual possession
- Suicidal ideation

Milton Keynes UK
Ingram Content Group UK Ltd.
UKHW041303270924
1887UKWH00007B/19